The Never

KRISTINA CIRCELLI

This is a work of fiction. Names, characters, places, brands, media, and incidents are either the product of the author's imagination or are used fictitiously. The author acknowledges the trademarked status and trademark owners of various products referenced in this work of fiction, which have been used without permission. The publication/use of these trademarks is not authorized, associated with, or sponsored by the trademark owners.

Cover Design © Sharp Cover Design
Edited by Juli's Elite Editing

http://www.circelli.info

Printed in the United States of America

First Edition: March 6, 2013
Second Edition: November 2013
Library of Congress Cataloging-in-Publication Data

Circelli, Kristina
The Never / Kristina Circelli – 2nd ed
ISBN-10: 0976372843
ISBN-13: 978-0976372844

1.The Never–Literature & Fiction. 2.Fiction–Fantasy
3.Fiction–Fantasy–Sword & Sorcery

For Renee

Never Stop Believing

THEY SAY THAT, in time, we all must grow up.

Keep your feet on the ground. Get your head out of the clouds. You dream too big. Such words force us out of childhood, out of our dreams, and into reality - if we let them. While our bodies may grow up and our minds may mature, our imaginations transcend the meaning of time.

To say that I grew up would be the truth. To say that I stopped dreaming would be a lie. My love for writing was born out of dreams, both waking and sleeping, that took me to worlds everyone else said could never exist. Perhaps this life is too limited in its possibilities, or maybe it is our lack of sight that keeps us from truly seeing.

You might even say that writing was, for me, an act of rebellion. Mermaids aren't real? People can't fly? Luck dragons are made-up creatures? Well, let me prove the many ways in which you are wrong. In books, there is no such thing as "impossible" - and that is what I love most.

The Never took hold in my mind many years ago, a story of what happens after we grow up, but cannot forget our dreams. Some of you may recognize its origin, the long-ago told tale of magic, or you may have heard my endless chatter about the boy who never says good-bye. The Never is not a story of what happens next, but rather, what happens when one woman decides to stop believing in the limitations around her and instead believes in herself - what she can do, what she can see, and what she can dream.

It is an unfortunate reality that we all must grow up. But, The Never has allowed me the rare opportunity to step back into a childhood that was all too short and be among the stories that keep my dreams alive, even during those pestering waking hours.

Even now, I am the one who stays on shore for fear of sea monsters. I am the one who looks for faeries in the flowers. I am the one who is terrified by the thought of being possessed, yet still hopes to meet a ghost or alien. I am the one who lives in The Never, if only in my dreams.

I hope you too enjoy the trip into the impossibly possible, and in the end, let your dreams take flight.

Prologue

A Child Dreams

THE CHILD SAT with her arms crossed, green eyes staring vacantly at the woman before her, mind and imagination in a world not of this realm. The woman, frustrated and bored, watched the girl carefully, tired of this game.

A clock ticked in the background, a steady *tick, tick, tick* of time that did not exist for the child, but drove the adult to her last frayed nerve. Not even the tranquility of her office, purposely decorated to best set every heart at ease with soft colors and peaceful seascapes, could ease the tension in her shoulders.

"Arianna, we have been through this," the woman said, speaking the first words of the day. Her voice sounded too high-pitched and nervous, betraying the stern expression her face had settled into. "You cannot keep lying to people. People don't like lies."

Those green eyes shifted ever so slightly, latching on to her in an eerie, unsettling way. The woman's breath caught in her throat, making her next question sound almost frightened. "Can you tell me why you make up these stories?"

The girl hardly moved when she answered. "I don't tell stories. I tell memories."

The answer only annoyed the woman more. "Memories of what?"

"Of the land I dream of."

"And where is this land?" At that, the girl unfolded her arms and slowly raised a hand, curling her fingers until just one was pointing toward the ceiling. "Up? Where is up? Heaven?" The girl only lowered her arm and narrowed her eyes in a way that told the woman exactly what she thought of her. "And who showed you this place?"

"A friend."

"Does this friend have a name?" The child didn't answer. "Is he nice to you? Or does he tell you to do bad things?" Another blank stare. "Are you afraid of him?"

"I'm not afraid of my friends."

"If he is a friend, why does no one else know him?"

"No one else can see him."

The woman smiled softly, gently touching the girl's arm. "Because he does not exist."

"Because they have forgotten how to see," the child retorted, bitterness in her voice. "He only comes to those who still believe in magic."

"I see. And who told you to say that?"

"I think for myself."

The woman sighed, rising to her feet and gesturing to the girl to do the same. "Magic is for children who cannot think for themselves, Arianna. It is time to grow up, and forget these stories. Then you won't have to see me anymore." The green eyes locked on her once again, sending a chill down the woman's back.

"I see you always. But you never see me."

THE GIRL ALLOWED her mother to tuck her in that night, obeying the soft commands to brush her teeth, put on her pajamas, and slip beneath the sheet. Bedtime was the best time for her, the time when dreams came, when she was visited by memories.

Her mother, a beautiful lady in every sense of the word, pulled up the comforter, smiling down at her daughter. "Tomorrow is a new day, sweetheart," she said, kissing her on the cheek. She held out her hand. "Here, take this."

The child looked down at the small blue pill, taking it in her slender fingers. "What is it?"

"To help you sleep," her mother replied, handing her a glass of water. Not a trace of anger or deception filled her words, as she was a good mother, one who knew what was best for her only child and refused to show distress. "So you won't have to visit your doctor anymore." As expected, the oath had her daughter eagerly swallowing the pill, never knowing what truths would come of the broken promises.

"Will I sleep better now?" the girl asked, settling down against her pillows.

"You will sleep like an angel, my beautiful little Arianna, with silk wings and a long, flowing white dress."

"Will I dream?"

"Of all the most wonderful things in this world." Her mother leaned over and kissed her daughter on the forehead. "Sweet dreams, my love."

But on that night, the little girl didn't dream at all.

An Artist at Work

BLACK MIXED WITH gray, an ebony sky threatening the tranquil land below it. Swirls of red created furious clouds, trailing across the canvas as the artist's brush glided smoothly from edge to edge. She knew not why Mother Nature was angry, only that something unspeakable had happened here, in this world crafted by her own mind, by her own unexplainable and unsettled emotions.

And now, the townspeople would pay the price.

Arianna sat back and observed her work, satisfied with the gloom and yet, saddened by the threat of destruction. The land below the sky was full of life, with gloriously green mountains, a sparkling blue river, the hint of magic hidden among colorful flowers and canopied woodlands. The contrast of light and dark fascinated her, allowing her to get lost in her own painting as she observed the scene, wondering if the sky would open up and swallow the world whole.

She often considered whether or not the sky in her own world would do the same, take her out of an existence where no one understood the thoughts and feelings swarming within her. Bring her to a place where being different, being herself, was celebrated, and dreams of the unimaginable didn't have to be tucked away into the corners of one's mind. It was in that dreamland that she felt truly alive, but it was also the land that so often got her into trouble.

A hand on her shoulder disrupted her pondering, startling her out of the dream world that she so often preferred. Arianna pressed her lips together as her fiancé, John, peered over her shoulder. Discomfort and nerves always distracted her whenever someone viewed an uncompleted work.

"Creepy," he asserted, kissing her on the cheek. "I like it."

Arianna frowned. "It's not creepy. It's...life, unfiltered."

John observed his fiancée as he set down his coat and briefcase. She looked cute with streaks of color staining her skin, ever the absent-minded painter absorbed in her craft. She was beautiful in a dark, mysterious kind of way, with thick chocolate-colored hair that tumbled down her back in waves, when it wasn't pinned up in a messy bun atop her head. Her almond-shaped eyes were a striking sea green, often glazed over with a far-away glimmer that saw things no other mortal in the human world could ever see.

Now she sat staring at her painting, lost in the colors and imagery. "Where is it?" John asked.

"Don't know."

"Some made-up place?"

"I saw it in my dreams."

He paused at that, the nonchalance in her voice, the acceptance of unexplainable sights. Though he was used to such absentminded comments, they always unsettled him a bit. "It's nice," he said easily, approaching her side again. "Did you take your meds today?"

Arianna spared a second's glance away from her painting to smirk at him, not at all touched by the concern in his dark blue eyes, the way he ran a hand through short, perfectly styled blonde hair. "Yes, Father."

"I was just asking."

"Checking up on me like I'm a child," she corrected, rising from the stool and setting her brush in a jar of mineral spirits. Her slender, if not slight, frame skirted easily around the wet painting as she walked to the window, which overlooked the river on this wing of the cabin. "Everyone keep an eye on the twenty-six-year-old dreamer, the girl who paints dark things and stormy skies. Everyone worry about the child with imaginary friends. Hide her away in a cabin in the woods so no one can hear her whispering to herself. Make sure she eats and takes her medicine, lest she wastes away while lost in her art."

John smiled and playfully poked his fiancée, wrapping his arms around her waist. "Sometimes I forget how much you love words just as much as you do painting. I've missed your monologues lately."

"I've been preparing for the show. No time for monologues," Arianna responded, forgiving him for his question by resting her head on his shoulder. He stood only three inches taller than her, the perfect height, with a businessman's build that spoke of his dedication to work and professionalism, two things she neither cared nor thought about regularly. Together they watched the river, enjoying a moment of peace in their little cabin in the woods.

Arianna never understood why John wanted to move from their city apartment to this woodland home, but also never asked questions. She preferred it here, feeling more at home than she ever did surrounded by concrete and cars. It was a sanctuary, where her dreams manifested themselves in the green of the trees, the blue of the lake, the gray of the shadows cast in sunset. She didn't dream of skyscrapers and corner offices bathed in fluorescent lights. No, she craved the natural world, the feel of grass and leaves beneath her feet, the sound of wind passing through the leaves.

Sometimes, when she closed her eyes, these woods brought her back to a place she could almost see in her mind's eye. A familiar place, and yet, nowhere she had ever been before. Her mother often said her dreams kept her from enjoying the world; John claimed it was simply chemical, and that her medication balanced out what her mind couldn't.

And so, here in her little cabin in the woods, she painted what no one would let her say, those desperate questions of place and self. All the while, she wondered who she once was that frightened her mother so badly, wishing she had the courage to find out.

A Soul for Sale

SHE GATHERED HER paintings the next morning, careful not to disturb the still-wet paint of her latest work. It was a long drive to the gallery, and, having lived in the cabin for nearly six years now, she dreaded the chaos of the city. The people, the rush, the questions, the fear. There was no escape in the concrete Hell, only the push forward to do more, make more, succeed more.

Still she made the trek every so often as the curator demanded, selling what pieces she could stand to part with at shows that were attended by the wealthy from across the globe. Arianna had known the curator since she was a child, an old family friend, and was proud of the gallery he'd built for himself, the reputation as one of the finest art dealers and discoverers the world over. She was his prized artist, and he made sure everyone who walked through his gallery doors knew of her paintings. They sold for the highest price at every show, allowing her to maintain her somewhat reclusive life-style without having to get the thing she dreaded most - a day job.

They made the drive in silence, save for the soft classical music that John preferred. Arianna kept her gaze out the window, watching the scenery change from towering trees to towering buildings. Though she wasn't fond of these travels, she did enjoy witnessing the transformation of the landscape. It fascinated her how the world changed, and the people with it, even as her stomach knotted itself in anticipation of what was soon to come.

In the city, she calmed her nerves by imagining herself flying around the tops of skyscrapers that loomed over the land, soaring through misty clouds, startling people in their offices as they sipped their morning coffee. She marveled at the sensation, to be carried by the wind, to smell the rain and clouds and sky, to be weightless.

To be free.

The wistful vision shifted to something else then, something almost more than a daydream. For a moment Arianna thought she could smell the sky and see the people with their morning coffee, a memory pushing through to the forefront of her mind that refused to be ignored. Such visions always reached out to her when she was stressed, feeling the weight of society pressed upon her shoulders.

Stifling a sigh, Arianna turned away from the window and smiled at John when he announced they were almost there. Discreetly, she swallowed a blue pill, already having forgotten her morning dose. She needed to be focused for the event, not lost in her daydreams.

THAT FOCUS CARRIED her through the day, encouraging her to charm the gallery curator, to arrange her pieces in a way that inspired viewers, to hold her head high as she carefully painted her face and slipped into a snug black dress that accentuated what few bony curves she had. She sold more than just her paintings at these events, all in the hopes of bringing home enough money to avoid another show. It was the curator who insisted she dress up for every show and wear makeup that covered the shadows beneath her eyes. It was her mother who told her men would buy her pieces if she looked attractive enough. It was John who agreed with them, and helped her select the perfect dress for the showcase.

Being forced to look her fanciful best didn't mean she had to schmooze, as the curator called it. Arianna wasn't comfortable talking to strangers, and so, she rarely did. From her place in the corner she watched as men and women dressed in their finest observed her work, murmuring to one another in hushed tones, gesturing to her art with hands grasping champagne glasses. She saw some nods of approval, a few smiles, some questioning frowns as they tried to decipher just what was going through the artist's mind when she painted such scenes. The *click*, *click* of heels against hardwood kept to the beat of her frantic heart, the swirl of movement from wall to wall, exhibit to exhibit, paced with the thoughts swarming her already frazzled mind.

Arianna waited until the crowd had thinned some to abandon her post, walking over to the piece she had just finished the night before. It called to her, seeking her gaze from its prime spot in the center of the room. She didn't enjoy being that exposed, but lost herself in the mix of color, the dark of sky, soon enough.

There was something about that sky that called to her, as if she could feel the rainclouds against her bare shoulders. She could smell the land, fresh with citrus scents and florals that welcomed her home. If she tried hard enough, she could hear birds singing in the distance, voices speaking to one another, loud clashes that she couldn't identify as either thunder or cannon fire.

"I do believe this one's my favorite," a voice said at her side.

Arianna glanced over indifferently, straightening a bit when she took in the man next to her, a man who looked as though he'd be more comfortable at sea than in a stuffy gallery. He was taller than her, but not threateningly so, with a lean build that reminded her of the father she knew only as a child. He wore a tailored, if not strangely styled, suit that fit him perfectly, a long coat with dark gold buttons and a wide collar, white shirt open at the collar, black pants fitted in all the right places, and black boots that looked as heavy as they did well worn. The boots defied his otherwise professional appearance, fitting over his pants and folding over at the knee, with wide straps and gold buckles. Shimmering ruby and emerald rings sparkled from the hands clasped behind his back, the same colors that reflected from the band that tied his thick, shoulder-length hair back at the nape of his neck.

But his eyes, those caught her attention most of all. A burning gaze, bright eyes that stared straight into her, straight through her. They were violent, tumultuous, frightening, familiar eyes that had seen a lifetime of sin and horror, and yet, were softened by the smile he offered.

She refrained from clearing her throat. "Um…why is it your favorite?"

He answered in a low voice, his tone raspy and inviting, his accent faintly British. "All of the pieces show a unique style, darkness and confusion mixed with innocence. But this one…" He lifted his right hand and gestured to the painting, one decorated finger hovering less than an inch over the surface. His touch was so close that it made her nervous, should he press skin to canvas and disrupt her finest work. "This one is real. This one comes from the heart. You can feel the terror of the impending storm, but also, calmness in knowing this too shall pass. It is quite spectacular."

"Some say it's creepy," she replied, thinking back to the day before.

"I say it's magnificent." He thought for a moment, eyes tracing over the canvas. "Out of nothing, we create something. And that something is a showcase of everything our world is, and everything it isn't." He eyed her then, and Arianna felt his gaze analyzing her very being, assessing her worth. "You must be the artist."

"Why would you say that?"

"Intuition. A perfectly painted piece by a perfectly painted woman."

Arianna turned back to the painting, uncomfortable yet tantalized by those bright burning eyes latched onto her, by that ever-so-slightly accented tone that spoke of faraway adventures. It annoyed her that her mother was right, men did take more notice when she wore makeup. “Your intuition is correct. I am the artist, Arianna.”

“Arianna.” He said her name like a caress, a threat, and a question all at once. She looked over at him when he shifted, taking a step closer. “My friends call me Jim. You may call me James.”

And then, with a single nod, he departed, leaving her alone with her work.

ONLY MOMENTS LATER, as Arianna was retreating back to her corner, the curator approached. He was a minuscule man, bony at every angle, with long fingers that spoke of his love and passion for art. Even in his old age he still walked with a spring in his step. “Your showcase piece sold, Arianna, and for an incredible price.”

“It’s not for sale.” The response escaped her painted lips before she realized what she said.

“What do you mean, not for sale? Arianna, this sale alone means you won’t have to hold another show for the rest of the year.”

“It’s not for sale.”

The curator sighed, clasping his wiry hands together and peering up at her through his glasses. “We’ve been through this, Arianna. You cannot keep every piece as soon as someone decides to purchase it. Not if you want to be a working artist, that is.”

Arianna struggled to keep her hands at her sides; she longed to shake the man by his protruding shoulders. “Who…who wanted to buy it?”

“A nice gentleman, by the sounds of his letter. He left a note stating he must have the perfectly painted piece by the artist who paints herself just as beautifully.” He winked at her as though she would understand the message. “He already left payment. The piece is sold.”

“To Jim? The man in the suit that made him look like a pirate?”

The curator frowned. “I saw no such man this evening. If I had, I would have introduced myself.” When she didn’t smile at the humor in his tone, he merely sighed. “You don’t have to work for the rest of the year, my favorite reclusive artist. This is a fantastic sale."

"Sounds like a good deal," John said as he came up from behind Arianna. He slid an arm around her shoulders, drawing her to him. "You'd enjoy the break from these shows, wouldn't you?"

"I suppose."

Eventually, she agreed to sell, though she didn't have much choice. As they drove back to their cabin that night, Arianna felt the empty longing traveling with them, knowing she had sold her dream.

Three

A Dream Awakened

THE EMPTINESS FOLLOWED her home, a shadow trailing behind her every step, seeping into her dreams until she could no longer find peace or restfulness in her slumber. Arianna slipped out of bed, careful not to disturb her fiancé, and retreated to her studio, where her paints waited impatiently.

The hours passed slowly as she mixed reds with grays, greens with blues, painting color across canvas in gliding brushstrokes. Frustration built when the colors wouldn't mix just right, blending beautifully but not creating the replica she envisioned. She wanted another painting like the one she sold. An exact copy, not a poor man's version that lacked the passion, emotion, and mysticism of the original.

Arianna threw the brush down in frustration, burying her head in her hands. "It's pointless," she muttered, rubbing her fingers over her face, not noticing that she smeared spots of grays and greens over her cheeks. Her hair caught on her engagement ring, tangling it even more than it already was.

With a sigh, she rose from the chair and cast a baleful glance at the easel and canvas, the remnants of what could have been the rebirth of a memory now long forgotten. Needing to get away from the failure, she stepped out the back door and lowered herself onto the stairs, staring out at the midnight sky.

The night was peaceful, a warm breeze traveling through the trees, which spanned up to a twinkling sky with nary a cloud in sight. She loved nights like these, surrounded by the sounds of nature - the gentle rustling of leaves, the chirp of crickets in the distance, Mother Nature settling herself down to rest. Midnight was always her most tranquil time, the hour between night and morning when she could almost feel the world rejuvenating itself, recharging in preparation for a new day filled with light and life and laughter.

Arianna sighed again, knowing what those thoughts meant. She resigned herself to the fact that another trip to the doctor was likely in order to up the meds that were no longer working as well as they used to, and pulled a blue pill from her pocket. A few loose pills were always kept on hand for moments such as these, just in case she had what her mother so lovingly referred to as "episodes," those times when reality and daydream merged together and she couldn't distinguish the two in her mind. Lately she was finding it harder to make that differentiation, even on the days when she remembered to take her medication on time.

She knew from years of begrudging experience that it would take a few minutes for her thoughts to clear, so she allowed herself a moment to simply sit and enjoy the night before retreating to the bedroom. Arianna leaned her head against the railing post, eyes tracing a pathway in the sky between the stars. Exploring them, imagining life among them, sparkling and glimmering, watching over the world below. A smile formed when one of those stars twinkled just a bit brighter than others, as though just for her.

"They remember you," a voice said from the shadows, deep and accented with the lilt of a foreign land, "just as you remember them."

Arianna's smile widened, her gaze never leaving the sky though exhilaration singed her nerves. She knew this voice; somewhere within her soul she knew this voice, had heard it before. As a child, she was, at first, terrified of the people who spoke to her in her fantasies. They told her to come away with them, to fight with them, to never go home. But the more she learned to control her dreams, her episodes, the more comfortable she was hearing the one who spoke to her most often.

That voice had changed over the years, aging with her, maturing from a child's curious tone to one that tingled down to her core. But, try as she might, after her mind and body matured, she was never able to match the voice to a face, especially when her medication had kept the voice at bay for over a decade.

"The stars are far too important to remember just one person," she answered softly.

"You are not just one person. You are Arianna of the Stars." She heard a rustling in front of her, saw a shadow forming in the trees. She blinked, but the shadow remained in place, not moving closer, but not moving away either. "You are lover, creator, dreamer."

"I am but a person, who dreams of the stars."

"And what of him? Does he dream of the stars with you?"

"...Who?"

The shadow didn't move, but Arianna swore she felt a brush of fingertips against her left hand. "The one who shares your bed. The one you call...fiancé."

The word sounded like a curse, one that sent shivers down her spine. "He...enjoys stories of my dreams, but doesn't often look at the stars." When the shadow didn't answer, she frowned and peered into the night. "He is a businessman, not a dreamer."

"And how does a dreamer fall in love with a businessman?"

Her thoughts drifted back to her teenage years, that time between growing up and longing to still be a child. "I met him in high school," she answered, her voice light and nostalgic. "He offered me a ride home from school after I missed the bus...stayed too late in art class. He made me laugh, and I felt safe with him. He didn't care that I was...different."

John had taught her how to trust, how to feel secure. "He asked me to marry him before I left for art school, and it seemed perfect at the time. Naturally, I said yes." John's request for her hand in marriage still made her smile, the sweetness of the gesture, the hopeful innocence when he lowered himself to one knee. “But you know all of this. You have always been here, somewhere, in the forgotten parts of my mind.”

“I have seen what you have seen,” the stranger agreed, voice still soft and mysterious, yet with the slightest hint of anger. *Or perhaps something else*, she wondered. Regret, or even frustration. “But not felt what you have felt, or what you feel now. Tell me, Arianna of the Stars, do you love him?”

Slightly taken aback, Arianna lifted her head and scanned the trees, searching. “Who are you to ask me such a thing?”

But there was no answer. The figure was gone, the dream awakened. Shaking her head at her own foolishness in arguing with a delusion, Arianna rose from the steps and walked back inside, back to the man she had promised to love until death do her part.

WHEN SHE AWOKE the next morning, John was gone. Next to her, laying on the pillow, was a note that read, *Work called, be back soon. Have a surprise for my talented artist.*

Arianna smiled and traced a finger across the words, imagining her fiancé as he tried to quickly, yet quietly, write the note before slipping out the door. He often left early in the morning, pulled away from a weekend rest to take care of business demands. She didn’t pretend to fully understand everything he did for his job, but could appreciate the fact that he worked hard and rarely complained.

Lifting herself from the bed, Arianna pulled on a thin, light-green sundress that hung just above her knees. It was a warm morning, which meant a hot afternoon was in order. Those days were her favorite, when she could explore the great outdoors without being bundled up, feeling the breeze against her skin, the grass beneath her feet. That’s where she belonged, tucked away in her own little world where nothing could touch her but the sounds and scents of nature.

Arianna slipped outside, relishing the morning time. The woods stretched out before her, surrounding the cabin in greens and golds.

It was rare to find this kind of paradise anymore, she knew, a forest haven that found a way to escape the growing masses of steel structures and bipedal traffic.

Sunlight filtered across her path as she walked, flickering with the wind, creating images in the dirt and grass that inspired visions of elves and fairies. Thoughts of fantasy creatures brought her attention back to the previous night. It had been a long time, too long a time, since the phantom figure had come to visit her. Years, in fact. There were moments when she almost thought she could sense him there in the background, waiting to be addressed, begging to be seen. Arianna felt a pang of guilt each time she took that little blue pill, as though she were forcing him into hiding, exiling him from an existence in the light, punishing him for a crime he did not commit. But her doctors, and her mother, had made it clear that speaking to the phantom would not be tolerated - not if she hoped to live her life outside of padded walls.

John gave her hope that what the others said wasn't true. He didn't look at her with pity, like she was something broken and discarded. He knew about her past, the voices she heard as a child, the places she claimed to have seen. But he didn't care. He loved her despite her faults, and encouraged her to simply be herself, the artist who dreamed. She tried to see his daily medication reminders as acts of love rather than an annoyance, helping her to be a better person.

Was it a kind of infidelity, then, to be seeking out the voice in her dreams, the one who came back to her after so many years of silence?

Arianna pondered that as she walked, circling the cabin slowly, hands grazing across rough tree bark, feet crunching over fallen leaves. She loved her fiancé; there was no doubt about that. But she was also fascinated by the voice, the figure in the shadows. She no longer remembered his face, but how he made her feel, *that* she recognized even when not in his presence.

Whole. She felt whole, after a lifetime of existing merely in pieces.

The man at the gallery, James, gave her a similar feeling. There was something about the way those bright eyes stared through her, something about the roughness of his voice, that called to her. She had never met him, neither in this life nor her dreams, but he was familiar in a way she could not explain. Arianna supposed that was why she let her painting go, though she still felt the loss of it deep in her heart.

With a sigh, Arianna finished her walk, disappointed to be alone. She was about to head back inside when she heard the crunch of footsteps over twigs behind her. She froze in place, not daring to look over her shoulder.

"Are…are you here?" she asked, her question nearly a whisper. A hand touched her shoulder, caressing it.

"Of course I'm here."

It wasn't the voice she expected, but it was one she recognized. Arianna turned, facing John with a wobbly smile. "You startled me."

"Expecting someone else?"

"Of course not. You just—" Her voice cut off when she saw the bundle in his arms, the wriggling, furry ball of golden fur. She looked up at John, who was grinning down at her. "He's for me?"

"She." John handed her the puppy, an eight-week-old mutt mix of lab and shepherd. "I know how much you hate the business trips I have to take this time of year, so I thought I'd get you a friend."

Arianna scooped up the puppy, burying her face in the soft fur. The puppy responded by licking her forehead. "Oh, John, she's such a darling. I love her."

John scratched the puppy behind the ears. "She needs a name."

Arianna held out the puppy, eyeing it with a tender gaze. Wide yellow eyes stared back at her, filled with unconditional love. "Lily," she decided, nodding to herself. The name surfaced in the forefront of her mind from some unknown place, feeling like the name of an old friend or perhaps a close family member. "Her name is Lily."

"It's a good name."

The hesitation in his voice had her frowning. She drew Lily to her chest again and looked up at John. “Is something wrong?” When he cast a glance down at the dog, she knew. “You’re leaving.”

“I’m sorry, Ari. I know it’s sooner than expected, but the boss needs me on a plane tonight. It’s just for a week, and I figured since you got such a big price for your painting, that you’d be fine here for a few days.”

Arianna sighed. She hated when he traveled, leaving her alone while he saw the world. Part of her distaste was purely out of jealousy, though the other, larger part was that she simply preferred his company over being by herself. Except this time, she’d at least have Lily. “Well…I guess I’ll help you pack, then.”

No Longer a Child

SHE SAW HIM off, making earnest promises to always remember her medication, putting on the happiest face she could manage until his car disappeared down the driveway. Lily the puppy pulled on her new leash, eager to explore her surroundings. Although the sun was setting, Arianna allowed the dog to pull her into the woods, taking her on an evening stroll before they settled in for a night of medicine, hot meals, and painting. Lily sniffed at the plants as she passed them, pouncing on flickering shadows and barking at nonexistent figures.

Arianna laughed softly as she watched the puppy play, giving her plenty of room on the leash to wander and explore. She'd always wanted a dog as a child, only to be told by her mother that animals were dirty and not meant to be kept as pets. The refusal only fueled her desire, as did the promises that, maybe, if she was good and took her medicine, then a puppy would one day be hers to hold and cherish. Now that she finally had a pet, she was going to spoil her rotten, even if that meant long walks through the forest. Their trek had already been lengthy, cutting it too close to her medicine dosage, which was already forgotten.

The sun slipped below the horizon, casting the woods in shadows. Arianna glanced over her shoulder and was comforted by the glow of lights in the cabin not too far in the distance. She tried not to wander too far from home at night, knowing what dangers lurked in a forest of heavy brush and wildlife. John didn't like her strolling through the woods at dark—or during the day, for that matter—so she tried not to upset him by staying close to home.

"A gift of life, to keep death at bay."

Arianna turned about, searching for the familiar voice. She saw only night and darkness instead. Her heart beat wildly, both at the surprise intrusion and the possibilities of what the voice's return may mean. "What…what death?"

"Death of love, of heart, of soul."

She took in a deep breath, grip tightening on the leash. She wanted to see the figure's face, *needed* to see it. Lily sensed her new owner's hesitation and barked once, taking a stance at her master's feet. "Who are you?" Arianna asked, narrowing her eyes.

"You know who I am. You have known me since you were a child."

"I knew a child as a child. You sound like a man." She felt a brush of fingers against her neck, as though a hand was pulling her hair back. She turned but saw only empty air.

"I have watched you, Arianna of the Stars. I have watched you, dreamed with you, grown with you."

Lily pulled at the leash and scratched at Arianna's ankles, eager to get away from what was agitating her master. Arianna let the leash slip through her fingers, not noticing the dog as she ran back for the cabin on four wobbly legs and waited on the back steps, whimpering quietly.

Free to wander on her own, the enraptured woman began to walk, slowly passing tree after tree. Her hands grazed over tree trunks, eyes grazed over leaves and shrubs. Moonlight streamed in through the canopy, creating a white glow that softened the night setting. "Who are you?" Her repeated question traveled a light breeze, laughter echoing back at her.

"I am the one you dream of, the one you seek."

She saw something then, an outline moving through the trees.

The figure was watching her, moving with her. If she looked hard enough, she could almost see a face, eyes. Not bright eyes, but seeking, piercing nonetheless. "Who are you?"

Those eyes, dark green and ever watchful, latched on to hers. They followed her as they walked, peering around leaf and branch, staring through the moonlight. "I am the dream. I am the reality," he answered, voice like a secret spoken in hushed whispers. "I am the eternal. I am the forgotten." They moved closer together in the woods, yet still at a distance. "I am the always. I am The Never."

Something inside her mind clicked. Arianna paused between two trees, one hand on either trunk. She knew that name. In the farthest corners of her mind, she remembered, and the memory hardened in her gut. Oh yes, she knew, and wished that her mind wasn't suddenly filled with recollections of salted shores and pale pink skies. "You are not The Never. The Never left me. The Never forsook me. The Never *forgot* me."

"No," came the soothing, reassuring croon. "The Never did not forget you. The Never could not reach you, Arianna of the Stars."

"Stop calling me that," Arianna snapped, taking a step back. "Stop pretending to be *him*. Tell me who you are."

"I have told you. You must believe me"

She heard the desperation in his request, but ignored it and instead slipped a hand in her pocket. "Have it your way. I know how to get rid of you." She swallowed the blue pill she'd forgotten to take earlier and he reacted fast, exploding into her line of vision and grabbing her wrist.

"What was that?" he demanded. "What is this thing I have seen you take so many times just before you slip out of my grasp?"

Unable to respond, Arianna simply stared up at him. This was not the boy she remembered, the boy who spoke to her as a child and led her on exciting other-worldly adventures. This was a man, perhaps a year older than her, perhaps even a year or two younger. There was something innocent about his forest green, almond-shaped eyes, and yet, something very sinister in the way he pressed his full lips together in a knowing smirk. His jawline was strong, as were his cheekbones, strong enough to take one of many hits she suspected he was used to enduring, and maybe even encouraged.

He was tan, the tan of a man who spent his days in the sun, with wild hair the color of the setting sun. For the briefest of moments she longed to run her fingers through those thick locks, which hung down to his ears in messy strands. Bamboo pieces decorated his ears, pierced through twice in each.

His clothing, if that's what it could be called, matched his eyes. His torso was wrapped in a soft, thin shirt that clung to his skin, with wide straps that crisscrossed at his shoulders to reveal finely toned muscle. The deep green of a material Arianna didn't recognize covered his legs with leaf-shaped designs, ending just below the knees. He was barefoot, which only added to his mysterious aura. Strapped around his waist was a leather belt, with a dagger sheathed at his side.

Boy had most certainly become man.

"What did you take?" he asked again when she only gazed at him. His grip tightened on her wrist, causing her to wince.

"Um…just, just my medicine."

"Medicine." He said the word quietly, as though trying to understand it. Then he took her by the shoulders, almost too urgently. "Medicine! You must never take it again."

Her brow furrowed. "I have to. It keeps me well."

"No. You must never take it, my Arianna. It is why I could not find you for so long, why we could not be together."

"But…you said you saw what I saw all these years. How could you see me, but not find me?"

"I could see through your eyes, my Arianna, but never would you tell me where you were. Only now have you allowed me to come to you."

Arianna hesitated, savoring the feel of his rough hands on her bare skin. She had never known this figure in her dreams as a man, and was fascinated by the creature he had become. "We…we had adventures together, as children?"

He smiled, gently brushing back a strand of her hair. "Yes, we did. You cannot remember them all now, but you will. Promise me you will not take your medicine again. Promise me, and I will return tomorrow to show you what you have forgotten. We will fly from this place, and have our adventures again."

An internal alarm was triggered, a familiar word, a familiar worry. Arianna ignored it and smiled up at him just before he faded into the night. "I promise."

Discover The Never

THAT NIGHT, ARIANNA dreamed of color.

Her world was a watercolor, soft and bright paints eddying together to form a gentle river. From that river stretched a verdant carpet spotted with wildflowers, a rainbow of colors reflected in a pink and orange sky. In the distance, carefully sculpted mountains waited to be acknowledged by the rising sun, peaks topped with white blankets of snow.

This was not a realm fully whole, but rather, still being created, painted stroke by gentle stroke so lovingly that Arianna could almost feel the artist's concentration and passion for crafting a true masterpiece.

Arianna had once known this place well, if not in person then in her dreams. But it had been a long time since she envisioned it, such images kept at bay either by medicine or will, and Arianna wondered how much she had forgotten. As familiar as this world was, she was also lost in it, confused by the swirling hues and surrounded by a landscape without definition.

When she awoke, nerves set in.

She stared at the blue pill sitting on the bathroom counter. It beckoned and demanded to be consumed, reminding her of the promise made to John just before he left, telling her to ignore the visions of the previous night and do as her doctor instructed. And yet, she longed to know what would happen if, just this once, she dared to defy what everyone else said was best to do. Would the dream-like stranger come for her? Would he show her the land she dreamed of? Or was this all just another delusion, setting her up for heart-ache?

Arianna stared at herself in the mirror, contemplating her decision. She looked tired yet determined, cautious yet carefree. Her long, wavy brown hair was unbrushed, her face unpainted, her eyes bright with excitement. She wore a flowing white skirt decorated with feathery blue designs, and a form-fitting cobalt tank top. It was the perfect outfit for spending the day outside, for exploring, for dreaming.

Making up her mind, Arianna turned away from the counter.

She scooped up Lily when she entered the kitchen, the furry golden puppy wiggling and licking with excitement. “Let’s build you something fun, shall we?” Arianna said with a laugh, hooking on the leash and leading her new companion outside. She was a small woman, considered weak by some, but Arianna had always been good with her hands and loved creating things—even things her fiancé couldn’t build. She considered art to be more than paint on canvas, but also in wood and craftsmanship, architecture and design.

Drawing the sketches in her mind, Arianna let the puppy play while she built. She wasn’t dressed for the occasion, but there was something pleasing, albeit vain, about looking pretty while she worked at what could be considered a man’s job. Though, she did tie back her hair; the long locks tended to get in the way.

Within a few hours, just before morning drifted into early afternoon, Arianna had constructed a high-walled run for the puppy. It stretched from the corner of the back deck at least twenty feet into the yard, attaching at the wall and expanding to the edge of the forest line. Sections of each side had been cut out and covered with fiberglass windows, allowing the puppy to see outside. Although she knew John would likely be furious, Arianna had also cut a hole in the back wall of the house that led into the run, with a thin sheet of plastic covering it so Lily could go in and out as she pleased, without the danger of escaping.

Inside the makeshift run, she set out plenty of food and water, and outside had covered the open top of the run with chicken wire so other critters couldn't get in. It wasn't the most beautiful of designs, but given the timeframe, Arianna was pleased with the result. Eventually she would paint it; for now the plain wooden sides would have to do.

She worked hard, never stopping for rest, never letting her mind wander from the task at hand. It wasn't until the run was finished that Arianna stood back and observed the day, realizing her thoughts were settled on the single fact that no one had come for her.

"The perfect place to play, my little darling," she said to the puppy, who was busy gnawing on the edges of her flip-flops. "Hey, chew on this." She handed Lily a rope toy that John had bought, holding it firmly and engaging in a game of tug-of-war.

"Just as nature calls to her, so too do the friends that walk on four legs."

Arianna took in a breath, just as Lily let out an impatient bark, wanting to play some more. The woman rose gracefully from the ground, facing her visitor. "You came."

He stood on the edge of the woods, not coming closer. But now, in the daylight, she could see him clearly. What the moonlight had shown her the night before, the sun magnified. He seemed to glow in the daytime, as though sunlight fueled his smile.

Yes, he was the boy she had known as a child, she realized as a memory began creeping into the forefront of her mind. A figure in the window, a fast flash of light darting around her room, a boy introducing himself with a cocky grin and smug swagger. There was something different about him now though. Not just age, but something…sadder. As she struggled to remember her childhood dreams, he only grinned an impish grin.

"Of course I came. I will always come for you." His green eyes narrowed slightly, wild hair blowing in the breeze. "And now will you come to me?"

She hesitated, not knowing why. Arianna wanted to go to him, guilt holding her back, curiosity encouraging her forward. It was foolish to feel guilty, she told herself. This was merely another delusion, an aberration from her usual life, finally allowing herself a moment to dream in a moment of solitude.

And so she picked up the puppy and set her just inside the cabin, closing the door firmly. Lily pawed at the glass, whimpering, before settling down on the mat and watching with wide round eyes.

Arianna closed the gap between them, her gaze never leaving his. He watched her with a hungry predator stare, jaw set firmly, arms tensed as though preparing to catch her if she fled. She was intrigued by his passion, even more so by the fact that he didn't move to touch her when she stopped before him.

"I'm here," she said, surprised at how breathy her voice sounded. "Now what?"

"Now, we go home."

"Where?"

"To The Never."

Arianna frowned. "But…you are The Never."

His eyes glistened as he gestured all around him. "I am The Never. The Never is me."

Normally she enjoyed a good riddle, but now she just wanted answers. "Where is The Never?" At that, he simply lifted an arm and pointed up. Arianna followed the gesture, eyes tracing the clouds, mind remembering her shrink's words so many years ago. Questions about Heaven, demons, voices asking her to do good or bad things. People thought she was sick, perhaps even possessed, led to say and do things by an evil voice that resided deep in her mind. No one ever celebrated her differences. No one ever dreamed with her.

No one except Malachi.

"The Never calls to you, Arianna of the Stars. It calls to its dreamer, wishing for you to return."

"Its dreamer?" Her thoughts were cloudy now as she struggled to remember. It was possible that he was lying, but Arianna wanted to believe he spoke the truth. She *needed* to believe his words. There was only one way to determine truth from lie, and so she nodded. "Let's go."

He smiled, pleasure and innocence and seduction in his expression. She couldn't look away, and grinned with him. "Then let us fly."

When he moved into the clearing and spread his arms, Arianna held up a hand. "Wait. I thought that was a figure of speech last night. You actually mean…fly?"

"Of course." His expression was quizzical. "Just as before." Arianna only stared at him. "You have forgotten."

Arianna lifted a shoulder. "It's hard to remember doing the impossible."

If he was disappointed, he didn't show it. Instead, he merely held out a hand in her direction. "Take hold of me, then. I will take you there."

Again, guilt wrestled with curiosity. She wanted to do what he asked, and yet yearned to see John, hear his voice. But curiosity pulled her forward and she approached him, wrapping her arms around his neck. She felt his hands on her waist, slowly sliding around her back. His eyes stared into hers as he pulled her closer, pressing body against body.

"You smell like the sky…and the sea," Arianna noted, hating that she sounded like some silly schoolgirl.

He only lowered his head, forehead touching hers. "Soon, you will too." His grip tightened, as did hers. "Hold on tight."

With his softly spoken command, he launched them both upward, into the sky.

Remember Thyself

IT WAS EXHILARATING. It was terrifying. It was natural.

Arianna clung to him, to the familiar stranger who smelled of the sky and sea, as they soared toward the clouds. She heard his laughter in her ears, laughter mixed with the roar of the wind. He was so carefree in his flight that she forgot her fear, allowing herself the joy of looking around and over his shoulder in wonder.

They climbed higher and higher until the trees were but green specks, until white clouds became mist that embraced them, until blue sky was their only existence. Arianna chuckled when they passed a flock of geese, which scattered at their sudden arrival and watched in shock at the strange creatures orbiting into the dark unknown above. Her laugh cut short when she felt pressure building against her chest, and fear began to set in again at the sensation of soaring into potential nothingness. She was just about to cry out when she saw the change in color, blue sky giving way to reds and purples that distracted her enough to ease the tension in her limbs.

They had left when the afternoon sun just began to rise, but now they were traveling into twilight. Arianna didn't understand how they passed through one time dimension to the next and started to wonder about her sanity, but when she felt his arms tighten around her, his fast heartbeat matching her own, she didn't care. She simply watched as the world around them transformed, twinkling stars flickering around a bright moon, blue-gray clouds set against a cobalt sky.

It wasn't a sky she was used to seeing in her daily life. Only in memories she didn't quite trust did she recall witnessing the magnificent sight of a white moon next to a dimmed yellow sun, both of which seemed to smile as they passed, neither of which outshone the other. They were content as friends side by side, surrounded by blazing stars that called out energetic greetings as the wingless travelers flew past. Arianna lifted a hand and waved to one of those stars, greeting what felt like an old friend, never feeling the foolishness one may have sensed in talking to a star.

Music erupted from all around them, little bells and flutes and wind-chimes singing their arrival. She felt them slowing down then, almost floating instead of soaring, but fast enough to keep her pressed against her pilot in this incredible flight. There was no other being in this sky-within-a-sky, only their own beating hearts and exhilarated breaths.

"Where are we?" Arianna asked, her voice a shout in the silence. "Where are we going?"

In response, he only pointed ahead of them.

She saw then where he was taking her, a sight that she remembered from a dream many years ago. They rocketed toward their destination, entering the atmosphere with a blinding flashing light that exploded all around them. Arianna could do nothing but squeeze her eyes shut and hold on tight, trusting her guide to lead them to safety.

When the brightness faded, it took a moment for her eyes to adjust. At first she saw only gray. Gray clouds, gray mist, gray trees. Then the gray gave way to white and a pale mix of color. Everything was subdued, as though she were looking through a tinted glass.

Arianna clutched at his shoulder as he flew her closer, toward what looked like a forest canopy breaking through the mist. One tree grew taller than the rest, jutting out in grandeur, sprawling above its neighbors with limbs wide enough for at least three to walk side-by-side. He set them both down on one of those limbs, waiting until Arianna had balanced herself to release her. She felt the draw of his hands across her back, then on her arm as his fingers trailed down her forearm and took her hand.

"Come," he whispered, gently pulling her out on the branch.

"Are you insane?" She tugged against his grip, casting a glance down. They may have been standing on an enormous limb, but that limb was stretched over an entire forest—and it was a long way down.

He only smiled. "I won't let you fall."

Arianna took in a deep breath, gathering her courage. She had never been afraid of heights, but walking out on a branch over a forest canopy with no safety net other than a man able to fly…it made her a little nervous.

Finally she took a step out and allowed him to lead her the rest of the way. She ignored the rush to her head that made her feel as though the entire world was dropping out from under her and instead held on to his hand and looked out.

The gray was starting to fade ever so slightly, giving way to a soft pink that lit up the clouds. In the distance, she could see the faintest of outlines forming high above the land, curious curves and summits peeking out from far below the sky. The mountains matched those she saw in her dream, but these were defined, real, able to touch and be touched.

When the sound of creaking tree limbs, rushing water, and a jumble of voices drifted in on a light breeze, Arianna turned to the man at her side. He was staring out at the vastness before them, a small, satisfied smile playing at the corners of his mouth. His eyes were an intense green, dark and determined, waiting for something to happen.

"What's going on?" Arianna asked when he shifted slightly, almost anxiously. He drew them both down to their knees to watch.

"It's waking up."

"What is?"

"The Never." He turned those steely eyes to her now, and she felt the gaze penetrate her, wrap her in a tight embrace. "It wakes for me, always for me. It wakes for you, for your return. It wakes for us, and our reunion."

He spoke of the land as its own being, and the more he did, the more that land responded. It stirred with his words, stretching and breathing, coming alive in the joy of his presence. Trees arched, the earth rolled, colors in the sky deepening before softening back into their pale hues.

"Do you remember this place?" he asked, gesturing with his free hand. He pointed to the right, where an open meadow gave way to an ice-peaked mountain range. "There, the Starlight Range. We used to play games in the meadow and race each other through the mountains until the sun could no longer light our paths. And there, the Gilded River, where we chased fish and built rafts that lasted but moments on the rapids. And over there, the lagoon that the sea creatures call home."

"Misty Marsh," Arianna whispered, creeping closer to the edge of the limb as the land came more into view. "Its name defies its very being, neither marsh nor misty, for the land where the sea creatures dwell is for those who see only in the darkest of clear waters."

Her wild-haired companion smiled, eyes shining in the rising sun. "You remember."

"Some of it." Memories were coming back in pieces, snippets of places she once knew, people she once cherished, before others intruded on her fantasies to tell her what was real, what wasn't. "I don't…I can't remember everything. It's like viewing the land through a veil, with so much still hidden from me."

Arianna didn't notice when he rose to his feet, shaken from her trance only when he pulled her to her feet."Come," he whispered, gently pulling her out on the branch.

"Where? Out there? I can't."

"I won't let you fall," he promised again. "I will always catch you."

"How?" Arianna kept to the center of the limb as they walked farther out. "How are you doing this? How is this possible?"

"I am The Never. The Never is me."

The repeated riddle failed to satisfy her curiosity. She kept her eyes on the landscape slowly revealing itself as she said, "You share the same name. That could get confusing."

"Then give me a name."

Arianna did turn her attention at that. "You don't have a name?"

"I did once, a long time ago."

"What happened to it?"

"It was forgotten, as was I." He stared out at the vastness before them. "Now you must give me a new one."

A curious smile crossed her face. "Any name?"

He moved closer to her, so close that she could smell the ocean on his skin. "The name that calls to you, that you call to."

There was something hungry in his response, and yet, playful enough that she grinned. "I'll think about it, and let you know."

The man to be named took hold of her arm and twirled her into him, pressing her against his chest. "You think, Arianna of the Stars. I'll fly."

Tipping them both sideways, he sent them tumbling over the edge.

THE FALL WAS fast, controlled, until they landed softly at the base of a tree. Finding her balance after detaching herself from her companion, Arianna craned her neck upward, taking in the gnarled limbs and knotted wood, the trunk so wide it would take at least ten of her to wrap her arms around its base. Her fingers traced over images carved into the tree, dogs and birds and creatures she didn't recognize, along with names - Kiddo, Snaps, Jimbo, Jokesy - that tugged at the corners of her mind.

She walked slowly around the tree, taking in the carvings, feeling the smooth, dark green leaves brush against her shoulders. The wind carried with it the scents of the land, jasmine and grass, innocence and youth, the smell of a land full of life. There was playfulness in the branches, she noted as she looked up. Small animals leapt from branch to branch, chittering to one another excitedly. Some dared to crawl down just out of arm's reach, observing the woman curiously. Arianna only stared right back, offering her new woodland friends a smile before moving on. The ground was soft beneath her bare feet, grass that felt like mashed potatoes, dirt cool like a fall morning, flowers that swept past her ankles like clouds.

Her airborne guide hung back and watched Arianna take it all in —the sights, the smells, the surroundings. He waited while she remembered, allowing her the time she needed to reconnect, rediscover who she was. When she had reached her starting point at the base of the tree, he stepped forward.

"You know where we are." It wasn't a question, and the subtle command to recall this place, this tree, had Arianna frowning.

"I…I do," she affirmed, reaching out and placing her palm on the trunk, her hand fitting over a carving that fit her own hand perfectly. She pressed down. "This is—"

She didn't get to finish her sentence. The wood moved beneath her hand, the trunk opening up, the ground shifting enough to throw her off-balance. He grabbed for her before she could fall but reached out too late, succeeding only in sending them both sliding downward into darkness. The passageway closed behind them, taking away any light to guide them in their fall, which, Arianna discovered as she bit back a scream, wasn't a fall at all.

They were sliding, taking twists and turns around what she could only guess were roots. In the darkness she saw only blurs of clay walls, though she slid on smooth wood arcing down at a steep angle. She couldn't gauge how fast she was falling, but, after a while, she started to enjoy the ride and laughed.

Arianna saw a dim light up ahead, but didn't have time to process her surroundings before the wooden slide dropped out from under her and she fell to the ground. She felt strong arms wrap around her in the air, cushioning her fall as he landed on his back, her strong and ever-present guardian keeping her form harm.

For a moment she simply lay in place, catching her breath. Only then did she notice that she was lying on top of him, his arms wrapped around her. He was staring up at her with a glint of humor in his eyes, dark auburn hair framing his face in a fiery halo.

"What…you can fly," Arianna breathed out, realizing that her hands were gripping his finely toned arms and not letting go. "Why did you fall?"

He lifted a brow. "I liked the landing." When she merely snorted, he lifted his head so that his forehead was nearly touching her own. "Give me a name, Arianna of the Stars."

Arianna took in a breath, feeling his body mold to her own as she did so. Her mind clouded, thoughts retreating into the corners of her mind as her skin tingled. A name, she managed to think, closing her eyes to get away from that piercing gaze. A name...a name.

John.

Her eyes flashed open then and she rose, turning away from him to free herself from his embrace. "John." She said it quietly to herself, but the grimace on his face told her that he'd heard.

"I don't think that name suits me. Besides, another has already claimed it."

"I know. I just, I…I need to think a minute."

He watched her from the ground, eyes never leaving her as she paced. "Think of the earth, and the home we made in it. Think of the days we spent here, playing our games, believing in magic."

"What? No. I was thinking about…" her voice trailed off when she looked around and realized what he was saying. A home within the earth, the place where they once played their games. She felt another shift in her mind, a memory clicking into place. Boys settling down after a day of energetic outings, telling bedtime stories to the little ones and singing songs to those too wound up to rest.

"You slept over there." She pointed above her head, where a hammock made of rope and vine swung from between two exposed roots. The hammock was old and fragile, not having been used in years. "I slept over there." She pointed again at a groove carved out of the earth where a mattress rested. "And the others…Where are they?"

He rose to his feet at the question, one fluid movement. "They have gone away. Others have taken their place. They wait for you."

"Where?" Her brow furrowed when he extended his hand. Arianna looked down to see a dagger in his palm, the blade as long as her forearm, the sheath and belt a menacing red. "What is that for?"

"Much has changed since you last dreamed in The Never. Much has stayed the same. Just as I vowed to always keep you safe when we were children, so too do I promise now." He reached out and wrapped the belt around her waist so that the knife rested against her hip. "So that you are always armed, and always ready to face what dangers lurk in the shadows." His face brightened then, a drastic shift in expressions. "But for now, we play."

The whirlwind of thoughts and emotions confused her, unsettled her. Arianna planted her feet when he attempted to drag her off again, needing a moment to collect herself. "No," she stated, pleased that her voice didn't waver. "You have taken me from place to place, messing up my mind with all your flying acrobats and words with hidden meanings and references to memories that I'm supposed to have. You want me to play? Tell me what I want to know."

He let go of her hand but stepped closer, not allowing her an escape. Arianna set her jaw and held her head high, staring him down when he gave her that captivating look. He didn't touch her, but she felt the heat of his presence burning against her skin. "And what do you wish to know?"

"Where are we?"

"The Never. The land we dreamed of as children."

"What does that mean?"

"You know what it means." He lifted a hand, pressed a finger against her forehead ever so gently. "You know who you are, where you are. You need only look inside yourself."

She brushed his hand aside. "You were young. You were a child, always a child. You said…" She struggled to remember those days, his visits at night, their adventures. "You said our youth was our savior. What happened?"

His eyes darkened, but in anger or sadness Arianna couldn't tell. "Some stories are not yet ready to be told, Arianna. Ours is only beginning."

Arianna stepped back again. "One more question. Why do you need me to give you a name?"

He smiled at that, almost a leer. "You are my creator, my destroyer. You are my everything and my nothing. You are my heart, and the arrow that pierces it. Only you can give a name to that which you desire."

"Maybe I don't desire you." His sudden laugh surprised her, challenged her, intrigued her. "You think you're smooth, and dark, and mysterious. Prove it."

He locked an arm around her waist. "I will prove nothing to you. But I will show you who you used to be. I will teach you to fly and to live. I will awaken that which now slumbers. And then, you will remember my name."

Give Me a Name

HE BROUGHT THEM to the edge of a forest, setting Arianna down in a meadow filled with bright orange and yellow flowers. She didn't let go of his hand when he started for the forest, but held him back.

"Where are we?" she asked, this place not familiar to her. The trees were a mix of colors, thin and twisting trunks of ashy green arching up toward the sky, short and squat trees no higher than her shoulders sitting proudly amongst bursts of verdant shrubbery. Branches arced out in circles and spirals, covering the canopy in layer upon layer of teardrop-shaped leaves that sparkled with silvery accents. The ground was soft, nary a twig or thorn in sight, and the air was sweet, an enchanting mix of fruits and ocean air and florals.

This was not a dark forest, but something else, some place inviting and enchanting and yet…unnatural.

"I have never been here before," Arianna said as she took a step closer, peering into the forest curiously. "This place…it's not in my memories."

"We never traveled here, to the Fae Forest."

She turned her attention to the nameless figure. Something about the way he was standing was familiar to her, so confident and cocky, so boyish and charming. But still, she had only snippets of who he once was, who *she* once was. "Why not?"

"Our adventures were with others, but never the fae."

"Then why did you bring me here now?"

"It is time you discovered who you are, Arianna of the Stars. Who better to unveil your very self than the ones who see life for what it truly means? Come." He led her into the forest just as the sun, bright and pinkish-orange, slipped below the horizon. The sky filled with purple and crimson clouds that drifted in a light breeze.

It was dark in the forest, light cloaked by the thick canopy, but he led her without hesitation, guiding her over logs, around rocks, playfully skirting around wide trees until he almost appeared to be dancing. Arianna laughed as she watched him, his body a moving shadow against the woodland backdrop.

Further into the thicket he led her with his dance, circling about her, hands trailing across her back, shoulders, stomach as he passed. She felt his breath on her neck, saw his eyes flash, heard the music that accompanied his grace.

She didn't question that music, its source or its meaning. Instead she only watched him, this strange figure with strange songs, wanting to know more, to feel what he felt in the forest of the fae. When he gave her that impish grin and gestured for her to follow, Arianna abandoned caution and raced after him.

Through forest and wood, around tree and bush, the duo played. Their laughter rang throughout the land, awakening the ones who dwelled within the trees, calling to the kindred spirits. Arianna saw only her playful target as she ran, ducking behind trees, running when he found her, squirming ever so slightly when he finally caught her around the waist. She let him pull her closer, feeling the rise and fall of his chest against her back.

"Look," he whispered against her ear, and she did.

All around them, the world was stirring. As the moon rose, the forest came alive, glittering silver glistening like veins on the plants, shimmering stars twinkling in the canopy.

Not stars, Arianna realized in wonder as the specks of light came closer, but hundreds of tiny winged creatures no larger than her hand glowing brightly from the inside out. Their thin, pale bodies were wrapped in coverings made of grass and leaves atop soft fabrics, much like what her wingless guide wore himself. Their strange clothing covered only what was essential, though for some, nothing at all. Golden hair glowed in the silvery atmosphere, translucent wings reflecting all the colors of the forest.

Arianna watched through wide eyes as the forest lit up, twinklings of bells and flutes sounding all around them. She breathed out in awe, lips curling into a smile of childlike wonder as the faeries twirled and danced in the air, gesturing for them to do the same.

"They have invited us to dance," her unnamed friend said, his arms tightening around her. "You must never reject an invitation from the Fae."

"I don't know how to dance," Arianna protested, awkwardness filling her limbs when she turned to face him. "Look at them. They are pure grace and elegance. They can dance upon the earth and air. You can ride the winds. I have no place in their celebrations."

He ran a hand down her hair, tucking a strand behind her ear. "There is always a place for you here, Arianna of the Stars." He backed up, pulling her into a small clearing carved out of the woodland. The area was decorated with thick vines wrapped around posts, flowers sprouting from logs crafted into benches, a silk-thin canopy covering the clearing and sparkling with hundreds of tiny lights.

Before she could ask why the benches were life size, or why the canopy was so high, some of those flickering pearl-colored lights burned brighter, bigger, until floating in the air were creatures of her own height.

"They can grow?" she asked her companion, who had taken the hand of a beautiful iridescent faerie to kiss her fingers. The faerie wore a sheer silken gown that left little to the imagination, her limbs long and lithe, her white-gold hair as smooth and porcelain as her face.

"Only in the Fae Forest, and only those who have learned how," he answered, his eyes never leaving the faerie. They shared a look so intense that Arianna could only guess they were having a conversation in ways she did not yet understand. And, despite herself, she felt a twinge of jealousy streak through her.

"Do you still want that dance?" She hoped her voice was light, and struggled not to square her shoulders when he turned to her, his hand slipping from the faerie's.

"Always." His own voice was deep and rough with the promise of the impending dance. He took her by the waist with one hand, positioning her arms around him with the other, then spun her in a circle. Arianna nearly giggled as the lights spun and music filled her thoughts. She had never been much of a dancer, but now found herself moving in rhythm with him, footsteps graceful, ballroom twirls seamless as he spun her, pulled her back, wrapped an arm around her and dipped her so close to the earth that her hair grazed the grass.

Soon all she saw was him, all she felt was heat, all she heard was the sound of their joined breathing. All around them faeries danced, some alone, some in pairs. They spun high in the trees, low on the ground, surrounding the pair in a blaze of white light that draped them in showers of color.

He tightened his hold on Arianna, the music slowing with him as he lifted a hand, brushed a finger down her cheek. She followed the movement, her head curving into the palm of his hand, eyes closed. "What makes you happy, Arianna of the Stars? What makes your heart take flight?"

"Why?" she asked. "Are you going to give me wings?"

"No," he answered softly against her ear. "I am going to give you a reason to fly."

Arianna sighed lightly, lost in the sway of the dance. "Adventure," she whispered, the hint of a smile playing at the corners of her mouth. "Art. Daydreaming and imagination. Believing in the impossible, and embracing the impractical."

"Will you believe in me, my Arianna? Will you embrace who and what I am?"

She opened her eyes at that, noting the worry in his brow, the truth in his gaze. He wanted, needed, her to say yes. The innocence in his need charmed her.

"With everything that I am," she answered. When he smiled and cast his eyes downward, she followed his gaze. A moment of panic struck when she saw that they were no longer on the ground, their feet dangling above the earth, having taken flight in their dance. Her hands grasped at his shoulders as she clung to him, her panic softening ever so slightly when he chuckled.

"You need not fear, my Arianna. Embrace your happiness and take flight." His hold on her loosened, just enough so that she realized she floated on her own, powered by her own self. Still she held on to him, lest she lose what made her take flight.

"Don't let me fall."

"Never," he promised. When she smiled, he leaned in closer.

"Never," she repeated. There was humor in the word, but none in his own when he spoke next.

"Give me a name, Arianna of the Stars," he whispered, lips hovering just above her own. "Make me more than that which I can never be."

And with the silvery trees embracing them, the sparkling lights encasing them, the dance of faeries surrounding them, he ignited a new dance.

His lips met hers, a soft kiss to warm the senses, a wanting kiss to beg for more, a passionate kiss to spark desire. Arianna let him take what he sought, the dance of lip and tongue and tooth burning through her, a memory taking hold in her mind, a child on the brink of maturity, not yet ready to want, but not able to help wanting.

"Malachi," Arianna whispered against his lips, feeling his hands fisting in her tangled hair. "Malachi of The Never."

He followed her words with another kiss. "And so I am yours, Arianna of the Stars. Never to forget, never to leave. Always to love."

Love.

The word seared through Arianna's thoughts, snapping her out of her daze. In an instant she was lost, fighting memory and truth, the internal battle sending her crashing to the earth. The newly named Malachi caught her before she hit the ground.

"My Arianna, what—"

"No." She pushed him away, crawling out of his arms. Her breath was heavy, lips tingling, as she rose unsteadily to her feet. If the faeries noticed the disruption in their dance, they didn't acknowledge it and instead continued with their celebration of the night. The movement that once captivated and entranced Arianna now made her dizzy.

"No," she said again, holding out a hand when Malachi stepped closer. Her mind raced, guilt seeping into consciousness as she struggled to hold on to an image, a name. "I…John. *John.* What am I doing? I need to go home."

"You are home."

There was no urgency in his voice, no anger. Simply a stated truth that had her shaking her head. "No. This, this isn't…"

"You would go back to him? Tell me, my Arianna, does your heart truly lie with him?"

Arianna moved back a step, a hand to her head. "Please don't be angry with me. I must go home."

Malachi grasped her arm. "You cannot leave, Arianna of the Stars. Not when you have finally remembered—"

"But I *don't* remember!" she cried, the shout finally disrupting the dance. The lights skittered and flashed, scattering about the forest and leaving them in near darkness. Her fear, anger, confusion, spread throughout the clearing, silencing those at play. "I only have pieces. Pieces of you, of me, of this place. I can't get it to all come together!" She saw the hurt in his eyes, hated that she put it there. "I need time, Malachi. You're asking me to remember an entire childhood of memories and put all the pieces together for us as we are now. I can't do that all at once."

Frustrated, Arianna stepped back and fought the urge to pace. "I'm asking you, Malachi. Please take me home."

Dream of Memories

JOHN ENTERED HIS cozy cabin home with a wide smile, eager to surprise his fiancée. The house was silent, but that didn't concern him. Arianna was quiet by nature. She rarely listened to the radio, and watched TV even less, preferring the solitude of her own mind instead.

"Ari?" he called out, clutching a bouquet of flowers in front of him. "I'm home early!"

He checked her studio, seeing only half-finished paintings and her usual clutter of brushes and paints. The bedroom and kitchen were equally empty. Not concerned, and knowing of her love for long walks outside, John ventured onto the back deck. He stopped short when he saw the newly fashioned run, and heard Lily scraping at the sides at the sound of his footsteps.

'What are you doing in there, girl?" he asked, opening up the side door and hooking on the leash that was hanging on the wall. Lily bounded out of the run, licking at his hands and wriggling as he pet her head. "What's your momma been up to out here?" He was impressed by the run, but not surprised. Arianna was crafty, and quick when she wanted to be.

John glanced around, searching the woods for movement. "Ari?" he called out again, letting the pup run around as far as her leash would allow. "Arianna!" Worry crept up in his gut when he saw her flip-flops at the edge of the clearing, looking as though they had been kicked off rather than gently left behind.

He began his search with a racing heart, cell phone in hand should he have to call for help. It was like Arianna to go on walks, but not like her to stay out of range from the cabin. Lily led the way, sniffing the ground and then the air, though he didn't know if she was playing or searching. Together they circled the cabin, then broadened their search.

"Shit," he muttered after the fourth pass, regretting allowing Arianna to talk him out of making her get her own cell phone. She wouldn't have left the cabin without leaving a note, as she always left behind information on her whereabouts whether he was in town or not. Such steps were a necessity due to her medication. That meant she was here, in the woods…somewhere.

There was one place he could look, deep in the woods where a lake was tucked nicely into the trees, where Arianna used to go when her paintings were frustrating her. She hadn't traveled there in a long while, after his stern lecture on the dangers of wandering through the woods without a cut path and without any type of safety weapon. He headed there quickly, not letting Lily stop to sniff or explore as they hurried down the overgrown path.

Rounding a corner, John's breath caught in his throat when he saw her laying on the ground just an arm's reach from the lake shore. He rushed to her side, dropping down to his knees as he gently touched her shoulder.

"Arianna? Ari, wake up." He shooed Lily away when she pounced on Arianna, but the puppy surged right back, licking the sleeping woman's cheek until she stirred. "Hey, Ari." John took his fiancée by the shoulder and shook her gently until her eyes opened.

Arianna blinked, brow furrowing. "John?"

He helped her to a sitting position, brushing dirt off her arms and back. "What the hell are you doing out here?"

"I was…" Arianna glanced around, getting her bearings. She saw the lake, the familiar woods, Lily nuzzling at her hands. What was she doing out here? She searched her mind for the answer. The last thing she remembered was dancing with Malachi. The lights, the faeries, the kiss.

Her lips tingled at the memory. Arianna fought the urge to run her fingers over them, and instead pushed the recollection from her mind before guilt could set in. She didn't remember what happened after the kiss and asking to go home. Somehow Malachi had brought her here, left her here.

"I was just taking a walk," she answered after a moment. "I laid down to rest and must have fallen asleep."

"Why didn't you take Lily with you?"

"I…I didn't think I'd be gone long." She hated how easily the lie came to her. "I just needed a walk to clear my mind. Painting frustrations, you know."

He did know, just as he knew Arianna wasn't telling the entire truth. Her feet were filthy, face smudged with dirt, hair tangled. She'd been "taking a walk" for longer than she was letting on. "Well, let's get back to the house. When I came back early I didn't expect to have my fiancée about give me a panic attack."

Arianna stared out at the lake. "Early? Why are you back early?"

John shrugged. "We finished the deal sooner than expected. Didn't think we'd get the terms agreed upon in just three days, but the other team was willing to negotiate."

Arianna nodded, then sat up straighter when his words sunk in. Three days. She'd only been gone for less than one…hadn't she?

"You okay?" John asked, concerned.

"Yes, of course. I was just thinking…we should camp out here this weekend, like we used to." Arianna reached out and pet Lily, who was chewing on John's shoelaces. "Spend some time together."

"Sure." John pulled Arianna to her feet and handed her the leash. "Come on, let's get back."

THAT NIGHT, ARIANNA'S dreams took her into the past.

A child sat on the windowsill, peering out into the evening. She was just a girl, shy and reserved, a dreamer who imagined things beyond this world. The night called to her, stars watching her, wind whispering her name.

A figure appeared in that night, a shadow against the sky. He was just a boy, wild and carefree, a playmate looking for a friend. The girl's dreams called to him, her wishes creating him, her smile transforming his view of the world.

It was the stories he loved most, he said, stories of his amazing self, of the brave boys he ran with, of this strange place called Earth he looked at with a grimace. And so she told him those stories until finally there were no more words to tell, only journeys to embark upon.

Together they explored the land he called The Never. Together they played with the sea creatures and pixies, the natives and children. Together they made a home for the ones lost in their dreams, where the imagined came to life, where fantasy was celebrated.

Again and again she went, always with him, always by his side. Again and again they flew, sharing laughs and stories in a land no one of her world could ever know. She liked him because he was different, a boy who loved adventure. He liked her because she was pure, a girl who made him whole.

But others weren't so welcoming, and refused to entertain talk of the boy, of The Never. Appointments were made, ultimatums were issued, worries expressed that the girl did not understand. So many came to help her live in this world properly.

She's got a demon inside her. The pastor.

She is a mentally disturbed child. The shrink.

She has a wonderful imagination. The teacher.

Together their words veiled her dreams. Together their medicine shadowed the light. Together their faith in reality shut out her beliefs in the impossible.

But the memories never left her. There, in the deepest, darkest corners of her mind, lurked The Never.

Adventure.

Danger.

Laughter.

Excitement.

Magic.

In her dreams, Arianna remembered. She remembered the child she once was, the places she once saw, the games she once played. She remembered him, the boy who refused to stop dreaming.

And when she woke, she waited for him to find her again.

Nine

Waiting for the Dreamer

MALACHI DIDN'T COME.

Arianna searched the stars the next three nights, listening for the sound of his voice calling her, the slightest change in the air. But she was alone. So now she sat opposite John, wondering if Malachi was angry, if she should be grateful she was seeing clearly. She still felt the power of the kiss and the shame in enjoying it, even knowing it wasn't real.

"Ari? You with me?"

Arianna shook herself from her thoughts, peering across the table at John. He was smiling over at her, wine glass in hand. "What?"

"You've hardly touched your dinner." He gestured to the plate of pasta. She was a creature of habit and ordered the same meal every time they frequented the restaurant, her favorite place, that rested on the outskirts of town. Tonight her meal went almost entirely untouched.

She forced down a bite of pasta, washing it down with a sip of white wine. "I was just thinking."

"So was I." Suddenly serious, John set down his glass and placed his arms on the table, taking Arianna's hands in his own. "I think it's time we set a date."

"For what?"

"For what?" He laughed. "For our wedding. We're both out of

school. Your art is doing well, I have a good job. What are we waiting for?"

"Oh." Arianna looked down at her engagement ring. The green center stone sparkled up at her, an emerald shaped like a teardrop. She loved her ring, its simplicity and elegance. "When were you thinking?"

John shrugged. "I figured you'd want to get married outside, so winter is out. Maybe springtime, when everything is just starting to bloom and it's not too hot. We could even have the ceremony at home, in the clearing by the woods. There are so many wildflowers and trees."

"And faeries." The quiet words slipped out before she could stop them. He only chuckled at the comment. "You don't believe in faeries?"

"Why would I?"

"Why wouldn't you?"

He knew better than to argue with her over such matters. John relented with a bow of his head. "Your imagination has bested me, my lady. The faeries will join us on our wedding day." To show he wasn't making fun of her, as he guessed she assumed by the look on her face, he quickly added, "Besides, I know a little something of faeries myself."

"What do you mean?"

"My great-grandmother, you know, the one who lived in London? She used to tell stories of faeries and mermaids and all kinds of creatures. They were our bedtime stories when we went to visit."

Arianna smiled, twirling pasta around the fork. The soft overhead lights reflected off the wine glasses, creating a glow that glimmered in her fiancé's blue eyes. "You never told me that."

"I just now remembered. She was an imaginative old lady, that's for sure. She wasn't a fan of the faeries, if I remember correctly. Said they were nasty little things that pulled her hair and called her names. I used to ask her where she saw all these creatures, but she never told me. She said if I was meant to see it, then I would."

His amused grin touched Arianna. She knew he was a family man, but unlike his other loved ones, she'd never met this great-grandmother. His story, and his reaction to it, soothed her nerves. "April."

"April?"

"That's when we'll get married. April."

John smiled again, lifting his glass. "April then, with the flowers and faeries."

They toasted to their future, and to their happiness.

IT TOOK FOUR more days for Arianna to get John and Lily ready for camping. Although she was a homebody at heart, she enjoyed sleeping amongst nature, and the lake always held special meaning for her. It was where John proposed, where she did her best thinking, where they used to spend many nights before life caught up with them.

As they made the hike to the lake with their gear strapped to their backs, Arianna tried not to think about Malachi. It had been over a week since she last saw him, and she now feared he would never return. When John wasn't looking, she hid her medicine, pretending to take it, only to lie when asked. Guilt ate at her, and yet, she felt as though she was seeing the world clearly for the first time since she was a child. Colors were brighter, days were longer, and for once, her mind was focused.

Lily trotted at her side while they walked, sniffing the ground and trees, yapping excitedly at a few lizards that crossed her path. Arianna let her explore the woods, laughing to herself at the puppy's curiosity and enthusiasm. John walked a few steps ahead of her, eager to get to the campsite.

"How about here?" John asked, setting down the tent and chairs at their old site. Arianna agreed with a nod, kneeling down and securing the leash to a post in the ground. She let out the lead a bit to give Lily more freedom to wander.

Arianna prepared dinner while John set up the tent, starting a fire before the sun dipped down below the horizon. It was an ordinary sun, in an ordinary sky, she noted with disappointment.

They ate by the light of the moon, cuddled together beneath a blanket in front of the blazing fire, and later danced to a slow tune under the stars. She liked it there, nestled against his chest, listening to the beating of his heart. Only when the music ended did they part, letting the night guide them into their tent, the last remaining embers of the campfire creating a sensual glow that lit the pathway for an evening of passion.

SHE AWOKE TWO hours later in darkness.

Her heart pounded against her chest, sweat causing her long hair to stick to her neck. What frightened her, she didn't know. But what caused her to awaken, she could only hope.

Arianna gently eased out of the covers, careful not to disturb John, who was snoring lightly beside her. Always a heavy sleeper, he rarely stirred when her insomnia struck.

The night was warm when she stepped outside the tent, bare feet padding across the dirt and grass. She checked the fire, then Lily, finding the puppy chewing on a stick, tail wagging even in this late hour. The pup rose when Arianna approached, pawing at her toes.

"Want to be my chaperone?" Arianna asked, peering around. She had never been afraid of the dark. In fact, she cherished it, loved considering the wonders it held. Now, she searched for a shadow—not just any shadow, but the one that had seemingly forsaken her. Seeing nothing but tree and star, she sighed and turned away from the woods.

Her attention focused on the lake, a sense of wild abandonment filling her. At the shore, she slipped off her silk nightgown and stood nude in the moonlight for a moment before dipping a foot into the water. The cold gave her a shock, enough to take her breath away, but she pushed forward. Lily stayed at the shore, watching her person through wide golden eyes as she strode out into the lake, ripples casting away from her bare body.

Arianna stayed in the moonlight, fearless in her midnight swim. As she floated, eyes tracing the stars, her thoughts strayed.

She remembered The Never in all its glory—and its darkness. Malachi found her that first night frightened and alone, retreated so far into her mind that she was lost, and brought her to the safety that The Never offered. There, she got to be a child again. For so many days she laughed, nary a concern in her mind as they met new creatures, explored new places.

Then came *him*.

The Never wasn't the same after that, when she let herself trust that all people of land were good at heart, and learned that innocence was too easily lost by blind faith. She couldn't see The Never like it was, though she tried hard with each visit only to realize that what she loved most about the land - its innocence untouched by the hands of grown men - had been forsaken. Too much like home, too different from reality, The Never was slowly stolen from her. Even though she hadn't been able to form the words, Malachi understood why and tried to punish the one who brought her harm, but could never get close enough.

Haunted by the memories of what once was, Arianna slipped beneath the lake's surface, relishing the feel of cold water against her entire body. It was safe under the water, a confined world where she neither had to see nor hear the truth. She stayed there for as long as her lungs would allow before drifting back up, brushing water from her eyes.

Arianna stifled a scream, panicked arms splashing water, when she saw the figure hovering just above the lake, hands on his hips, eyes shining in the moonlight. She couldn't read his expression, ever watchful and serious, curious and eager. Suddenly self-conscious, she wrapped an arm around herself while treading water although she knew it was too dark for him to see past the water's surface.

No words passed between them, the only sound coming from his cape that waved in the wind. He watched her swim; she watched him fly until finally he lowered himself, crossing his legs so that he was floating just above the water's surface in a sitting position. Closer now, she saw that he wore clothes much like his last visit, only these were darker and showing more of his sculpted self. A cape was strapped across his chest, a belt at his waist holding a bone-handled knife. His hands, smudged with dirt and small scabbed nicks, rested on his knees.

Annoyed by his silent presence, Arianna lifted a brow. "So, you came back."

"Did I say I would not?"

"It's been over a week."

Malachi shrugged. "Today, yesterday, a week, now. Time makes no matter to me, or to The Never."

She believed him, as much as she didn't want to. Time *was* different in The Never, a land where age didn't exist and clocks never worked. "What do you want now?"

His gaze deepened until she felt herself blushing. "Just you."

Arianna kicked away, putting distance between them. Her eyes narrowed as she treaded water. To her surprise, he followed her, lowering himself into the lake and sliding through black ripples. With every stroke forward, she moved back, circling him, watching him.

"You said we would be young forever," she said, accusation in her voice. "You said we would never stop dreaming."

"You said you would never leave." His tone matched her own as he swam with her, a dance all their own in the night's water.

"Is that why you're here now? To bring me back?"

He made a move toward her but she matched it. Malachi cocked his head to the side, interested in her actions. "I am here to dream with you, Arianna of the Stars. You are the light. You are the dark.

You are the dreamer. Without you, there is no me. Without me, there is no forever."

"Forever is a long promise, Malachi."

"Forever is love. It is the here and now. It is what you make of it, what you wish it to be." This time when he swam forward, she stayed. He moved within inches of her, eyes never leaving her face. "Believe in yourself, my Arianna. Take the adventure. It is only what you make of it, for as long as you wish it to be."

Arianna looked over her shoulder at the shore. Lily was sitting patiently, but warily watching her. The campsite was quiet, John still slumbering heavily. In the morning they would make plans for their wedding, decide menus and décor, dresses and guests. And here was the promise of forever, one more night of freedom.

"One night," she stated. "Then you'll take me home?"

"If you wish it."

"One adventure," Arianna decided. "And then The Never finds a new dreamer."

Malachi nodded once, reaching up and snapping off the cloak. He draped it across her bare back and she wrapped the cloth around her, crisscrossing the straps at her shoulders so that it would hang like a dress when she left the water.

The night stilled, no wind or cricket or breath to be heard. But somewhere in the distance flutes played a low, almost melancholy tune that filled Arianna's thoughts. She allowed Malachi to embrace her, looking up at the stars as he shot them out of the lake and into the sky.

Today, We Battle

HE BROUGHT HER back to the underground treehouse, their old home and playground as children. They took the makeshift slide down together and landed, this time, with more grace. As soon as her feet hit the floor, Arianna heard the excited chatter all around them that signified their arrival.

"You're back!" a mix of voices exclaimed. A rush of bodies flowed past her and gathering around Malachi. Arianna turned as they ran, seeing a group of boys no older than ten or eleven, several as young as perhaps six. They crowded Malachi, some jumping up and down, others spinning in circles. He matched their movements, and it was only when Malachi held up the dagger at his waist that Arianna realized all the children held weapons tightly fisted in their hands.

Malachi laughed as the children, all boys, chattered about their day, sharing stories of battles and adventures as they gestured wildly with their weapons. He listened to them all before finally interrupting to ask, "Boys, why have you not yet introduced yourself to your new friend?"

Their attention turned then to Arianna, the boys seeming surprised by her presence. Some gripped their weapons tighter, others rushed to her side. She knelt down to their level.

"Hello, little one," she said to the smallest of the bunch, with his unruly curls that framed a freckled face. “What’s your name?”

“Little One!” he exclaimed proudly, eyes twinkling at the joke.

Arianna laughed and turned to the skinny child next to him. “Well, aren’t you a slightly little fellow. And you are?”

“Fellow!”

Beginning to understand the game, Arianna accepted a hug from a very solemn, and very round, little boy. “And you must be… Solemn Sam.”

“Solemn Sam I am, ma’am."

She introduced herself to the others in much the same fashion, the boys reveling in their names and dancing around the underground treehouse with their weapons.

There was Caps, who always wore two hats, one forward and one back.

Then came Sandy, the munchkin who always had dirt on his toes.

Next in line were the nearly identical Two, Three, and Four, who insisted there was no such person was One.

With a giggle, Chuckles introduced himself, followed closely by Cowboy, then Shooter, the biggest of the bunch who enjoyed pretending to shoot his enemies.

And finally there came Croc, with a long face and round nose.

There were more boys milling about the treehouse, fourteen total, but these were the ones who surrounded Arianna the closest. She looked up at Malachi. “How long have they been here?”

“As long as they’ve needed to.”

“Why are there only boys?”

“The girls never stay, as you well know.” He looked at her from the corner of his eye. “They could use your guidance.” Malachi stepped forward and the revelry ceased immediately.

“They love you, and fear you.”

“As they should.” Malachi put his hands on his hips, stance firm. “Boys! Are we ready for an adventure?” The resounding cries of approval answered his shout. “Tonight, we have a guest seeking danger! Tonight, we embark on a great battle! Tonight, we play a game with the natives and show them what we're made of!"

As the children gathered their things, Arianna gathered her nerves. "What exactly is this game, Malachi?"

He faced her squarely. "This morning the north natives kidnapped the daughter of the south natives' chief. We are going to get her back."

"I thought you said we were playing a game."

His grin only deepened. "We are."

THEY GATHERED AT the outskirts of the forest, all wearing their finest battle gear. Malachi led the way, strutting to a large rock that overlooked an encampment. He gestured for the others to follow and keep low to the ground. The boys, dressed in loose earth-colored garments with their weapons fisted, eagerly approached. Arianna took the end, holding a knife in one hand and carrying a bow across her back. Malachi had assured her that she once knew how to use it, and was an excellent shot. She vaguely recalled target practice during their childhood games but couldn't quite perfect the movements now.

"What's the plan, Malachi?" Fellow asked, crouching down next to Solemn Sam and Chipper, two boys who contrasted one another in every way but were the best of friends.

"The north natives are keeping the chief's daughter there." He pointed to a small hut in the center of the camp surrounded by spear-tipped gate posts. "We are going to get her back."

"Why can't the other tribe get her back?"

Malachi regarded her almost irritably. "Don't you remember, my Arianna? This is the game. They steal the chief's daughter, and we get her back. It has always been this way. It may be a bit different than you remember, since this tribe came after your final visit to The Never, but the games are just as exciting."

It didn't make sense to her, but she decided to accept it. After all, this was her one night, her one adventure. "Tell us what to do."

Malachi pulled her closer to his side. "You are with me. Fellow and Little One, you skirt off to the east end and draw their attention. Caps, you head off to the west and set fire to their stock hut. The rest of us will attack from the north." He quickly finished outlining the rest of the plan. "And remember, it's every man for himself out here, boys."

They waited for the three fighters to make their way to the battle stations. Arianna watched them for as long as she could, and when they finally disappeared in the trees, she turned back to Malachi.

"What's her name?"

"Whose name?"

"The chief's daughter," Arianna said, exasperated. "Did I know her?"

"No. She came after your final visit to The Never." He started to say something else, but was interrupted by a shout. Malachi peeked out over the rock to see smoke rising from the west side of the village. Tribesmen were racing to the hut, yelling to one another and gathering together to start a search for the intruder.

"Shoot true, Arianna of the Stars," Malachi said with a wink, then leapt out from his hiding place.

CHAOS SURROUNDED HER. Chaos filled her.

Chaos excited her.

Arianna raced into the village, only steps behind Malachi. Instinct took over, the part of her that remembered this race, this game, leading her headfirst into battle. Together they led the boys into the camp. The wind rushed past her ears, the stars lighting her path, energy surging through her with each footstep and breath.

A native appeared in front of her, spear raised as he shouted at her in a language she didn't understand. Arianna dodged his attack but used his momentum against him, slinging him to the ground with ease. The man grunted as he hit the earth, and again when her foot connected with his back as she ran over him.

Into the battle she rushed, her body reacting with each attack, knowing what to do and responding accordingly. She arched backward when a spear was stabbed at her throat, then grabbed an arrow and sent it into her attacker's arm. A grim smile crossed her face when he howled in pain.

Bare feet raced over mud and burning embers, never feeling pain as adrenaline took over. Arianna ducked beneath a dislodged log from the stockhouse, with its flames reaching up toward the night sky, and leapt over a fallen native, somewhat surprised to see a dagger sticking out of his back.

The sight and scent of blood had her hesitating. She'd expected some amount of fighting and had, indeed, been the cause of another's injury, but this man was dead. Arianna paused and looked around, taking in the fighting scene by scene.

She saw Solemn Sam scowling as he rolled away from a native boy about his age. They were engaged in an intriguing game of cat and mouse.

She saw Shooter mimicking gunfire with his hand, and Cowboy throwing knives with each fake bang. The blades were thrown true and always found their mark.

She saw Fellow locked in battle with a native twice his size, kicking the man's shins and biting his wrists, even though the experienced fighter only looked on in amusement.

All around them smoke billowed and suffocated; fires burned and scorched; villagers screamed and raced for safety, and the intruders laughed gleefully as they trampled over destroyed homes and crops.

"Arianna!"

She heard her name shouted from behind, and turned to see Malachi pointing as he raced toward her. She followed the direction of his finger to see Little One in the clutches of a tribesman. Dread rose in her stomach, curdling sourly when the man lifted a knife.

"Arianna! Shoot him!"

"What?" she yelled back, surprise causing her voice to break. "You can't be serious!"

He reached her then and grabbed her by the arm. "Shoot him!"

"Malachi, it's just a game! No one was supposed to her hurt!"

"The game has somehow changed, my Arianna." Malachi spun her around, shoving an arrow into her hand. But it was too late.

The world around her ceased to be as Arianna took in the sight, the fallen child and the warrior standing over him, grinning. The knife in his hand dripped red, the body at his feet lifeless. Her eyes shifted then to the burning hut, watching black smoke twist and tumble up into decomposing clouds. The wind stilled and the air thickened, shouts and cries and snarls surrounding her. Fellow, still fighting the man twice his size, now bared a face mixed with fear and horror. The chief's daughter cried out in pain. Malachi took a knife to the shoulder, stumbling to his knees.

Yes, the game had changed. This was no longer a fun battle between amiable enemies. This was a fight to the death. The scent of war and blood consumed her, overtaking her worries about the children's safety, shoving aside fear of injury or death.

Like second nature, she nocked the arrow, aimed, and let it fly. The arrow buried itself deep in the chest of the man who stood over Little One. Not allowing herself a moment to accept what she'd done, Arianna released another arrow and saved Fellow from his almost certain demise.

As she struck, so too did Malachi and the boys. Warrior after warrior they took down, dirt and blood and soot smudging their cheeks, glee filling their eyes as they bled. They took the village for themselves until the prisoner was in Malachi's arms and the natives accepted their loss, retreating to the forest to lick their wounds.

"Victory is ours, boys!" Malachi shouted, lifting an arm in triumph. The moonlight glinted off his knife, casting the victors in a white glow. When the light struck them, the boys celebrated with howls and crows, stomping their feet as they cheered. Malachi matched their crow, throwing back his head so that his voice traveled to the treetops.

"To the south, boys!" he cried, then took for the sky with the formerly imprisoned woman clutched to his chest.

Eleven

How Things Have Changed

ARIANNA TOOK THE lead, at times walking, other times racing the boys through the woods until they reached the north village. They broke through the encampment line shoving and playing with one another until finally stumbling to a stop.

A bonfire reached toward the star-filled sky, stacked high with wood. The smell of cooking meat permeated the air, and only then did Arianna realize how hungry she was. She accepted the plate of food placed in her hands, using her fingers to eat just as the children did. Only when Malachi approached did she pause to breathe and wipe her mouth with the back of her hand.

"We have been welcomed for the night," he told her. "The chief thanks us for saving his daughter and offers us this meal and this night to commemorate our bravery."

Arianna offered him a bite of meat. He accepted, leaning down and taking the piece with his teeth, lips lingering on her finger. "Well then, let us commemorate ourselves and celebrate the lives that were lost as though they still live among us."

Malachi took the plate from her hands and set it on a rock, then swept her toward the fire. There, the boys were reenacting their battle, thrusting knives into empty air and faking injury when a pretend weapon pierced their skin. The tribesman laughed and cheered, clapping with each victory and feigning fear at each wound. Arianna and

Malachi joined them, hoisting the smallest of the boys onto their shoulders and leading them in a dance around the flames.

Their feet beat to the rhythm of the drums, movements both graceful and uncoordinated as they stepped around one another and sent their crows of self-triumph into the bonfire. Arianna let the sound of celebration consume her, closing her eyes as she danced, holding tight to Fellow, who still rode atop her shoulders.

For a moment she forgot who and where she was and instead allowed the sensation of such abandonment fuel her, guide her. No one knew how long they danced, only that it was a well-deserved party to celebrate their bravery. When she opened her eyes again, she saw that Malachi had left the circle and was standing in the shadows, head bent down as he spoke with the chief's daughter.

Arianna watched them converse as she slowed, gently sliding Fellow off her shoulders and sending him to play with the others. She frowned when the chief's daughter, an attractive young woman with sleek black hair, seductive black eyes, and a perfectly curvy figure, traced a finger down Malachi's arm and sent a knowing smile in his direction. Malachi returned the grin all too willingly.

A flutter of jealousy announced itself in Arianna's gut when he leaned over and kissed her lightly on the cheek, but that flicker of unjustified anger was quickly extinguished when she heard the chief call out to the village. Her breath caught in her throat when she saw that he held the body of Little One in his arms. The battle came rushing back to her, and shame filled her heart when she realized that, in the excitement of their revelry, in feeling so invincible in the face of her enemies, she had forgotten about the loss of their youngest warrior.

The chief began to speak in a tongue Arianna didn't understand, but the others seemed to. He gestured about, the boys nodding with tears in their eyes and the adults looking on solemnly.

"He says we must give him a proper burial."

Arianna glanced over at Malachi as he approached her side. "We should have protected him."

"Little One understood the dangers of the game."

"He was a child, Malachi. He understood only that we were going to have fun. You can't have expected him to have known he might die. *I* didn't even know that. Our games were never like this as kids. We fought, and we bled, but we *never* killed." Arianna still couldn't grasp that fact. Had The Never changed so much since she was little that it had turned its inhabitants into murderers? "We should have protected him," she repeated as the chief placed the body in a small coffin made of thatched leaves and branches.

"We will protect the others."

"We?" She spared him another look. "You and the chief's daughter, I assume?"

She left him standing there alone, confusion and a hint of irritation in his frown. She needed to get away from the scene. The sight of the child's funeral, the knowledge that she could have prevented his death had she not of hesitated, weighed too heavily on her soul.

Arianna pushed through the forest, not knowing where she was going, keeping her knife in hand should she come across an unwelcome visitor. She pressed forward until the sounds of the village were no longer overcoming her senses. Eventually she stumbled into a small clearing filled with wildflowers lit up in the moonlight. With a sigh, Arianna lowered herself to the richly colored ground and fell back, crossing her arms at her stomach and staring up at the sky.

She wanted to say the sky was beautiful, with clouds that welcomed her warmly and twinkling stars that brightened her spirits. The truth, however, was that she felt cold and despondent beneath a changed sky, one that laughed at her trials and tribulations. More than just their battles had changed.

Arianna of the Stars, he called her. As though that meant something, or *should* have meant something to her.

Her first visit to The Never when she was but a little girl had seen a fierce fight, the enemies' faces painted like tigers and their bodies lithe to stalk through the forest like the beast they worshipped. Arianna clung to Malachi that night, her hand never leaving his, eyes wide as they took in the new world around her. The boys, different boys back then, were brave, never letting fear fill their hearts and instead chasing down the enemy until they saw only their retreating backs.

Her second visit introduced a new kind of danger, not native or beast, but found at sea. A ship that was neither welcoming nor reclusive, a captain who was neither jolly nor vile—Arianna was fascinated by this new development in the creation of her world. Malachi showed her how to rile up the pirates and bring them into battle, and how to fight sword to sword simply to feel the thrill of metal sparking in the air.

Games were fun back then, when she didn't have as many worries and didn't understand the dangers of such freedom. Getting hurt was never a thought in her mind, and so she simply didn't. She merely returned home with grand stories that no one believed, with no evidence except her memories and the truth buried deep in her heart of what she witnessed. But now, reality was a hard thing to forget and she was beginning to wonder if she needed to do just that —forget.

But she wasn't sure what, exactly, she should be forgetting.

"You are angry with me."

The disturbance in the night's silence startled her. Arianna twitched at the sound but didn't turn her head as Malachi landed softly on the grass at her feet. He sat down next to her, stretching his legs out and leaning back on his hands. "Have I done something to offend you, my Arianna?"

She rolled her eyes. "You asked me to come here, Malachi. You asked me for this…this adventure, as you called it. Maybe I just don't know how it works here in The Never nowadays, with children being killed for sport, but I would have thought you would refrain from your little side dates while I was here." She hated how pathetically jealous she sounded, and was even more annoyed that he didn't understand. Instead he only looked over at her curiously, eyes crinkled with the ghost of a confused grin. "The chief's daughter, Malachi. If you would rather be with her, why am I even here?"

At that, he laughed. "You are jealous, Arianna of the Stars! You never were jealous before."

"You never flirted so openly before."

He forced his smile to a frown, though the corners of his mouth twitched. "I never wanted to before. We were children, Arianna. Things have changed."

"Why? Why have things changed?"

"Because…they must."

Arianna sighed, deciding the chief's daughter wasn't worth the time to argue. "Do you remember when we were little, and we'd have our crazy adventures without a care for the world? We promised each other we'd never grow up and never have to deal with grown-up things… School, love, jobs. We didn't want any of that. We just wanted to have fun, always. What happened?"

He did turn somber at that. "You left me," he answered, casting his eyes downward. "I searched for you every night, at every star, calling your name as loud as I could, until I finally found you. You were in your room drawing a picture of a pirate ship, and you were sad though I do not know why. But I watched you from the window, wondering what had happened and why you were upset, wondering if you had forgotten about me, and just when I was going to knock someone entered the room. You called her Mother, and were happy to see her. She gave you something, to help you sleep, she said, and I remember…you said you hoped you'd dream of The Never again." He pressed his lips together at the memory. Arianna's brow furrowed, her silence encouraging him to continue.

"I knew then that you remembered me and wanted to return, but something was keeping us apart. I kept trying to reach you but you were always too far away and couldn't hear me calling you. So I vowed to wait for you, to watch you and wait for the moment when we could be together again. But then one day you weren't in that room anymore. Someone had taken you away, and I didn't know where." He dared a look at Arianna, who was staring back at him. "It took many years, but I found you, Arianna of the Stars. I will not let you go again."

"You found me," she repeated softly, turning her eyes back to the sky and the bright pearl-white moon. "Watching outside my window, wondering if I had forgotten you. Perhaps I am drawn to you, as all other women seem to be."

"They may be drawn to me, but I am drawn only to you." Malachi slowly lowered himself to his back next to Arianna. "You see only what your fear allows you to see. Now you must let yourself see the truth."

"And what truth is that?"

"That The Never is no longer the place we knew as children. But with your return, we may be able to restore the world we created for ourselves. I have looked forward to The Never's return, as have the ones who wait for you."

"Ones?" Arianna turned her head, a bit startled to see those green eyes so close to her own. A chuckle caught in her throat despite the gravity of the discussion. Malachi was filthy from head to toe, with smoke stains on his cheeks and blood matted in his hair, and she imagined she looked much the same. What amused her, though, was that neither of them cared. "There are others?"

"Of course. The boys, the natives. They have heard stories of your greatness and have long since wished to meet you. Others wish to settle old business, and those I would advise you to stay away from."

"Like who?"

He shrugged as best he could when lying down. "The sea creatures. The pirates. We were a bit…mischievous in our days with them."

Arianna laughed, remembering their games well. Tails pulled, sails let loose, children at play with not a care for being told otherwise. "Perhaps I should visit them and apologize. Start off on new terms."

"No." Malachi gripped her wrist and raised himself to his elbow. "You must promise me, Arianna. You will not go back to Misty Marsh, or to Pirate Port. The Never is not as you once knew it. Old rules and boundaries are not always respected as they once were. Promise me you won't go to the lagoon."

She saw the worry in his eyes. "Okay. I promise I won't go to the lagoon."

Relieved, Malachi lay back down, shoulder to shoulder with Arianna. They watched the stars twinkle and listened to the sounds of the village as the wind carried with it the last of the celebration. When he reached over and took her hand in his, lacing their fingers together, Arianna only smiled and knew that Malachi was hers, and hers alone.

A Woman Gone Missing

WHEN JOHN AWOKE the next morning, he knew instantly that something was wrong.

Arianna had always been a late sleeper, especially on camping trips. The simple fact that she wasn't next to him when the sun rose was cause enough for concern. But more than that, the tent was open, Lily sitting patiently in the opening and watching him sleep. Arianna's side of the tent was undisturbed, the sleeping bag and blanket folded over, her belongings next to her pillow where she'd stored them the night before. Those belongings made him frown, as they served as a reminder that wherever she was, his fiancée wasn't keeping to her promises.

John rose and dressed quickly in loose jeans and an unbuttoned white shirt, stepping out into the cool morning air to scan his surroundings. The campfire was out, all their gear still in place from the night before. Morning sunlight dappled in through the trees, creating golden droplets on the ground as he walked over it barefoot. Lily sauntered at his side, nipping at the ends of his jeans and wriggling with the excitement of exploring new places. Together they approached the lake, staring out at the mist that rose up from the water.

It would have been a peaceful morning had he not of been worried about his missing fiancée and her precarious state of mind. He'd seen the medicine bottle next to their bag when dressing, in the same spot as where he'd packed it, which told him she didn't take her meds the previous night or that morning. He was beginning to suspect she hadn't been taking them for a while now, which would explain her increasing - and lengthening - bouts of daydreaming.

"Ari!" John shouted, starting to pace the shoreline. He wasn't sure if he should be fearful or irritated. For the moment, he decided to be both. "Arianna, this isn't-"

He stopped when he saw the pile of clothes on the ground only a couple feet from the water's edge. "Ari!" John yelled, this time letting that fear take over his call. Lily matched his voice by barking wildly, running around trees and bushes with John, leaping in the lake when he ran in up to his knees.

The two looked everywhere, letting their cries echo throughout the forest, silently praying this was just a nightmare. John's frantic shouts turned into demands to be answered, furious cries of frustration mixed with fear, until Lily could no longer match his panicked rage.

But no matter how loudly he called, Arianna never answered.

LILY SKIRTED THE shore, both nervous and excited as police officers searched. She watched them pace the woods through wide golden eyes, listened to them call to one another and talk on their radios, whined when John held her back from joining them in the lake. When he tied her leash to one of the tent stakes, she simply sat and kept up a determined vigil. Her gaze shifted from the uniformed strangers to her male master and back again, trying to access the situation.

An officer approached John, clutching his hat in his hands. "There's no sign of her yet, sir. We've got officers combing the area here and back closer to your place. No signs of a disturbance or evidence of foul play on land. We have a team coming in to search the lake more thoroughly than we're able to do."

John nodded and swallowed hard. He'd been trying to keep back sheer terror for the better part of the morning, but as the day wore on it was harder and harder to keep his composure. "Do you…um, do you really think they will find anything? I mean, wouldn't we have found her, if…" He couldn't finish the sentence.

The officer nodded, compassion in his frown. "We're just covering all our bases. This is a big area to cover, and considering her mental state-"

"Don't make it sound like she's some crazy person," John cut in, holding up a hand. "Her mental state is none of your concern."

"Begging your pardon, sir, but if she hasn't taken her medication, as you stated you suspect, then it is our concern. We need to know what to expect just as much as you do."

"You should concern yourself with finding her. Not with—"

"John."

John turned at his name, seeing the sheriff approaching. Some of the tension in his shoulders relaxed. "Jason," he greeted the man who had been a close friend for going on twenty years. "Have you found anything?"

"Not yet. The divers just got here and are about to start their search." Jason, a tall and thick man with warm brown eyes and close-cropped blonde hair, gestured to the lake, where a crew was gathering with scuba gear, nets, and a small boat. "They are going to start closer to the south judging by the wind and current from earlier."

"They won't find anything. She's not there. She's fine. She's alive."

Jason regarded his friend, never having seen him this distraught before. "I'm sure she is, but we have to take as many precautions as necessary. But, John…where were you last night?" He held up a hand at John's harsh glare in response. "I have to ask, I'm sorry."

"Are you kidding me? Jason, how could you ask me that?"

"John, we're looking at a missing woman, a pile of clothes by the lake, and a fiancé who is perfectly fine and holding said woman's unopened medicine container. Questions will be asked, if not by me, then by others. Who would you rather have asking the questions?"

He wanted to rage and argue, but after letting his friend's words sink in, couldn't manage an argument. John was a businessman, and a good one at that. He knew how to look at a problem from all sides, how to formulate an argument and determine a solution. At this moment, with these facts, it didn't look good for him.

But the very idea of it, of him doing something to hurt the woman he loved most in this world, was downright insulting.

When Jason simply regarded him with a look that spoke of years of friendship and trust, he knew he had to set aside his pride. John blew out a breath and shoved his hands in his pockets. Lily whimpered at his feet, sensing his apprehension.

"Jason, be honest. Do I need to call an attorney?"

Thirteen

Broken Promises, Broken Bones

THE MOON WAS low, slowly sliding beneath the horizon in preparation for dawn. Arianna watched its leisurely journey across the sky before turning her head to the man sleeping at her side. She allowed herself a moment to observe him, the wildness of his hair not tamed even in sleep, the soft lines of a mature yet still-youthful face, that full mouth always ready for a grin or smirk. She marveled over how innocent he looked when sleeping, knowing that when those green eyes opened, mischief would be waiting for anyone who glanced his way.

They'd talked all night, hands intertwined as they reminisced over the old days. Life had been simpler then in The Never, when they could go wherever they dreamed and be whoever they desired.

Their adventures had been plenty - soaring high in the skies to race among the clouds, battling their pirate enemies on the open seas, racing through the woods with the natives so close on their trail. Every game a child loved most, they made greater, bigger, grander. They laughed, planned great escapades, and promised one another they would never grow up and never do grown-up things.

She'd broken that promise, just as she was about to break another.

Assuring herself that Malachi was deep asleep, Arianna rose and quietly stepped to the center of the clearing. She wasn't planning on breaking her promise entirely - she wouldn't go to the lagoon, but instead to the mouth of it, on the shore - she needed to know the truth. Some truths, she was quickly learning, were better left discovered on one's own.

Closing her eyes, she remembered what Malachi had asked her in the Fae Forest and envisioned those things that made her happy. And, just as easily as she pictured those things, her feet lifted off the ground. Flight was a fascinating sensation, one both familiar and foreign, making her weightless as she hung suspended in the air. It took her a moment to figure out how to control and direct herself, but soon, she was off.

The Never was not too large an island, though large enough to comfortably fit all the creatures that called it home, and so she reached her destination of Misty Marsh within the hour. From her place in the sky Arianna could see the outskirts of the lagoon, starlight reflecting off the dark water. She could hear the rush of the waterfall and the trickle of the Gilded River as it babbled from the lagoon and into the ocean. But she wasn't going to the lagoon; that was her promise to Malachi.

She set foot down on the shore, only steps from the mouth of Misty Marsh. In the night she couldn't see farther than a few feet, shadows and rock outlines in the distance. Arianna half jumped, half flew from one algae-covered rock to the next until she was in the middle of the river, the ocean at her back as she faced the lagoon's inlet. Taking in a deep, nervous breath, she whistled a low, haunting note.

It wasn't long before she saw ripples in the water, ringlets that broadened the closer they got to her narrow rock. When the first one appeared, Arianna squatted down and offered a welcoming smile.

"Hello," she greeted, not at all taken aback by the creature's appearance. The sea creature was a woman, with sleek white hair slicked back from a long forehead. Almond-shaped eyes the color of a snowy sky stared back at her with a mix of malice and mischief, eyes that were pointed to match her small, narrow nose. Her lips were full and tinted with an opal hue, skin so pale it was nearly translucent. The sea woman's long hair pooled around her as she lifted herself from the water just past her bare breasts, and Arianna could see the tip of a pearl-white tail flicking in and out of the water for balance.

Arianna knew that each of these creatures were unique, with their own color that was their defining feature. She remembered that much from her childhood in The Never. But, she didn't recall this particular member of the merfolk.

"My name is Arianna," she said, not able to break her stare with the woman. She could almost swear she heard music playing softly, a haunting humming of flutes. At one point in The Never's history, the merfolk were known for their beautiful songs, songs so lovely that the entire world responded to each note that rung throughout the earth and sky, but she hadn't heard those charming tunes since she arrived.

"You don't know me, but I…I used to come here and play. Malachi and I, we came up with games and songs with the sea creatures. The merfolk, they called themselves then. We didn't always get along, but we had our fun." She was babbling, but couldn't seem to stop. The woman's intense gaze lured her in, encouraging her to speak.

"Malachi told me not to come, said your kind was different now." Arianna leaned closer as the woman rose out of the water just an inch. "I want to know what happened, why our kinds are no longer partners in building The Never. I want to know why I don't hear your songs, why what I hear now speaks of sadness and despair. I want to know why the games have changed between the boys and the natives, why they kill and are killed. I want answers." Her last words were nearly a whisper. The woman of the sea parted her lips ever so slightly, a soft smile forming on her translucent face. She reached out and took Arianna's hand, a promise in that simple gesture.

"I want answers," Arianna whispered again, searching her mind for the reason why Malachi didn't want her here, searching the creature's eyes for the truth behind The Never, and the darkness slowly forming at its core. "I want to know everything."

The darkness deepened around her, the melancholy music of the merfolk entrancing her. Arianna didn't notice when the she-creature's fingers tightened around her wrist, or that she was being gently pulled toward the water. When the woman's eyes narrowed slightly, Arianna could only breathe out in wonder.

"What is it?" she asked. "What do you know?"

She never got her answer. Just as the last question was asked, the creature shifted and jerked, pulling Arianna under the water.

The shock of the cold water forced Arianna from her trance. She kicked at the river, forcing her head above the surface for a gasp of now-bitter night air. Her arms flailed at her sides, searching for something, anything, to hold on to, but the grip on her wrist only tightened. Fear welled in her throat when she realized she was being dragged down by a force far stronger than her own feeble strength, but before she could cry out for help, Arianna was tugged beneath the surface.

Frantic bubbles raced upward, her chest already tightening. She saw nothing but black water all around her, battled the freezing sea as it struck against her like thousands of pin needles against her flesh, heard only low-pitched laughter and the sound of a dozen angry voices accusing her of crimes she did not commit.

She felt their words pierce her skin, their fury taken out on her defenseless body. Slice after slice, crushing hands against bruised bone, jagged teeth biting into tender skin. Her own hands grabbed at what enemies they could find, only to be shoved aside. Her feet kicked at unseen threats, but could not keep her from sinking further into the abyss. The cold sucked away the last of her breath, the smallest of bubbles escaping from behind clenched teeth. Arianna could only pray for help in silent pleas no one could hear.

Her world started to fade then, her struggle lessening as the lightness in her head spread to the rest of her body. It was only in the dream of near-death that she realized the black water had been disrupted, a blur of bodies racing past her as another form grabbed hold of her by the arms. Her eyes barely recognized their surroundings, disrupted by water that blurred the nighttime vision and cleared only enough for Arianna to realize she was no longer beneath the surface. Somewhere in the distance she heard a man snarling and fighting, sounds of a sharpened blade and hissing threats slicing through the air, but his grip on her never faltered.

And then, when she felt safest in the stranger's arms, she allowed herself to sleep.

WHEN SHE FIRST opened her eyes, she thought she was blind.

Arianna panicked, lifting herself to her knees and immediately stumbling. Her breath hitched in her throat as she tore at the binding wrapped around her head, hands shaking and heart pounding as her head struggled to make sense of where it was.

"Easy," a familiar voice said in her ear, calming her.

"Malachi?" Arianna shot out a hand as though to defend herself, fist striking a man's chest. He didn't seem to notice, or at least budge, but she felt his fingers on her scalp, untying the knot of the fabric around her head. "What's going on?"

"Nothing that's not of your own doing."

She heard exasperation and bitterness in his voice, but didn't need to wonder at it. With the panic subsiding, Arianna was starting to feel the pain. All over she hurt, her pride perhaps the most of all. She had deliberately done what he'd asked her not to do and was nearly killed as a result of it. He had every right to be furious, and yet…

"You saved me," she said as he unwrapped the material. When her eyes were clear, she blinked, surprised by the harsh sunlight that contrasted the dark of night that filled her last waking memory. "How did you know where I was?"

Malachi lifted a brow. "I know you, Arianna of the Stars. You always were too curious for your own good. I knew you would go to Misty Marsh eventually and quicker so if I told you not to. I am only glad I got there in time, to save you at least. The rest I was not able to defend you against."

Her brow furrowed at that. Arianna sat up, woozy and unbalanced, to inspect her wounds. It was only then that she realized just why she hurt as much as she did - with good reason. Her arms and hands were littered with nicks and bruises, finger marks wrapped around her wrists and shoulders. Across her chest, from sternum to left collarbone, was a deep gash that someone—Malachi?—had crudely patched with a mixture of mud and leaf. Dried blood had scabbed around the wound.

Her pants, once made of a comfortable cotton-type material blended with sinew, were in shreds, and through those tears she could see the reasons why. Nail marks, bite marks, all covered her, and she felt matching teeth patterns along her jaw as well. Her right eye was tender, her forehead cut, and the back of her head throbbed.

"Why?" she asked quietly, gingerly touching the gash on her chest as she observed the rest of her body.

"The merfolk have become tainted," Malachi answered, squatting on the soft grass across from her. "A darkness has come to The Never, my Arianna. I thought I could shield you from it for as long as possible, let you see only the beauty that is our home in hopes that you would want to stay. I'd hoped that even if you went to Misty Marsh that the merfolk would remember you and perhaps show themselves as they used to be, but now you see the truth of what your years away have brought."

"My years?" She shook her head. "The Never has never answered to me. The Never was always yours. It responded to—"

Arianna's lips parted when she looked up at Malachi, truly saw him. The left side of his face was bruised, his bottom lip scabbed, part of his hair matted with dried blood. His clothes were torn, though not as badly as her own, and his bare feet showed evidence of a battle with teeth - or possibly a fast trek across rock, she mused as she glanced at the rough landscape around them.

"What's the other guy look like?"

Malachi frowned. "I don't understand. They were the sea creatures."

"I know." Arianna waved him off, wincing at the movement. "I was joking, trying to lighten the mood." She sighed when she saw that he didn't appreciate the gesture. "For what it's worth, thank you for saving me. I didn't think...well, I don't know what I thought. I just wanted to know why things were different and didn't expect to be almost murdered."

"I didn't expect to have to rescue you. I had other plans for our morning."

"Like what?"

"It doesn't matter now." Malachi rose and took a few steps away, his back to her. She saw the tension in his shoulders, and did wonder about that.

Arianna followed his gesture, slowly rising to her feet and biting down on her lip at the soreness the movement produced. He stiffened as she approached. "Hey," she said, placing a hand on his arm. "I'm sorry, okay? I never meant for you to get hurt, or me. So just...don't be mad."

"I'm not mad."

"Yeah, right." She huffed and took back her hand. "I know how that one goes, so fine. If you're going to be mad, then be mad. I get it, okay? And I'm sorry. I—"

His lips against hers silenced Arianna. She had barely registered the fact that he'd spun around before he was pressed against her, one hand on her back and the other cupping her face lightly.

Guilt had her shoving Malachi away, an expression of angry hesitation in her eyes; curiosity had her allowing him to take hold of her again, his mouth silencing her protests. There was tenderness in his kiss, but also desperation; she tasted it on his lips, felt it in his breath. The mix of emotions made her crave more, and so she took what she wanted from him.

What was it about Malachi that made her want so deeply, so fiercely? Never before had she felt this fire in her gut, this rush in her head, this ache in her heart. He was the unattainable, the forbidden, and yet, here he was, the savior. Without him she was lost in The Never, a world she no longer recognized. With him, she was lost in her own mind, forgetting the promise she'd made to another.

And still she wanted more.

It was Malachi who pulled away this time, resting his forehead against hers to catch his breath. "I am not mad," he repeated quietly. "You frightened me, my Arianna. I cannot lose you again."

She opened her eyes, seeing honesty in his gaze. "Okay. Then tell me what I need to know, so this doesn't happen again."

Two Worlds at War

HE BROUGHT HER to a ridge overlooking the western ocean, setting her down carefully to avoid further injury. Taking her hand, Malachi gestured to the edge and to their surroundings—Misty Marsh to the east, the native village to the south, their own home tree far off in the distance just peeking out over a mountaintop. Arianna saw nothing out of the ordinary.

The pink-orange sun was high in the sky, lighting the clouds in color. Two suns hung perfectly balanced, one at each end of the dome to watch over the land below.

The sea was a beautiful blue, revealing the ocean floor and all the life it contained. At one time, that sea life had frightened her, but she'd grown accustomed to the scaled and tentacled beasts that roamed the waters.

Trees and grasslands were a verdant green, and the wind carried with it the sweetest of scents. Flowers, fruits, meats roasting over open fires, all met her senses with each breath.

The Never was alive and bountiful.

"It lurks beneath the surface," Malachi cut in, seeing into her thoughts. "It is a crafty darkness, sneaking in while we sleep and taking over our hearts."

Arianna turned to him, puzzled. "What is it?"

"No one knows. Most do not even know it is here."

"Then how do you?"

"Because I left The Never, to find you." He spared her a glance before looking back out over the land. "After you left, I did not bind myself to The Never as I once did. Every time I came back, a little more of our home was changed, and I did not know how to stop it. Trees didn't grow as high, flowers weren't as colorful, the sun not as warm. Our battles with the natives grew more vicious, the pirates became greedier. Everything changed; even the boys became wild."

"The boys were always wild," Arianna huffed. "*We* were wild."

"Not like this," Malachi protested, sounding both despondent and hesitant. "They became indifferent instead of innocent, and no longer cared when one of their own died or disappeared. They played and fought like they always did, but never saw the dangers in their new games…I lost them all, my Arianna, one by one, until new boys came and took their place. Tougher children, but children all the same. And now, they are dying too."

Arianna couldn't respond, didn't know how to. She couldn't imagine the loss of the boys she once loved. Even now, years later, she remembered their faces, their innocent questions, their playful pleas for bedtime stories. They weren't bad children, or naughty, only lost, forever separated from the ones they called mother and father. To watch them disappear, and know not a thing could be done to stop it—just the thought of it brought tears to her eyes. The pain of such memories was written across Malachi's face as well.

"I fought our enemies alone," Malachi continued, "searching for the answer to why these changes were happening, and finally one day an old woman came to see me, a native from a western village that destroyed itself after the darkness came. You may remember her from our days feasting with the chief. She was a frail woman, crippled with age, limbs as gnarled and knotted as her hair. I helped her sit when she came to me, then listened to her speak for an entire day. She had a way about her, much like you did when telling stories, that made you listen without even realizing you were trapped by the stories she painted with her words.

"She told me that darkness had come because the light was gone, a darkness that no one could see and only the chosen could feel. She said this darkness would reign until the stars were lit once more. Two had created this land, but only one could be the dreamer who leads The Never to its rebirth."

Arianna didn't need further explanation. "So that's why you came back for me. To be the dreamer," she concluded. "Not to be with me."

"No." Malachi faced her, hands on her shoulders. "I came back for us, and for The Never. We are three, we are one. We exist as part of ourselves, and each other. The Never does its job by sustaining life and giving us a canvas for our dreams. I do my job by bringing you here, and showing you who you are. Now you must do your job."

"And what is my job?"

"Only you can answer that, Arianna of the Stars." Malachi tucked a strand of hair behind her ears. "But I suggest we start there."

She looked where he pointed, eyes widening when she saw the bow of a ship, carefully carved into the shape of a beautiful, long-haired mermaid, curving around a mountainside and into the channel. There was a small port on the shore where the more nefarious of residents lived in The Never. That port had been home to many of their battles as children, fighting the pirates who wanted to claim The Never as their own.

This ship was familiar, frighteningly so. The curve of the sail, three perfectly straight masts with the mainmast topped with a crow's nest, dark stained wood, a black flag with those threatening skull and crossbones. And the name, scrawled across the side of the ship in blood-red letters. She remembered that name, could still hear it being laughed into her thoughts during her last visit to The Never. The memory merged with visions of the ship sailing after her and Malachi, cannon fire erupting from the ballasts, a shadow watching the war from his cabin windows.

"Is that—"

"Yes."

"Captained by—"

"His son."

Arianna couldn't tear her gaze away from the ship sailing closer into The Never, out of the foreign seas. "His son?"

"The captain is dead." The leer Malachi cast her direction answered her next unasked question. "And now his son seeks his revenge."

Enjoying the sudden rush that flooded through her, remembering what had happened on that ship through no fault of the new captain, Arianna narrowed her eyes. "Then perhaps it's time for vengeance."

JOHN'S LEG SHOOK as he waited for his attorney. He'd been ushered into the office only a few moments ago, and in those moments of silent solitude he'd realized just what could be at stake.

Arianna had been missing for nine days, the only sign of her being the pile of clothes on the bank and a hair tie found floating in the lake. Police had scoured every inch of the woods and even their home, suspicion mounting with each passing hour.

Accusations were yet to be made, but John knew how this game worked. And so did his friend, the sheriff, who had advised him to speak with an attorney before anyone else, especially the media. He'd been approached already by two local news stations and refused comments both times, but that only made those suspicions worse. Despite his better judgment, he read a few articles covering the disappearance of a local artist, words like "mysterious" and "no trace of the woman" and "fiancé allegedly asleep in the camping tent" sticking out like a prison sentence.

So now he was seeking advice, all while fearing that the woman he loved most would never return to him.

He never imagined he'd be in this situation. Ever since he was a child, he'd known he was a family man, having grown up with a mother and father who loved each other dearly, and doted on their son as much as they did one another. They enjoyed being together, being a family, and as a boy, John wanted that same love for himself with the woman he would one day hold dear.

He thought he'd found that love in Arianna. From the moment he first saw her in high school, that instant after classes were over for the day when her green eyes randomly locked on his and saw things within his soul that no one else ever could, John knew she was the one for him. Others spoke of her strange behavior, the way she talked to herself and never really seemed to live in reality, but that only added to her appeal. He loved the way she talked, the way she dreamed, and wanted to be the one she looked for when she did finally root herself in reality.

There were times when he wondered if she wanted the same things, marriage and children, a life away from daydreams. Part of him waited for the day that Arianna would realize her potential and no longer need to sedate herself with medication and even her art; the other part accepted that she was, at heart, a woman with her head forever in the clouds.

Still, he never did wonder about her heart. She was honest, loyal, the kind of woman he'd wanted since he was a child. He often felt secretly frustrated by her lack of drive or desire to rise above that little blue pill, despite having to be the one to constantly remind her to do so for her own protection. But he loved her nonetheless and was heartbroken over her disappearance. He couldn't imagine the "what ifs" that were being wondered about by others and instead chose to believe that wherever she was, whatever she was doing, Arianna was safe.

John jumped to his feet when the office door opened, but he wasn't expecting who stepped through.

"Georgia." His greeting was grateful and welcome. He always enjoyed seeing Arianna's mother, albeit not under such dire circumstances.

Georgia was a tall woman, willowy but strong, elegant but fierce. Her almond-shaped eyes were a somber brown that matched her hair, which was cropped close along her angled jaw. Everything about her was fluid, from the long lines of her body to the flow of her dark green dress. She looked nothing like Arianna except for the dreamy, sometimes doe-eyed stare. Right now, that stare was locked on John, and it wasn't dreamy. Hostility glared back at him, hostility and impure thoughts.

"You were supposed to watch her, and take care of her." Georgia's normally calm tone was harsh. "You know she sometimes forgets to take her medicine. You are her fiancé. You should know when she needs help." Despite her words, she gathered him in a hug, forehead wrinkling as she forced back her tears.

"I'm sorry," John said as he accepted the hug, then took a step back. "I don't know what happened. She was fine, acting completely fine. Then she just…disappeared. And now the police—"

"The police are fools," she cut in, waving her hand. "You would never hurt my Arianna. Everyone knows that."

"Apparently not." Suddenly restless, John started to pace the large office. "Before you came in, I was thinking of when Arianna and I first met, back in high school. She had stayed after school to work on a painting, and I was just leaving practice. We rounded a corner and ran right into each other."

Georgia knew the story, but smiled anyway, allowing John the moment he needed to reflect.

"She didn't even say anything, just stared up at me like realizing for the first time ever that other people existed in the world." John laughed softly, recalling the look on her face, a mix of surprise and annoyance. "She took my breath away, she was so beautiful. But she didn't even seem to notice me."

"But you didn't give up," Georgia put in, matching his smile.

"Arianna often acts like she doesn't remember or notice much, but she came home that day and told me about the annoying guy at school who wouldn't let her pass by without telling her name. And the next day, I'd never seen her so giddy when that annoying guy asked her to go out to lunch with him."

"Really?" John hadn't heard that part before, or any sort of reaction Arianna had to their introduction. "I always figured I just irritated her into going out with me."

Georgia chuckled. "That may have been part of it. But mostly, she was excited that someone actually wanted to talk to her, let alone spend time with her."

John started to reply, but was interrupted by the office door opening a second time. They took their seats when the attorney entered, hands full with a thick file. "Afternoon, John, Georgia," Michael Waters greeted. "It is good to see you both again, although I wish the circumstances were different."

John could only nod. He'd known Waters for years, as had Georgia, though Arianna had never met nor even heard of the man. The attorney was a closely guarded secret, one that was never mentioned in front of her daughter. Their first meeting had been in regards to Arianna's mental health nearly six years ago, and their last had involved discussing turning her care over to John upon their marriage.

There were times when he felt guilty going behind Arianna's back to meet with her mother and attorney, but ultimately he knew it was for her own good. Georgia was right—she did forget to take her medication, and in the past, she'd allowed childhood delusions to overtake her, to the point that her physical health was in danger as well. Georgia lived several states away and couldn't always be there, and so John would be given the power to make important decisions, should the need arise. Waters had nothing to do with her actual medication, but was their safety net should something happen that required one of them to take control.

But this was all assuming Arianna would return home.

"I know last time we had discussed your legal options should Arianna have another episode, and whether or not you would have to make medical decisions on her behalf. But, I think right now we have more important matters at hand," Waters began, placing the file on the desk and taking a seat. "First of all, I'm very sorry for what's happening. It can't be easy knowing she is missing, and it's even harder knowing blame is being shifted."

"You can see it in their eyes," John admitted, running a hand through his hair. "The way the police talk to me, the way people stare at work. They all think I did something to her. And, now that I'm here, they'll just think I have something to hide even more. But I didn't know what else to do."

"You are right to be here. You have to protect yourself first, and not concern yourselves with the opinions of others right now." Waters clutched his hands together, staring at the two intently. "We are going to make two plans. The first, what happens when Arianna comes home. You need to make serious decisions about how to handle her in the event that she refuses to go back on her medication. The second, if Arianna doesn't come home, then my job is to prove your innocence." He held up a hand when John started to cut in. "Everyone here knows you are innocent. Now, we prove it."

Georgia placed a hand on John's arm, comforting him as best she could when her own nerves were already frayed. "Okay, Mr. Waters. Tell us what to do."

Fifteen

Enter the Pirates

THEY WAITED UNTIL nightfall before making their way to Pirate Port. Blending in with the dark, Malachi and Arianna perched on the rooftop of what she guessed was an abandoned schoolhouse, judging by the desks she could see through the broken windows. They pressed themselves against the rotted wood and peered at the activity below.

Drunken men staggered from tavern to bench, bench to concrete, reeking of a day's, or week's, filth. Their clothes were muddy, hair tangled, faces bloated, tones belligerent yet strangely jolly as they fought with one another. Women with dresses two sizes too small stood in doorways and at corners, long locks in curls around painted faces. They smiled sweetly at any man who paid them attention, as their hands slipped into pockets to take what coins they could find.

From the steam-filled alleys came a stench unmatched, nearly palpable in its offensiveness. From the dimly lit buildings came shouts and cheers, a chaotic mess of male voices. From the docks came a pack of burly sailors intent on spending the evening with ale in hand, and those drunken men and sneaky women moved out of the way for them.

This was not a pleasant place where happiness dwelled. This was a pit, a small, secluded world for heathens and blasphemers. The more Arianna watched, the more she was fascinated and repelled by what she saw. The more Malachi watched, the more she realized he longed to race out into the masses and slice into every gullet he passed.

But they remained on the rooftop.

"What are we looking for?" Arianna asked, her voice a whisper.

"Nothing," Malachi answered. "We are waiting." He shifted slightly and gestured to the ship currently docked. "The darkness began spreading through The Never when *they* came back."

"Who? The pirates?"

"They don't call themselves pirates. They call themselves the Sea Killers."

Arianna scoffed. "They can call themselves whatever they want. They're still pirates."

"Call them what you wish, but they are not like the pirates we used to know. Those pirates had a sense of honor, even as they killed. They took part in our games and adhered to the rules of The Never. But these…they don't respect The Never. They abuse our land and take away its magic, stealing it for themselves. They must be stopped."

"How?"

"I don't know," Malachi admitted. "But I know it has to do with their captain. They call him The Hunter. I have never seen him, no one has, but they say he holds a dark magic. That if you look upon him, you will never look away, and will forever be trapped in his seductive embrace."

"Uh-huh." Arianna watched the men marching back and forth from the ship to dock, loading and unloading supplies. They certainly looked the part of hardened pirates, but then, she had fought such men as a child, back when The Never's original pirate captain sailed the waters. If his son was now leader of the ship, then she was in no hurry for a meeting. Games they may have played as kids in this incredible realm, but, as Malachi insisted, The Never was a different place now.

"So what's the plan?"

Malachi gripped his knife. "I'm going to cause a distraction. You're going to scout the ship and see what you can find."

Arianna grabbed hold of his shirt when he attempted to leap off the roof. "Are you insane?" she hissed. "After what you just said, you want me to fly over there and start peeking in windows?"

"There is nothing to worry about, Arianna of the Stars. You have the advantage of flight and the night. I will draw them away, and when I can no longer distract them, you will escape." His eyes shone in the moonlight, excited for the impending game.

Arianna opened her mouth to argue, but the words never came. Instead, a smile formed, her excitement matching his own. "Okay," she agreed. "I'll head down to the outskirts, and you cause the distraction. What are you going to do?"

Malachi grinned. "Oh, you will know."

ARIANNA DIDN'T HAVE to wait long to realize Malachi was right. She knew—the blinding orange flames bursting up toward the sky, the thick plumes of black smoke, the chaotic swarm of men racing for buckets of water, all told her that it was her turn to act.

Flight came naturally to her now and she lifted off the ground with only the slightest twinge of pain from her lagoon encounter. She headed straight for the ship. It was dark save for lanterns scattered across the upper deck and in some of the lower rooms, pale yellow light flickering out of the windows. Her heart thumped in her chest as she approached slowly, weightless in the air. That air was fresher now that she was over the ocean, smelling of fish and freedom rather than pillaging pirates.

Arianna gripped the outer ledge of a window and carefully peered in, seeing that it was empty except for a few rows of barrels. The rum stock, she guessed. In the next window she saw bunks, with dirty clothes and empty bottles strewn about. Frustrated, not knowing what she was even looking for, Arianna moved to the next window—and there she finally found something worth stopping for.

A lone figure sat at a workbench, its back facing the window. The figure, which she guessed to be a man based on his outline, wore a long black cloak with a hood that hid his face from the rest of the world. Strong black boots matched the cloak, well-worn but sturdy nonetheless.

Arianna tried to see his face, perhaps in the reflection of a glass or mirror, but the room was covered on all walls by lush red curtains. She briefly wondered what those curtains were hiding, as the rest of the room was unnervingly bare except for the workbench, but her attention remained on the figure. He was hunched over something, hands and arms working, and even from her place outside the window she could hear the sounds of ripping and tearing, banging and sanding.

Her brow furrowed at the movements, creasing even more when she realized what he was actually doing—making a canvas. Then, confusion turned to interest and she began to ponder the nature of this person. Was he the sensitive type she'd so often met, eager to discuss the deeper meanings of life? Was he arrogant and rude, able to appreciate only his own talents? Was he the kind who went about his day unsure of his every move, taking each mark of criticism as a personal affront?

Any of his personal characteristics would have fascinated her. She simply wanted to know more about this mystery man locked in the hull of a pirate ship, and was tempted to call out to him, perhaps even save him.

Arianna had nearly gathered the courage to tap on the window when the door to the room opened and a second figure entered, head also cloaked. Startled, she floated down a little lower and hoped that neither of the two looked her way. Her wide eyes never left the scene as she watched, a dozen scenarios racing through her mind, a dozen ways this moment could end. All of them entranced her, scared her, excited her.

But then the man who entered threw back his cloak and lifted his head, and fascination quickly shattered into fear.

She knew that face, with its scars cut deep across the cheekbones. She knew those eyes, black pits that were always narrowed until just before the kill, when they widened like saucers in anticipation of blood. She knew that frame, huge and hulking, never able to back down from a fight. And worse, she knew his name, a name so simple that not even he could spell it, a name that inspired terror in all who had the misfortune of meeting its maker.

"X."

She said his name before realizing what she was doing, at the same time as the second figure greeted the man. Her voice merged with the other, but was loud enough that they both turned. Quickly, she ducked down beneath the window, silently cursing herself as she flattened against the wood and floated closer to the water until her feet just skimmed the surface. Shadows played across the window, and she imagined them both looking out, searching for a possible intruder but seeing only the nighttime sky instead.

Arianna breathed a sigh of relief when the shadows pulled back, footsteps matching their retreat. Cautiously, she rose again but this time stayed out of sight as she listened.

"What's happening out there, X?"

"Nothing we can't handle, Captain. Just the usual, the locals wanting to have a little fun."

Arianna grimaced at the sound of that rough, grating voice. Even after all these years, the chill still went up her spine.

"The usual?" the captain repeated. "So then our flying friend has returned?" There was silence then, and Arianna imagined the two conferring through glares. "Am I to assume *she* has returned as well?" Arianna's head turned at that and she inched closer as X replied.

"Aye, Captain. Word has it that the Wild One brought her back, and that they have already clashed with the savages. Got one of their boys killed, all for the sake of sport."

"Their little games are of no concern to me. I want the girl, X.

Bring her to me, and then the real fun begins."

Her stomach dropped as Arianna heard the words. There could be only one *her*, and the fact that they were looking for her frightened her to her core. Just as she pushed off the boat to escape, she heard the captain, The Hunter, call after his first mate, "And X, for the last time, just find Malachi—and kill him."

JUST FIND MALACHI—and kill him.

The words echoed in her mind as she soared to their meeting place. Arianna didn't worry about being seen; the chaos below her was nearly entertaining in its muddled messiness, drunkards falling over themselves or into one another and splashing water on the wrong buildings. A few of those drunkards had drawn weapons, abandoning the fire in favor of the fight.

In the center of the melee was Malachi, sword to dagger with one of the few men not overcome by drink. A smile was wide on his face, and he was laughing with each strike and clash. Blood dripped from an open wound on his upper arm and his jaw was bruised, but his newest injuries didn't slow him down.

She couldn't land amidst the battle and didn't have a weapon that would match those of the pirates', so instead Arianna simply shouted Malachi's name as she passed and raced for their meeting place. Out of the corner of her eye, she saw him shove a man on his back, then launch himself into the air with a gleeful crow that echoed from port to mountaintop.

They hit the ground together on the outskirts of Pirate Port, faces flushed from the heat of the fire and the rush of battle. "We have to go," Arianna breathed out, heart pounding. "They are after you. They want to kill you."

"They always want to kill me!" Malachi cried back, taking her hand. “That is the game, my Arianna!” His nonchalance mixed with excitement amused her, and she nearly giggled when he cast a wink her way. “Come, it is time we retreat.”

Together they took off for the woods, the still-burning fire at their backs and the scent of madness surrounding them. They could have flown, but chose to race barefoot across the soft forest floor.

Sometimes, it just felt good to run.

Sixteen

The Truth Comes at Morning

THEY RETURNED TO base, their own makeshift treehouse, to the sound of excited chattering. The boys surrounded them when they entered, marveling over their wounds, demanding to know what happened, asking dozens of questions about the battle at Pirate Port that was already the talk of The Never. Arianna and Malachi answered their questions with the same energy, settling down only when the oldest of boys, Shooter, ushered them to a crudely crafted table littered with knife nicks and years of abuse.

"Tonight, we feast to our fearless leader, and to his mighty partner in crime!"

The boys cheered and raised glasses, then scrambled to grab steaming bowls and scatter them across the table. For a moment the only sounds to be heard were those of chewing and grabbing food from bowl or plate, Arianna joining in with the rest of them. Prim and proper had no place here, where fingers were the utensils and belches spoke of a satisfied stomach.

Arianna had no idea where so much food came from or who had prepared it, but didn't allow herself to be concerned with such details. During the meal she forgot what worried her, for once enjoying a meal without having to converse or make difficult decisions, but simply be in the company of others just like her. It wasn't until the boys' eyelids began to droop that her joy started to fade.

"Bedtime!" she announced, much to their disappointment. Even the sleepiest of them protested, but climbed into bed without a fuss when she pointed to their respective bunks. Softened though by their child-like complaints, she went around to each of them and tucked them into bed with a whisper good-night and kiss to the cheek or forehead. Promises were made for stories the next night, stories that told of their greatness and of The Never before their time.

Although she'd insisted on the boys washing up before bedtime, Arianna didn't have the energy to spare. She climbed into the only bed left after blowing out all candles except for the one by her bunk, thankful for the soft furs and feather-filled pillows. Her eyes closed as soon as she laid her head down, and then opened immediately when she felt the bed move and someone else settle down.

Malachi sat next to her, leaning back on his hands as he looked out at the sleeping boys. He'd removed his tattered and smoke-ruined shirt, and for the first time Arianna found herself observing new parts of him. His arms and shoulders weren't the only toned muscles, she noted, casting her eyes across his muscle-lined stomach and strong chest. Scars lined his torso, some thin and white, others dark and uneven—evidence of battles past.

The scrawny boy she'd once known had become a man, in more ways than one.

"They aren't so bad," his voice cut into her thoughts, bringing color to her cheeks.

Arianna diverted her eyes, but was charmed that he thought she'd been staring just at his scars more so than anything else. "What, um…what are you doing? Here."

Malachi sent her a quizzical look. "You climbed into my bed, Arianna of the Stars. The better question is, what are *you* doing here?"

What *was* she doing here? Was it simply that the boys had taken every other sleeping place, or was it something more? "I'm going to sleep," she answered. "I'm exhausted."

"As am I." He laid back and shifted so that his arm was beneath

Arianna, who allowed herself to be cradled into the crook of his shoulder. She settled against him, one arm draped casually across his chest, her other hand resting lightly beneath his. He smelled of campfire and sweat, the ocean and blood, and the scent intoxicated her.

"Goodnight, Malachi."

"Sleep well, my Arianna," he replied, and was asleep within moments.

Arianna listened to the sound of his steady breathing for a while before her thoughts turned to the day's events. She was confused more than she was frightened, even though she knew that the future didn't bode well for her in The Never.

Clearly, she'd been wrong in assuming the man in the empty room was a prisoner. No, that man was the captain, the feared leader of the Sea Killers, and he'd been making something meant just for her - canvases. She knew the sound of canvas being torn and stapled, frames being constructed. And he knew that she was an artist.

But why did that matter? How did he know she was an artist, and what did he want from her as a result of her only true talent? She liked her paintings, as did others, but they were no more special than any other found in a gallery. Briefly she wondered if the captain wanted her only because he wanted to bring down Malachi, or perhaps as revenge for his father's death, but that still didn't explain why he was making the canvases, and why X was the one reporting her activities to him.

The thought of X nearly made her shudder, even though she was safely tucked against Malachi. Never before had such a name, such a simple letter, inspired such fear in her that just the sound of it nearly made her sick to her stomach. But this was more than fear, more than just a child's precaution at the sight of such a large, scarred, and threatening man.

She'd been captive on the ship once, her hand ripped out of Malachi's as they took off in flight, a hook grasping her ankle and dragging her back down to the main deck. She'd been thrown below before Malachi could rescue her, given to X as a prisoner. He'd been ordered to watch her until the captain came to fetch her.

He'd done much more than that.

Arianna couldn't bear the thought of X, of ever having to be in his guard again. But this new captain wouldn't stop until she was found, and he would send X after her, after Malachi, after the boys. She wasn't safe in The Never; she knew they would find her at home.

Home.

This wasn't home, in this bed of furs with this man who smelled of fire and blood. Why did she keep forgetting home, forgetting John, when in Malachi's presence? He held a power over her thoughts that even he didn't know he had, giving her an escape into magic and adventure when she should have been home. Arianna couldn't even remember what she'd last been doing when Malachi brought her back to The Never, or how long she'd been gone.

A day, she decided. Surely it had only been a day, perhaps two. John would be worried sick, and might even call her mother. She had to return home for their sake. She had to return to The Never for Malachi's.

As she lay against Malachi, cherishing the feel of his warm skin against her cheek, she planned her return—both there and back. This couldn't go on, disappearing from home at will and playing in The Never until she remembered she had someone waiting for her. But The Never needed her, and she had to see this game through until the very end.

Quietly, Arianna rose from the bed, careful not to disturb Malachi. She tiptoed out of the treehouse and into the cool night, staring up into the sky to get her bearings. She'd never made the journey alone and hoped she'd be able to find her way home again.

"Where are you going?" a small voice called out to her just before she could lift herself from the ground.

Arianna turned, seeing little Fellow at the base of the tree gripping a teddy bear. She walked over to him and knelt. "Just on a little trip. I'll be back," she promised.

"Malachi says you never come back. He has to go and get you, because the other man you say you love won't let you visit."

The statement interested her, brought forth a flash of irritation that she pushed it back. Fellow watched her through wide yet sleepy eyes, hands tightly clutching his bear. "I will come back. I just need to get a few things so we can make The Never even more fun and exciting." Hope filled his face at that, and she smiled while brushing back his messy hair. "Will you do something for me?" Fellow nodded eagerly. "When Malachi wakes up, tell him that I've gone to get help. Tell him that if I'm not back in a day's time, to come and find me. Can you do that for me?"

"Yes."

"Good. But remember, not until he wakes up." She knew Malachi would follow her, and needed time to do what she was planning. Fellow wrapped his thin arms around her in a tight embrace and she accepted the hug, then released him. "Back to bed, little Fellow. I will see you soon."

She waited until Fellow disappeared back inside. Alone again, Arianna took a deep breath and prepared for flight, thinking of all the things she dreamed of, what made her happiest of all. Her hands gripped the edges of her shirt nervously, and she had the passing thought that her ragged and worn clothes wouldn't survive the tumultuous winds before throwing caution to the night and letting it take her away.

JOHN SAT ON the back porch, staring out into the woods as though his endless vigil would make Arianna magically reappear. He'd kept watch every day and every night, taking a leave of absence from work so that he could be here, at home, waiting for her. Not that he wanted to be at work anyway.

Suspicion had grown since he last spoke to his attorney, and talk of Arianna's disappearance spread as locals aided in the search. A few of the local news stations made mention of Arianna's past, digging deep into her life and somehow discovering her tendency to forget her medicine. John didn't know where they got their information from, and it bothered him that they were mostly correct, even if they did exaggerate their claims of her mental issues.

Despite talk of her past, though, the scrutinizing eye was always on John. No one had accused him directly yet of harming, or worse, killing, her, but he heard it in their voices and saw it in their eyes. The media had hinted at it as well, posing questions about how a young woman could simply disappear, why only her clothes were found, why she had disappeared at night while he had been left untouched.

He didn't have the answers, which only made him look more at fault. Sometimes he couldn't blame people for what they thought, other times he longed to lash out at the ones who dared to knock on the front door. Georgia had done her best to keep the wolves at bay, but even she was wearing down to the constant threats and questions.

The quick ring of his cell phone startled John from his trance-like watch on the woods. He never took his eyes off the trees as he answered, greeting the caller with a monotone "hello."

"John? It's Jason."

His friend's worried tone had John getting to his feet. "What's wrong? Did you find something?"

"No, still nothing. Look, I shouldn't even be calling you. I'm risking my job, but…"

"But what?"

"I can't hold them back anymore. The detectives are on their way. They are bringing you in for questioning."

"They've already questioned me." John ran a hand through his hair, frustrated.

"No, John. They are bringing you in for questioning, and charging you."

At that, John did manage to tear his eyes away from the forest. He clenched them shut, fingers prodding at the headache forming at his temples. "They can't do that, Jason. It hasn't been that long. We aren't done searching for her. I didn't *do* anything!"

"I know," Jason assured, his tone indicating that he really did believe his longtime friend. "That's why I'm calling you. You deserve a heads-up."

John realized then the purpose of the call. "You want me to run. You really think that will make things better?"

"I don't know, John. I just thought that you—"

"I won't run," he stated firmly. "I haven't done anything wrong, and I'll prove that with my dying breath if I have to."

"John—"

"No, Jason, I can't. I have to face this head on. Look, I—"

But then he stopped, mouth parting in shock when he saw the figure emerge from the woods. He could hear Jason asking questions, but John couldn't move as he watched the woman walk slowly toward him, filthy and scabbed, and completely naked.

"Ari," he whispered, a sob catching in his throat. In his ear, Jason repeated the name as a question, then louder when he didn't get a response. "Jason…call the detectives and tell them to meet us at the hospital. She's back."

He all but threw the phone down and ran to meet Arianna as she stepped away from the edge of the woods. Her eyes, tired and confused, met his as he approached, wrapping her in a hug. "Ari! Where the hell have you been? What happened to you? Are you okay?" He couldn't stop the barrage of questions, or the tears forming in the corners of his eyes. "Arianna?"

John pulled back, hands gripping her shoulders. His breath hitched at the wounds on her chest and arms and face, and he wondered at the dirt and smoke-smudged stains covering nearly all of her skin. Her long brown hair was tangled and she was shivering. Quickly, he wrapped his jacket around her.

"Arianna, where have you been?"

It seemed a lifetime before she answered. "On…on an adventure."

"An adventure?" he repeated, anger taking over his joy and worry. "Are you kidding me? Where were you?"

She lifted a hand and gestured to the sky. "Away."

He noted the breathlessness of her voice, how lost she sounded. "Did someone attack you? Were you kidnapped?"

"Of course not."

"Then where did you go?"

"On an adventure."

"Jesus Christ, Arianna, they thought I fucking killed you!" He was yelling now, furious at himself for doing so.

Arianna didn't seem to notice. "Kill me? You would never hurt me."

He couldn't respond, not wanting to yell and knowing he would never break through her state of mind. Georgia came running out of the house then, shouting her daughter's name. Arianna's attention drifted for only a moment before she slumped against John, unconscious.

Hurt Her Never

SHE AWOKE IN a bed, a blanket tucked around her waist. Her vision was blurry for a moment, but as the sights came into view she realized the curtains were drawn, letting in only the last bits off sunlight as dusk approached.

A beeping sound had her turning her head, seeing a machine at her bedside with wires and tubes attached. With some amount of horror, she realized those tubes trailed down to her body, attached to her hand by a needle.

A hospital. She was in the hospital—but why? Arianna sat up and glanced over herself. She wore a thin, white cotton gown and had gauze taped to her chest and parts of her shoulders. A touch to her face told her more bandages ran along her jawbone. Her wounds were quickly forgotten though. She needed to get home and gather her supplies, then race to save The Never.

Carefully, Arianna lifted the tape from the back of her hand and slid the needle out, wincing. She took off the heart monitors and the clamp around her pointer finger, not noticing the change in beeps from the machines behind her. Just as her feet touched the floor, a nurse rushed in.

"Miss Arianna, you're awake! We were worried about you."

"Worried? How long have I been asleep?"

"Oh, only a day. The doctor got you patched up and gave you a little something to help you sleep." She guided Arianna back to the bed and had her sit. "He will be in shortly."

The door opened again, John and Georgia entering. Both rushed to her side, offering kisses and hugs.

"Oh, honey, we were so worried," Georgia said, her arms around her daughter. "We looked everywhere. You just disappeared."

"You scared the hell out of me," John put in, kissing her firmly. "I just want to know what happened."

I had an adventure in The Never. I battled the natives and played with the children, then spied on the pirates and saw an old enemy, Arianna thought, thinking all the things she couldn't say out loud in her head.

"I…I don't know."

Georgia pursed her lips, taking a seat next to Arianna. "How can you not know? Sweetie, something awful happened to you. You were attacked. You have bite marks on your jaw and claw marks on your chest. Something must have attacked you, some kind of animal. The police are searching the forest right now for the beast."

Beast. The word both amused and annoyed her. It wasn't a beast, but a beautiful sea creature overcome by the darkness. She didn't want any of the merfolk harmed because of her; they knew not what they did when under the influence of an evil force.

"The wounds will heal," Arianna said in return, looking over at the nurse when the woman lifted her hand. "What are you doing?" She pulled her arm back, but the nurse held tight.

"Just some medicine, dear. We wanted to wait until you woke to give you this dose, to be sure the fluids were working."

"I don't want any medicine," Arianna argued, jerking and freeing her hand. She glared at John accusingly when he spoke up.

"Ari, it's okay. Just relax. The meds will help you get better faster."

"I'm fine, John. Let's just go home. Get off me!" she yelled when the nurse touched her again.

The doctor entered then, accompanied by a male nurse. "Good evening, Arianna. I'm Doctor Barrie. How are you feeling?"

"Like I want to go home."

Dr. Barrie only smiled. "We are going to keep you overnight for observation, but I see no reason why you can't go home tomorrow if things go well tonight." He nodded to the nurse, who reached for Arianna. "The medicine will help you relax and clear your mind."

"I don't need to relax. I'm fine." Arianna rose, but was held back from moving by the male nurse and by her mother, who gripped her upper arm. "What's going on?"

"It's for your own good, sweetheart," Georgia answered, her eyes full of regret. "Don't fight it."

"Don't fight what?"

Her question was answered when she followed her mother's eyes and saw the straps attached to the side of the bed. Horror filled her face. "John?"

"We're worried, Ari. We are just trying to get you well."

"I am well," she insisted. "But I have to go home. I have to save—" She stopped, knowing that what she was about to say next would only strengthen their suspicion. "No!" Arianna yelled when the nurses took her by the arms, one on each side. They pushed her onto the bed, a third nurse appearing to grab her ankles when she kicked out.

"Get off me!" Arianna struggled against their hold, tears forming when the doctor slid the straps around her wrists and ankles, tightening them. Her limbs secured no matter how hard she fought, Arianna could only clench her hand into a fist and strain against the strap as the doctor slid a needle into her hand. "Don't do this. Please, stop," she pleaded, thinking only of The Never and her promise to Fellow. "I have to go back. I have to go back!"

She heard a thump at the window, saw a shadow beneath the curtain. "Malachi!" she yelled, desperation and relief in her cry. She didn't see the way the others looked around in confusion, or the sadness that crossed John's face in hearing her call out another man's name. "Malachi!" she screamed again, her roughened voice breaking and filling the room, carrying down the hall. Out of the corner of her eye she saw the doctor stick a syringe into a plug and press the plunger, sending its contents down the tube.

It hit her fast, the lightheadedness, the bewilderment. "Malachi! Please…"

But she could say no more as the medicine took over her mind, severing her connection with her savior.

JOHN SAT OUTSIDE Arianna's room, head cradled in his hands. How long he'd been there, he couldn't say. Minutes had turned into hours, hours into days, days into endless questions and interrogations by police officers who still didn't believe he had nothing to do with Arianna's disappearance and sudden—and suspicious—reappearance. His attorney, Waters, did his best to fend off the wolves, but even his claims of Arianna's previous medical problems did little to quell the lingering skepticism.

He didn't move until he sensed someone taking a seat next to him on the uncomfortable wooden bench.

"She's sleeping," Georgia said. Exhaustion lined her face, matched with sorrow. "She screamed so much her throat is bleeding. The doctor says she probably won't be able to talk much for the next few days."

"She screamed for another man," John replied, turning his head enough to look up at Georgia. His blue eyes were bloodshot and tired. "I don't know who he is, or where she would have even met him. She doesn't go anywhere and never leaves the house unless I make her, or unless she disappears in the woods. It never even occurred to me that she may have been meeting someone out there, but now…"

Georgia listened, hating what she would have to say next even though she knew it may bring some amount of comfort to her future son-in-law. “He’s not another man,” she told him, not able to meet his gaze. “Well, I suppose he is, but not in the sense you’re thinking of.” She sighed then and rubbed her brow. “I haven’t heard that name in a long, long time.”

“What do you mean?” John sat up straighter, wondering if he was now finally going to get the story he’d been waiting for since he first met Arianna in grade school. Georgia and Arianna had always been tight-lipped about what exactly happened in the past, sharing only what details were necessary. No amount of questions and pressure had garnered additional information, and after a while, he’d given up. He accepted Georgia’s concerns and eventually came to see that her worries were justified, even if he did doubt whether or not he was doing the right thing by being her daily medication reminder.

Georgia was quiet for a moment, eyes glazed over as she thought about her daughter as a little girl. Arianna had been a precocious child, full of fire and life until the day she’d gone inward, retreating within herself to a place Georgia couldn’t reach. A little girl with bright green eyes and curly brown hair and more energy than her limbs could contain was subdued, preferring the company of shadows and secrets to those right in front of her.

When Georgia did finally speak, her voice was reminiscent. “Malachi was…is…the reason why Arianna takes her medicine. She used to dream of a figure in the night. She saw him in the shadows. She heard him in the stars. He called to her, she said, he chose her. I used to ask what he said, what he chose her for, but she only said that he was her friend and that he kept her safe. They told stories together and went on adventures.”

“Adventures,” John repeated, trying to wrap his mind around what he was being told. “That’s what she said when she came out of the woods, that she’d been on an adventure.”

“That’s what it always was. These great adventures with mermaids and pirates and Indians. There were other children, the boys, but she never called them by name. Only Malachi had a name." Georgia remembered those nights clearly, listening to Arianna recount her fun, terrified by the thought of what her dreams meant. "He was her closest friend. She loved him dearly. At first I thought these were merely dreams, since she only spoke of them in the morning and looked forward to going to bed. I even encouraged them at one point. After all, what's the harm in letting your child have an active imagination?" Georgia shrugged, attempting a smile and failing.

"But then she started getting these…marks on her. All over her. Bruises in the shapes of fingers, little cuts that looked like scratches, bite marks on her legs. She was hurting herself, either on purpose or unknowingly." Georgia pressed her lips together, her memories dark.

"My husband at the time, Arianna's father, couldn't handle it. He used to bring his friends over for late-night card games and drinking, these worthless men who'd steal your money before they bothered trying to earn it, and he said he couldn't bring them around such an embarrassment. He said he wouldn't let his daughter make him look like a fool in front of others. He refused to accept that something might have been wrong with her, and got so angry with me every time I brought her to the doctor for a checkup. He kept saying I *wanted* something to be wrong, that I was just imagining it, that she was fine. But she was getting hurt somehow, and there was no denying that even if we never could figure out what exactly she was doing."

Georgia took in a deep breath. "So, he left. He packed a bag and walked out the door. His drunken hulking friends helped him, even encouraged him. I remember him looking back at the house and waving once to Arianna, who was looking out the window, and then he just drove away. We never saw him again. After that, Arianna got worse. The self-inflicted injuries stopped, for the most part, but she would just sit in her room staring out the window, looking for this Malachi. I…I thought she was sick…mentally…and took her to more doctors."

And they saw so many doctors. Mental health specialists, child psychiatrists, the list never seemed to end.

"Some of them thought she just had an overactive imagination and was crying out for attention. One…one thought she needed an exorcism. Said the devil had invaded her soul." Georgia nearly scoffed; John could only listen. "The rest said she needed professional help and medication. They listed a bunch of big names and diseases, and it all made sense. They seemed to know exactly what was wrong with her, and so one night I gave Arianna her first pill. That night was the first night she didn't dream of Malachi."

Georgia sighed again, tucking her slender arms around herself. "After all these years, I thought she had finally forgotten him."

John swallowed hard, processing the information. "Perhaps he hasn't forgotten her."

Eighteen

Good-Byes Mean Never Coming Back

ARIANNA STARED BLANKLY at the television across the room. A morning talk show was on, but she was barely able to follow the discussion. The medicine flowing through her veins, combined with hours of struggling against the restraints around her wrists and ankles, had exhausted her.

Tired as she was, Arianna barely moved when the door to her hospital room opened. She knew by the heavy footsteps that it wasn't John or her mother, so she didn't bother looking at the stranger to greet him. Soon enough he appeared, taking a seat in the chair by her bed and resting a notepad on his knee.

Arianna looked him over without enthusiasm. He was a short and pudgy man, balding at the top of his head, eyes very serious behind round glasses. A white coat covered khaki dress slacks and a pale yellow shirt.

"Hello, Arianna. My name is Dr. Peters," he greeted her, smiling warmly. "We met when you were first admitted."

She didn't remember, but then again, she hardly remembered anything after walking out of the woods. "What do you want?"

"I am just here to talk," he answered.

"About what?"

"About whatever you'd like to discuss."

Arianna lifted an arm as much as she could. "Can we talk about why I'm strapped to a bed?"

Dr. Peters glanced at the straps, then at Arianna. "The doctors and your family thought it best that you are restrained, for the time being. When you were admitted, you displayed potentially self-harming behavior."

"Like what?"

Instead of answering right away, he wrote something down on his notepad. Arianna watched, curious, then diverted her eyes when he looked back up and gestured to her. "Your injuries. Can you tell me how you got them?"

"No."

"Why not?"

"Because I don't remember." She sighed again and shifted uncomfortably. "Look, I get it. You're here to figure out all my secrets and figure out what's going on in my head so you can report back to everyone else. I've seen dozens of doctors just like you since I was a kid. Like I told them, it doesn't matter what I say."

"And why's that?"

Arianna regarded him plainly. "Because one, you wouldn't believe anything I say. And two, I can't tell you something I don't even remember. Maybe if I wasn't so drugged up all the time I could actually make sense of my thoughts."

Dr. Peters sat back, clasping his hands together. "What kind of thoughts?"

"I don't know. Wanting to see lights in a forest. Laughing over little boys running around. Wishing I was at sea. I think lots of things, but I don't know what they all mean."

He could see the frustration in her face and knew it was genuine. Dr. Peters had spoken with Arianna's family several times and read her files. The woman was often confused and unable to make sense of the things she saw in her mind.

"Tell me, Arianna, do you believe that what you see is possible?"

"What do you mean?"

"I mean, do you believe men can fly? Do you believe there are pirates out there sailing for gold and silver? Do you believe there is a world where children never grow up?"

Yes, Arianna thought. She did believe in those things, but she knew what would happen in saying so. More medicine, more frowns, more hours talking to the shrink. So she didn't answer, and instead asked a question of her own. "Do you believe in God? In angels?"

Dr. Peters smiled lightly, understanding her ploy. "You're asking about my spiritual beliefs, Arianna?" She affirmed with a shrug. "Are you saying that this is your spiritual belief, in a flying boy who takes you to a magical world?"

It sounded stupid the way he phrased it, and she didn't appreciate being mocked. "All I'm saying is that what one person believes in may be illogical to another, only because they choose to believe in something different."

Dr. Peters set the notepad aside and leaned forward. "Arianna, I'm trying to help you get out of here, away from the restraints and medicine you hate so much. But you have to work with me, give me something I can use to help."

Defeated, Arianna turned her head and looked back at the TV. "How can you help," she asked sadly, "when you've already stopped believing?"

THE DOCTOR LEFT soon after, promising another visit when she was feeling up to it. John entered the room only moments after, taking the seat Dr. Peters had vacated.

"How did it go?" he asked.

Arianna shrugged. "Just another shrink asking all the wrong questions."

"And what are the right questions?" When she simply gestured to the restraints, John nodded. "I know, Ari, but they are for your own good. What you did to yourself…you can't keep this up."

"What makes you so sure I did it to myself?"

"How else do you explain the wounds?"

Everyone kept asking her that, she thought. She had an answer of sorts, but not one they would accept. She had visions of being pulled underwater—in the lake, perhaps? - and attacked by the beasts that lurked beneath the surface. Claws against skin, screams piercing her ears, hands pulling her from the water - she couldn't explain any of it, and if *she* couldn't, then the doctors certainly wouldn't have answers either.

At least, none that she was willing to accept.

"I don't have a way to explain them," she replied. "But I hope that maybe one day you'll stop asking me to try."

John leaned over and kissed her forehead. "If you remember anything, please let me know. I'll be here first thing in the morning. They're kicking me out for now. Visiting hours and all that."

Arianna mustered up a smile. "I understand. Good-bye, John."

His gentle expression changed to something sad and worried. "Never say good-bye," he responded, brushing back her hair. "My great-grandmother, the one I told you about who lived in London? She always said good-bye means you're never coming back, and I hope you'll always come back to me."

"Until tomorrow, then," Arianna answered.

"Until tomorrow."

It was only after the door closed behind John that Arianna whispered, "Good-bye."

IT WAS THREE more days before Arianna was allowed to go home, three days of medication, counseling, and tears. After her last meeting with the hospital shrink, Arianna hadn't said much, instead choosing silence over words that may incriminate her. That silence had frustrated the police, who came to her in hopes of determining exactly where she'd been, but even the possibility of clearing her fiancé's name hadn't sparked the desire to speak until she left the hospital walls. By the time John led her inside their own cozy cottage, her eyes were dim and her movements sluggish.

"Can I get you anything?" he asked, setting her bag down on the floor. Georgia came in behind them, closing and locking the door.

She wanted to take a nap, but didn't have the energy to say so. Arianna just looked toward the bedroom and let John help her there, then tuck her in. Lily leapt up and curled at her side, her snout on her master's stomach. Woeful chocolate eyes stared up at her. Arianna was somewhat surprised by how big the puppy had gotten.

"She's excited to see you," John said, kissing Arianna on the forehead and offering Lily a pat. "Get some rest. I'll cook up your favorite for dinner, greasy cheeseburgers and curly fries."

With a week's worth of hospital food still causing her taste buds to grimace, a cheeseburger sounded delicious. Arianna managed a smile before she fell asleep.

John observed her for a moment, then rose and left Lily to watch over Arianna. He made his way to the kitchen, where Georgia was cleaning. "You don't have to do that."

"Of course I do. We've been worrying our heads off lately and cleaning has taken a back burner. Arianna is going to wake up to a spotless home."

He could have been offended, but she was right. They hadn't done much lately in the way of cleaning or even tidying up much, and the results of their carelessness showed in piles of dirty dishes and laundry. So he let Georgia take over, knowing she likely just needed to keep her hands busy.

"The detectives called," he informed her while pulling ground beef out of the freezer. "Said they'd be over in a couple days. They want to talk to Arianna about everything. My guess is they still think I had something to do with it and want to hear firsthand from her that it either was or wasn't me."

"They don't like being wrong," Georgia replied, wiping furiously at a spot on the stove. The bangles on her thin wrists clattered against one another as she did so. "We know the truth. We'll get rid of them."

"And then what?"

"Then, we just move on. I'll go back home, you and Arianna can get married. We go back to normal life, make sure she stays on her meds this time. Just put this whole awful experience behind us."

John glanced over his shoulder toward the bedroom. "Are we doing the right thing, Georgia? Upping her dosage like this? She's so tired and out of it."

"She'll get used to it eventually. Her body will adjust."

"What if it doesn't?"

"Would you rather her believe in her delusions? Go wandering around the woods naked?"

"Of course not. I just think…well, there has to be a better solution."

Georgia tossed the rag into the sink. "When you think of it, let me know. Until then, we make sure she never remembers who Malachi is again."

ARIANNA EYED THE detectives from her studio the next morning. She sat at the easel, brush in hand, attempting to ignore them but unable to do so. She'd retreated to her studio as soon as they arrived but knew that soon enough, they'd want to talk to her.

They came early, the men claimed, to get it over with and let her get back to her life. John knew they were merely hoping for the element of surprise, to catch them unprepared. First they spoke to Georgia and then John, but about what, she neither knew nor cared. She wanted only to give her statement and have them leave her alone. The only reason she'd agreed to speak with them at all was because she didn't want John to get into more trouble than he already was, and it was her responsibility to clear his good name.

When she heard footsteps coming her way, Arianna turned back to the canvas. She had a flash of something, a memory perhaps of when she was younger, when she did so. A figure headed her way, a hand on her bony shoulder, the brush being taken from her hand. The image passed as quickly as it appeared, and so for the time being she ignored it, dipping the end of the thick brush into dark gray paint and sweeping it across the top of the canvas.

Her hands worked fast, mind not really comprehending what she was painting. She simply needed to work and painting usually helped clear her thoughts. It didn't surprise her that after only a few minutes, the piece took on a dark theme.

"Looks like a storm is coming."

Arianna refrained from rolling her eyes, instead picking up a smaller, narrower brush and coating it in black. She traced a few lines in what was becoming a ferocious sky, with tumultuous gray clouds and flashes of white lightning hidden behind the mist. Indeed, a storm was coming.

"Arianna, my name is—"

"I know who you are," she interrupted, speaking her first full sentence since coming home. Her back remained to the two men. "You are the ones stupid enough to think John would ever hurt me."

"That's what we want to talk to you about." They came into view then by approaching her on either side. One of the men was tall and lanky with slicked-back blonde hair; the other was rounded with a face framed by brown curls. The contrast between them was so stereotypical that it nearly made her laugh. "We need a full recount of what happened, in your own words."

She made them wait, absently painting the greens and browns of a forest floor. It would have been easy to forget they were there and simply let the painting take her away. When she finally did turn to them, the outline of a fallen tree and a strike of lightning were waiting to be filled.

"What do you want to know?"

"Everything you remember."

That won't take long, she thought grimly. The new medication she was on had effectively blocked out the majority of the past few weeks. "I was camping with John and Lily," she began, letting her mind remember as much as it could. "We ate dinner, danced, and went to bed. I don't sleep well and woke up in the middle of the night, like I usually do. I didn't want to wake John by tossing and turning, so I got up and went to the lake." That much of the night was crystal clear.

"Lily came with me and we walked along the shore for a bit. I was bored and decided to go for a swim, so I stripped down and got in the water."

"According to your fiancé, you aren't a strong swimmer," one of the detectives put in. "Why would you go swimming, alone in the middle of the night, if you can't swim well?"

Arianna nearly hesitated, wondering where that information was coming from. She wasn't a weak swimmer, never had been. John knew that, as did her mother. Her movements remained fluid as she answered, the lie coming easily. "I didn't plan on going far. I didn't even plan on going past where my feet couldn't reach. It's just the lake. I've been in it a hundred times."

"So you got in for a swim, and then what?"

And then what?

The question rang through her mind. Arianna took in a deep breath, focusing on her painting again. She added a shadow to match the fallen tree. "And then I…disappeared. I don't remember a lot. I have…flashes." Her brush lifted to the sky and created two stars side by side. "The smell of the sky." She painted a light gray cloud. "The feel of wet leaves beneath my feet." Her brush dappled brown leaves to the forest floor. "Thrashing in the water as something bit me." Shaky gray lines were added to the river winding off the canvas side. "A fire, and chaos around it." Black smoke rose in the distance behind the river. "The kind of safety you feel curled against a warm body." Moonlight broke through the dark clouds.

Arianna lifted her eyes to the detectives. "And then I remember walking out of the woods and seeing John on the porch. He ran over to me, crying, asking me where I'd been. He brought me to the hospital, but after that, I...I only remember coming home." What had happened at the hospital? She had the fleeting feeling that she should be angry, but her mind was blank.

The detectives didn't seem to care either. "What about your injuries? You claim you disappeared and that your fiancé would never harm you, yet you were covered in bruises and lacerations. Medical record state they were wounds caused by an attack of some kind."

Arianna looked herself over. Her wounds were healing, although they still looked and felt tender and fresh. "Something attacked me in the water. I remember going under and feeling teeth tearing at me."

"How did you get out of the water?"

"I don't know. Maybe I walked out, maybe someone saved me. You're the detectives. Why don't you figure it out."

The men scowled, though they tried hard not to show their frustration. After consulting with one another, they accepted her answer and bid her farewell, informing John that they would be in touch. Once outside the door, they offered each other a skeptical glance.

"What do you think?" one asked the other.

"I think the woman is bat-shit crazy," the second replied, closing his notebook, "but the guy and her mother refuse to believe it."

Embrace the Never

FOUR DAYS PASSED by peacefully.

In those days, Georgia went home, giving her daughter a tearful goodbye and promising to visit again soon—next time, under happier circumstances. Unbeknownst to Arianna, she also went with John to their lawyer, giving him the rights to make medical decisions on Arianna's behalf should she have another episode. John wasn't thrilled with the trip, or with keeping it from his fiancée, but did what was best for them all.

Arianna spent her time in her studio while John worked, catching up on lost hours as best he could. He worked from home a lot now, and it was then that she felt trapped, always being watched, always being judged. Alarms were set to remind her when to take her next dose, her mother called to make sure she was feeling well, and even the hospital shrink made a house call for an hour-long session that left her exhausted and depressed.

For now she sat out on the back porch, having brought her easel and paints outside to enjoy the fresh air. Lily sat at her feet, alternating between napping and nipping at her brushes, which rested on a small table next to her.

"What do you think?" Arianna asked the dog. "Too dark? Not dark enough?" The painting was a mix of grays and navy blues, with swirls of speckled light mixed in. The ocean was raging, waves pounding against one another, the lights of a port in the distance nearly faded. It was a painting without hope, as many of her pieces had been lately. She'd already decided it would be part of her new series, which she'd titled *Chaos in the Calm*.

She observed the painting carefully, staring at the faraway port, wondering why she'd painted it on fire. Usually she could only paint things she'd personally seen, whether they be people or places. The accuracy to this depiction surprised even her.

"It reminds me of your last piece that sold at the show," John said, handing her a mug of hot chocolate. "The storm, the clouds. Except this one is at sea, and the other one was on land."

Arianna considered that. Surprisingly, she'd forgotten about that painting, the one that the man with bright eyes had purchased and that she'd tried so hard to recreate. That painting had been calm in the chaos, but this one…this piece held no hope.

"There is darkness in the world," she told him, gesturing to the painting with her brush. She had black paint smeared across her hands, speckles of color on her face. "Someone must defeat it."

She wondered at the statement as much as John did. Darkness in what world? Who was its savior? Did she know something about this painting that her own mind realized subconsciously?

A timer sounded in the house, buzzing twice and disrupting her silent questions. John rose, but she stopped him by grabbing his arm. "Wait. I want to show you something." Arianna replaced the painting on the easel with another, a smaller canvas. "I painted this last night, just before dawn. I kept getting this image in my head, over and over again. Do I know him? Or do you?"

John wasn't sure how to feel about the man who stared back at him from the canvas. Jealousy waged war with sadness that melted into uncertainty. He certainly did not know the man with the dark yet fiery red hair, wild hair that framed a strong and tanned face and accented triumphant green eyes. The man was smirking, hands on his hips as though claiming victory over an unseen battle. He wore an outfit made of leaves and cotton that clung to muscle, and he was barefoot despite a forest floor of brambles and twigs.

The man was painted in such detail that he could have been a photograph, and John found himself thinking that he wouldn't be surprised if the figure simply walked out of the painting and stood before them a real person. He was bothered by this stranger's cockiness, the way he stood in such self-assured splendor, the way he seemed to know something no one else knew.

"John?" Arianna poked his arm with the end of a brush. "Do you know him? Why are you looking at it like that?"

John cleared his throat. "Um, no. I don't know him. I was just…admiring how detailed he is."

"He is, isn't he? I don't know why. I don't usually paint people unless I have a photograph. Maybe I saw him in passing somewhere." Arianna shrugged and set the painting back on the ground, leaning it against the side of the house. She glanced over her shoulder when the timer sounded again.

The chime got John moving. How long had he been staring at the painting? The timer only went off twice, fifteen minutes in between dings. "I'll be right back," he told her, then hurried inside. He'd already put the first dose of her medication in the hot chocolate, though she didn't know, and the second needed to be administered soon after.

Outside, Arianna brushed off John's strange reaction and picked up the thickest brush, tucking two smaller ones behind her ears and another in her back pocket for future use. She started to reach for the hot chocolate, but recoiled when Lily bounded off the deck suddenly, knocking over the table and mug.

"Damnit, Lily," Arianna cursed under her breath, rising and stepping over the spilled drink. The pup disappeared into the forest and she followed, stopping just on the edge of the clearing. "Lily! Come on, girl! Where the hell did you go?"

The sun was rapidly falling below the horizon, making sight near impossible. With a sigh, Arianna stepped further into the woods, one hand on a narrow tree trunk and the other still gripping her brush. She squinted and peered into the growing night, annoyed that she would have to disrupt her painting to get a flashlight and find the dog. “Come on, Lily. You’re gonna get me in trouble.”

“She’s a sweet little thing, once she gets used to you.”

Arianna took a step back when a voice sounded out from the trees, but its familiar lilt had her hesitating. “Who…who’s there?”

“Have you forgotten me already, Arianna of the Stars?”

Then he came into view, all wild hair and playful smirk. She knew him instantly—the man from her paintings. “Malachi.” The name came out of nowhere, a flash in her mind. Malachi. Fellow. Caps. X.

The Never.

“Where have you been, my Arianna?” Malachi asked, coming into view. Lily was at his feet, eyes droopy. “You did not return as promised. I couldn’t find you.”

“I was…here,” she replied, brow furrowing.

“You left me again.”

“No. No, I left to…to get help. I was going to return, but then…” What had happened? Her memories were faded, slowly unraveling and impossible to hold on to. She pointed back at the house, confused, then at the sky, trying to retrace her steps. “There was a fire.”

“At Pirate Port.”

“And then…the boys, we had a battle with them, with the natives.”

“That was before the fire, Arianna.”

“I slept next to you.”

“Until you left.”

Arianna shook her head, pulling Lily away from Malachi and setting her on the ground next to her feet. The pup stirred, nuzzling against her ankles. “I wanted to return. I was injured and they brought me to the hospital. They gave me medicine.”

He snapped to attention. “Medicine! I told you to *never* take medicine!” Before she could answer, Arianna heard John calling out to her from the house. Malachi's expression turned urgent. "Come back with me now, my Arianna. It is your only chance."

Arianna hesitated, wondering if this figure was real or if the hospital doctors were right, that he was just a delusion that needed to be wiped away. "How can I trust you? Everyone says you're nothing more than a figment of my imagination. That you're just a dream, fading in and out at twilight, never letting me wake up."

Malachi leaned in closer. "And what do you believe?"

John's voice came closer as he stepped off the porch. Arianna glanced over her shoulder, then back at Malachi. "I don't know."

"He's doing this to you, Arianna. With all his *medicine*." Malachi spoke quickly, fiercely, taking her chin in his hand when she started to look for John again. "Do you want to be trapped by medicine that confuses your mind, or do you want to embrace the part of yourself that dares to believe in the impossible?"

John was close now, only steps away from the edge of the woods and nearly within sight of her. Arianna stared up at Malachi, this maybe-delusion who seemed to know her. She was starting to feel parts of her former self slipping back into place, settling down in her mind and hoping to stay.

Did she want the fantasy, the dream, or could she settle for the average, the expected that was as dependable as the daily timer? What was best for her, the right decision?

Did it even matter?

"Embrace the impossible," she declared, and took Malachi's hand. "Take me to The Never."

"WE MUST GET to the fae. They will help you."

Arianna allowed Malachi to drag her through the thick forest, around tree and bush. He was breathless, as was she, but worry didn't tinge her voice like it did his. She was still fuzzy, her mind cloudy and her heart beating wildly.

The race to The Never had been frantic, neither of them speaking as Arianna struggled to hold on to her memories and fight against whatever medicine was still pulsing through her veins. Malachi never let her go; had he of released his hold, she surely would have slipped away into the sky, disappearing yet again.

Now on land, she was at least able to put her feet beneath her, though her movements were sluggish and confused. After a long while, they reached the place where they first danced beneath the starlight. Like before, it was empty, but as soon as they arrived the forest came to life. Faeries swarmed around them, sensing that one of their visitors was in trouble. Arianna stumbled as one of them came closer, not quite able to make out its form.

"Who is that?" she asked, shielding her eyes from the bright white light. "What does it want?"

"It is the fae, Arianna." Malachi sounded confused. "Can you not see her?"

She saw only a blurry outline, a flash of light. "I…I don't know. Almost?"

"It is the medicine. We must draw it out of you." He grabbed her wrist and pulled her into the center of the circle. "It is keeping you from connecting to The Never. We must get it out, before he takes you back."

"Before who…" *John*, Arianna thought, barely able to picture the man she called fiancé. She could almost hear him calling to her, panic in his voice. "He…he only wants what's best for me."

"No!" Malachi whirled around, taking her by the shoulders. "*He* did this to you, Arianna! *He* took you away. *He* lied to you and forced you to believe you were wrong, and made you forget. *We* want what's best for you, my Arianna. You must let us help you."

He was right, Arianna realized as she took in his words. *He* did this to her. *He* was the reason why she was so confused, why she couldn't make sense of her dreams. *He* made her forget.

John was the enemy.

"Get it out of me. Get it out of me," she ordered, grabbing Malachi by the shirt. A strange sudden urgency overcame her. "Now."

"As you wish."

She released her hold and took a step back, bracing herself for whatever was to come. When two of the fae appeared at either side in a flash of blinding white light, her eyes narrowed and her mouth formed a tight line. Malachi stood just before her, head slightly down, watching her with a fierceness she'd never seen before.

Arianna started to ask him what to do, then balked when strong hands gripped her wrists. On reflex she jerked, but their hold only tightened. "Let go," she demanded, looking at both in turn. "Hey! Get off—"

But they dragged her to the ground, flat on her back. She kicked out, connecting only with air, arms stretched out at her sides with strong bodies holding her down. She felt fingernails digging into her flesh as she struggled, white light disorienting her.

And then Malachi was hovering over her, straddling her legs, gripping her face in his strong hands. "He did this to you," he said again, voice deadly calm. "He took you away from me. He made you forget."

"I know what he did!" Arianna shouted, throat straining with the effort. She felt something hot course through her veins, looked at her arm to see a golden glow starting from her wrist and traveling throughout her body. The fae held tight, emitting the same glow, eyes closed as they concentrated on healing her.

Arianna's body seized when the fire within her reached her core. Pain radiated throughout her body and her back arched, neck muscles bunched. "Malachi," she croaked, hands curling into fists. "Malachi, what…make it stop. Make it…stop."

Malachi lowered himself, knees digging into the dirt. His body kept her from convulsing again, his forehead touching hers as he fought against her struggles.

"Malachi…what's happening to me?"

“You are healing, my love,” he answered, letting his words whisper into her ears, and her ears alone. “You are the earth. You are the sky.” He pushed back her hair, wiped away tears. The white glow of the fae brightened, caged them. “You are wild. You are savage.” Malachi gripped her chin, turning her face to meet his and gently kissing her tightly shut eyes. Arianna’s muscles strained against his hold, arms shaking, jaw clenched. “You are free, my Arianna.”

“You are free,” he repeated. “Embrace who you are.”

And so, she did.

Her eyes flew open, shining in the night. Malachi jumped back, the fae releasing her. He watched as she rose to her feet in one fluid motion, taking in her surroundings. There was no confusion in her stare now, but a kind of clarity she hadn’t felt since she was a child. She knew this place, the fae who once spurned her, the boy who had become a man. She remembered the scent of a land alive, the sight of the unknown becoming reality. She wanted them all, and wanted nothing.

“Stay,” she ordered Malachi, then left him behind in the Fae Forest as she took for the sky.

Together As One

SHE SPENT THE evening soaring the sky, hiding in the clouds and exploring The Never. Having embraced every part of her that celebrated being in this world, Arianna finally remembered everything Malachi had been so desperately trying to rebuild in her memories.

She flew over Misty Marsh, recalling the beautiful songs that used to lull her to sleep while she sunbathed on the rocks. Skirting Pirate Port, she saw in her mind's eye herself and Malachi engaged in a laughing swordfight with the captain at that time.

Arianna sailed around the snow-tipped evergreen mountains next, enjoying the chilly air against her cheeks and the way the wind rushed through the ravines.

Colors were subdued and scents masked, but even the growing darkness couldn't dampen the wonder that The Never held.

When she finally returned to the treehouse, she felt at peace with herself. She loved The Never and all it contained, and even in its despair could see the light that once pulsed through the land's veins. It was up to her to bring that light back, and to do so, she had to embrace every part of herself.

Arianna slid down into the underground lair, surprised to find it empty. She stepped into the round room and saw Malachi sitting on the edge of the table, one leg propped up, elbow on his knee.

"I sent them away," he told her casually, peeling an apple with a flint-sharpened knife. "The boys will return tomorrow."

"And tonight?"

Malachi lifted himself off the table, taking a bite of the apple and tossing the rest over his shoulder. "Tonight is for us."

Her eyes never left his as he approached, the apple forgotten on the floor. "For us," she repeated. "For me, finally free. For you, who always knew what I was, but never told me until it suited you."

"I could not tell you what—"

"You could have told me everything," she cut in. "You could have helped me remember faster, so that I didn't have to wait for all the pieces to finally come together the longer I was here. You could have told me that the captain wants *me*. That he knows who I am, and what I can do." She took a step toward Malachi. "You could have told me about X. But you played the fool, Malachi. What else are you hiding from me?" Arianna shoved him, then again until his back hit the wall. "You are a fool, Malachi. You are a coward, and a child."

Malachi grabbed her wrist when she moved to strike him, holding her only hard enough to prevent the attack. His face was hidden in shadows, shadows that flickered in the candlelight and cast his green eyes in a fire that blazed through her.

His eyes held no soft seduction now. Instead they were filled with desire. Hot, fierce desire. This was the Malachi she knew, the boy who always wanted, even before he understood what that wanting meant. This was the man she'd come for, the one who called to her in her dreams.

In a single swift turn, Malachi spun Arianna around so that she was against the wall, pinning her there. He never let go of her wrist, instead holding her arm above her head. Arianna responded by pushing against his shoulder with her free hand, fingers digging into muscle as his own worked their way up her side, grazing her chest, taking hold of her chin just before his mouth met hers.

She struggled against him, lips parting even as she clawed at his shirt. He took the kiss deeper, breath hot, hips pressed against her own. With a snarl, Arianna freed herself from his grasp and shoved him back, breathing heavily and glaring at him. He moved to her; she stepped to the side, lashing out when he caught her by the waist.

Again he captured her hands in his, working them behind her back as he brought his mouth to her throat. She arched her neck, letting him take what he wanted. "Fool," she rasped out, trying to regain control. "You are a fool."

He pulled back only enough to take in her face, her closed eyes, her swollen lips. "You are the dreamer of fools," he whispered back, pressing her against the edge of the table. He felt every part of her, every muscle and curve, every shudder that worked its way up her spine when his hands met her flesh.

In a teasing leap Arianna bounded away, powering her jump with flight. He followed, catching her, releasing her, tumbling to the floor, pulling her down by the ankle and latching an arm around her. A smirk worked its way across her face in her capture, one that defied the leg she managed to work between them, the foot she struck against his chest, sending him crashing into the wall.

"Just another game, Arianna of the Stars," Malachi growled, voice heavy, eyes flashing.

"If you want me," she replied, body graceful and sinuous as she hovered mere inches above the ground, "then come and take me."

And so he did, soaring across the room and shoving her against a post, both of them taking pleasure in pain, in the bite of teeth against lip, fingernail against flesh. Malachi wrapped her long legs around him, tearing off her top and feasting on every part of her. Her hands worked over his chest, the strong lines of his shoulders, the firm muscle of his back.

Arianna fell back when he threw her to the bed, arching up to meet him when he landed on top of her, one arm on either side, his mouth already covering hers. She felt the growl work its way up his throat when her hands searched his body, seeking out every part of him, and finding him ready for every part of her.

His hand gripped her hair, tugging as they kissed, touched, explored. Her legs tightened around his waist, urging him, teasing him. She felt his mouth tracing down, discovering the tender flesh of her breast, the sensitive dip of her hips. When he ripped off the cloth covering the last bit of her, Arianna had the fleeting thought that this was wrong, and she should reclaim control.

But he was already inside her, and she let him take her.

SUNLIGHT STREAMED IN through a small opening in the tree trunk, washing over the sleeping bodies intertwined around one another. Arianna woke slowly, blinking in the golden glow, realizing where she was, who she was with.

Rising to a sitting position, she wrapped a fur blanket around herself and cast a look down at Malachi. He was sleeping soundly on his back, one arm to his side, the arm that had been cradling her while she slept. Arianna hid a grin when she saw the scratches on his shoulder, on his sculpted hips, made by her own nails just last night. With some amount of surprise, surprise that mixed with a renewed desire, she saw that she too held evidence of their union—fingermark bruises on her upper arms, a light but distinct bite mark on her shoulder, knotted hair that tumbled down her back.

She didn't regret a single moment of it.

Arianna saw a new side of Malachi last night, and of herself. They were wild, they were savage. They were one with each other, matching curve to curve, desire to desire, melding violence with gentle caresses in a dance of passion. She'd never experienced that kind of love before, that kind of wanting.

She wanted more.

Her eyes dark with desire, Arianna shifted and straddled Malachi, lowering herself so that her flesh just teased his own. He stirred at the touch, and she felt his strong hands grip her thighs even though his eyes never opened. She let him guide her body, arching down and kissing his throat, breathing in the scent of him. The earth and sky, ocean and forest—scents that tantalized her.

There were no fleeting thoughts of wrongness now, as she closed her own eyes and moved with him. There was no guilt in letting another take every part of her as Malachi's fingers fisted in her hair. There was only pleasure, hot, gasping pleasure that burned through her with each thrust.

Breathless, Arianna fell over onto her back next to Malachi, who rolled to meet her.

"I worried you would not be here in the morning," he told her, kissing her shoulder. She only smiled at him. "It seems our nightly playtimes have grown up with us."

Her grin widened at that, a bit of color rising in her cheeks. As children, they'd spent their nights staring up at the stars and finding images in the dots of color like many would find in clouds. As children, they pretended to be bandits racing through the forest, hiding in the shadows and leaping out in pops of color to startle the other. Their games had been innocent.

Their games had changed.

"We should get up," she told him, avoiding talk of who they had become, not wanting to admit how often she'd imagined this very moment. "I'm sure the boys will be back any minute. It's almost breakfast time."

"Let them wait outside." Malachi positioned himself at her feet and threw the blanket off her, crawling up her suggestively. She only laughed and pressed a hand to his chest, pushing him away. They dressed in time to hear footsteps and energetic voices, and soon the boys appeared in a tumble.

"You're back!" Caps shouted, pumping a fist in the air. The others agreed excitedly, all except one.

Fellow approached Arianna cautiously, lower lip stuck out. "I waited like you said," he told Arianna quietly, words strained as he held back tears. "I didn't tell him 'til morning, but then it was too late. He couldn't find you."

Arianna squatted down so that she was eye level with the child. She lifted a hand, squeezing his shoulder. "You did just fine, little Fellow. I'm here now and that's all that matters."

Fellow grabbed her in a fierce embrace, then pulled back and announced that they were all to spend the day playing the best game The Never had ever seen.

Together the group tromped outside and began that game, a battle of boys against grown-ups. Malachi and Arianna hid behind wide-trunked trees, crouching down so they would not be seen. Shooter named himself the scout, sniffing out their trail and sending telling calls into the forest for the others to follow. Fellow took the role of team leader, ordering the boys on where to go and what to do. Caps and Cowboy named themselves warriors, taking hold of their weapons and slinking through the forest to find their prey. Solemn Sam stated how he wished he too were smart enough to find the grown-ups, but alas, he would simply follow behind the others.

The grown-ups took to the air when found; the boys catcalled and named them cowards. Malachi allowed Caps to catch him by the ankle and feigned fear when Cowboy came at him with a spear. Arianna blocked the blow with a sneak attack, wrapping her arms around the boy and tackling him softly to the earth. The grown-ups and children ended up in a rowdy heap, pinching bare skin and pulling loose hair and head-locking anyone within reach.

For hours they raced, tackled, chased, wrestled. Some battles took place in the air, children holding on tight to their flying counterpart; other battles were held on land, feet pounding dirt and grass. One by one the boys lost interest in the game, distracted by other sights or engaging in war with a fellow friend until finally the grown-ups were all but forgotten.

EXHAUSTED, ARIANNA FLOPPED down on the bright green grass and let the boys continue their fun all around them. Malachi joined her, taking a break from the revelry, laying back and staring up at the cloudless blue sky.

"Antelope."

Arianna looked over at him, then back at the clouds. "Antelope leaping over a log."

"Antelope leaping over a log and chasing a rabbit."

"Antelope leaping over a log and chasing a rabbit with two heads."

"Antelope leaping over a log and chasing a rabbit with two heads wearing a polka dot dress."

They burst out laughing, remembering their many days spent doing just this, dreaming up outrageous images in the clouds and outdoing one another with each reveal. It was refreshing for Arianna to know that while their minds, bodies, and desires had matured, this much stayed the same.

"I forgot how much I missed this," she said, letting her memories take her back. "I hate that I forgot what it was like to lay here with you and see our dreams in the clouds."

"But you remember now, my Arianna. That is all that matters."

"I know why I forgot, Malachi, but I don't understand what has happened to The Never. Sometimes it seems like the world we knew as children. Other times there is a darker feel to the air. Right now it is peaceful and beautiful."

"Because the Sea Killers are gone." He spared her a moment's glance. "They went out to sea a few days before you returned. Whenever they are gone, The Never is at peace. When they arrive back at Pirate Port, the darkness returns."

"And you know why."

Malachi lifted himself to his elbow, peering down at Arianna. "All I know is that The Hunter is interested in you. But I don't know why."

"Is that why you came back for me?" Arianna's eyes narrowed. "Did you want me for me, or only to save your precious Never?"

"For you," he answered without hesitation. "I have searched for you since you left when we were children. The darkness did not come until recently, when The Hunter took over. I learned that X was looking for you, but chose not to tell you. I thought it would upset you and wanted to let you adjust to The Never first."

She couldn't be mad at him for hiding that much. Malachi, of all people, would understand why she needed to be protected from certain truths. "When will they return?"

"Hard to say. No one knows why they go out to sea, or when they will return. But now that you are back, my guess is that they will come back to port soon. Word of your return will have traveled fast, as it did the first time."

Arianna rose, pulling him up with her. "Well then, let's not waste our days in the light."

Making Deals, Making Enemies

MALACHI'S WORDS PROVED true when, just three days later, there came a change in the air.

Arianna sat watching the boys play, grinning over their youthful antics. It had been so long since she simply enjoyed kids being kids. She'd forgotten how much fun it was to watch them race around, trying to catch one another, screaming obscenities and insults that made the others laugh. She wasn't entirely sure what their game was, but that was part of the fun.

Fellow and Caps were on a team together, chasing Solemn Sam and Chuckles around the field. All four boys were shouting and giggling, having a great time beneath a bright blue sky.

Until one of them pulled a knife.

Arianna saw the movement just as she noted a cold wind that blew in from the sea. It took her a moment too long to process what was happening, a moment in which she watched the scene through a foggy lens. Caps drew his blade on an unsuspecting Chuckles, and when the smaller boy's back was turned, slid the knife deep into the child's left side.

"Chuckles!" Arianna leapt to her feet as Chuckles fell to the ground, groaning and clutching his side. Blood seeped through his fingers. Caps and the other boys only laughed and pointed, brandishing the knife like a celebrated war weapon. "Caps, what have you done?"

"I have won!" the boy responded, red-stained fingers fisted around the blade. "I have defeated the enemy!"

"It was just a game, Caps! You might have killed him!" Arianna dropped to her knees, fighting back tears and not understanding how the child could be so indifferent. Caps merely shrugged and turned away, racing away with the others.

"Chuckles, hold on, buddy. I'll get some help." She pressed her hands against the wound, distressed by the warm liquid that refused to lessen. Arianna was just about to yell for help when Malachi appeared, worry written across his face. "Malachi! We have to help him. We have to bring him somewhere. Anywhere. I don't know what to do," she rambled, but Malachi only picked the boy up, not appearing to notice that Chuckles had gone limp.

"Follow me to the natives," he ordered.

She did just that, fighting back tears the entire way. When they landed in the natives' camp, it seemed word had already spread, as the chief was waiting for them. An old woman stood at his side, stepping forward when Malachi landed.

"Let me see boy," she demanded in her foreign accent, kneeling slowly after Malachi had set Chuckles on a narrow bed made of intertwined palms. "You step back. I work now."

Malachi did as directed, gently taking Arianna by the arm when she made no move to do the same. She stood clutching her blood-stained hands together, eyes wide.

"Just like Little One," she whispered. "They were just playing, and then…I don't understand what happened."

"*They* have returned," Malachi replied in her ear, drawing her away from the scene. "Did you not feel the change?"

She did, Arianna realized. She felt the cold wind, smelled the foul breeze, saw the shift in the boys' faces. "He didn't even care. Caps. He just stabbed him and walked away."

"It's getting worse. The darkness," Malachi explained when Arianna only glanced at him, then back at the old woman, who was leaning over Chuckles. "The boys used to simply fight. Then they began drawing blood. And now…" He gestured to their fallen comrade, sliding an arm around her. They watched the woman work until she finally sat back on her heels and said something to the chief, who nodded and walked over to them.

"Chuckles will live," Malachi said after the chief spoke in his native language. Arianna breathed a sigh of relief. "The wound is deep and they are worried it might get infected. He will need to stay here until he is healed. For now, all we can do is let him rest."

The chief placed a comforting hand on Malachi's shoulder, then turned and walked back to the hut where Chuckles was brought. Arianna sank down on a log, burying her head in her hands.

"Part of me hoped you were exaggerating," she confessed. "I thought maybe you were using The Never as a way to get me back, blaming the pirates for the way things have changed. But you were right. Something must be done." Arianna looked down at her hands, rubbing them together and doing nothing to wipe away the dried blood. Malachi watched her, considering her words.

"What do you propose to do?" he asked. "Did you learn anything in our trip to Pirate Port?"

"Only that they are looking for me and want you dead. And that the captain wants me. He was making a canvas, which I can only assume is for me. He knows I'm an artist, and somehow, that means something in all of…this." Arianna waved a hand at the sky, which was a strange bluish-gray. "That's…that's why I went back," she remembered. "I went back to get my brushes, because they are mine, and not his. I thought I might need them."

Malachi frowned, processing her statement. "Why would you need your brushes?"

"So that if I am forced to paint, I can do so using my own tools, my own power."

"Why would you be forced to paint?" His confusion seemed to match her own when she looked over at him. "The only way you would be forced to paint is if the captain captures you. I will not let that happen."

"I know." Arianna let out a deep, nervous breath. "That's why I am going willingly."

Malachi leapt up, hands immediately going to his hips. "You will *not* go willingly."

Arianna also rose. "Malachi, I understand that you're worried. But you have to trust me. This is the best way. If I go willingly, pretend that I want to be away from all of this, away from you, that I want to be a pirate, then I can earn his trust. If I earn his trust, then I can figure out how he's destroying The Never."

And if I earn his trust, she added silently, *then he will have no reason to turn me over to X.*

But Malachi didn't agree with her assessment. He shook his head vehemently, pointing at Arianna. "This is not the way to do this, Arianna of the Stars. You do not know what he is capable of. You will not survive him."

"I *will* survive him. And I will save The Never."

"No," he said again. "I forbid you to do this."

"Forbid?" Arianna repeated, eyebrows raised. "You forbid me? You don't have the right to forbid me." She pressed a hand to his chest and pushed him back a step, not noticing that the sky had turned dark with threatening clouds. "I am going, Malachi. With or without your approval."

Malachi grabbed her wrist, lightning flashing across the sky when his flesh touched hers. "You cannot leave me again."

Her immediate instinct was to yell, but the desperation in his voice softened her just a bit. "Malachi, I'm not leaving you. I'm trying to save us, and The Never. I'll come back."

"You *never* come back!" Malachi shouted, thunder rumbling. In the distance, the chief emerged from his hut and peered at the sky. "You always promise to come back, and you never do! Why would this time be any different?"

His words cut deep, because she knew they were true. She made empty promises, and yet, expected others to still believe them. "Listen, Malachi. I know you're scared. But I promise I will come back. I have no intention of being one of them. I don't really want to be a pirate. It's just pretend."

"There is no pretend with them, Arianna. You do not know them."

"I know them better than you may think."

He saw the pain in her eyes, heard it in her voice. That pain matched the cold rain that began to fall, coating them in freezing slush. "My Arianna, we must fight them together."

"We *are* fighting them together."

"No." Again, he shook his head, holding up a hand. "We do this side by side, or not at all. If you go to them, if you go to *him* and fall prey to his power, then we are done."

The argument fell into silence then, the two staring at one another through narrowed eyes that reflected all the hurt feelings and fears felt within them. Their heavy breathing matched, as did their clenched fists. They stood as mirrors of one another, hair and clothes soaked by the cold rain, each fighting off shivers and resentment.

Finally, Arianna spoke. "You don't mean that."

"I do."

"Fine. Then we are done." Her voice broke at that, but she didn't let her face show her pain. Instead, Arianna bent her knees slightly and took off for the sky, leaving Malachi behind before he could see her tears.

SHE MADE TWO stops on her way to Pirate Port, partly because they were necessary and partly because she was hoping to delay what was coming next. First she went back to the treehouse and retrieved her brushes. Four of them, all different sizes. That was the easy trip. The second one she dreaded, convincing herself that this time she would be more careful, and that the sea creatures held no power over her.

Arianna approached the lagoon cautiously, peering through the icy rain, her breath clouding out in front of her. Misty Marsh was quiet, the water still save for the ripples created by the falling rain. There was no moonlight here, only glowing orbs beneath the water that cast an eerie light from rock to rock.

She stepped out onto one of those rocks, toes gripping the edges of stone as she leaned over the water, searching for a sign of life. "I know you're here," she said through the rain. "We're going to talk. And this time, no games."

For a moment nothing happened and Arianna began to wonder if she was being ignored. But then the water stirred and a figure approached her solitary rock in the middle of the lagoon.

"You," Arianna accused indifferently, her face emotionless. The sea woman who had nearly drowned her last time stared back, her eyes filled with amusement. Arianna lifted a hand and pulled down her collar to reveal the scars she would always bare. "Your work, I presume." The woman of white only smiled, revealing a set of pointed teeth. Her angular face looked even sharper in the glow of her pearly hair, which clung to a willowy torso.

"I know why you attacked, and why you feel no remorse." Arianna took a step back when the woman placed a hand on the rock, too close to her feet. "I know that I used to come here to play, and that I was welcomed even though I also caused the kind of trouble only a child can get into. But The Never has changed, and I aim to change it back."

The woman pulled back, head cocked to the side curiously, lips parting slightly as though asking a silent question.

"You heard me," Arianna stated firmly, placing her hands on her hips. "This is not The Never we once knew. I am going to save our home, even if I have to sacrifice myself to do so. Although, I'd rather not die at the hands of the captain, this…Hunter everyone fears so much. That's why I'm here. Are you with me, or against me?"

At first Arianna feared the woman of white chose the latter, but then realized the sea creature had sent out some sort of silent call. She nearly gasped when the others appeared, heads of blue and green and pink appearing in the distance. The sea creatures joined the woman of white, listening eagerly. They were silent, but at times Arianna could swear that she heard their thoughts rolling off them, across the water, into her ears, her mind. Confusing thoughts, jumbled into images of The Never.

She saw sunlight bouncing off crystal blue water, reflecting off a flurry of scaled bodies swimming around Misty Marsh. Some of those bodies were laid out on rocks, enjoying the warmth, their tails swishing ever so slightly; others splashed about, their laughter echoing off stone and waterfall.

She saw human children swimming with the finned creatures, diving off the rocks and pretending to be mermaids like their new friends. There was a boy, with wild red hair and bright green eyes, a wiry frame and a cocky strut. And there was a girl, with long brown hair that tumbled down a skinny back, eyes wide as they took in the magnificent sight.

She saw the lagoon many years later, no longer filled with sunlight and children. The water was clouded and dank, the sea creatures hateful for what their land had become, what they had become. Songs had been silenced, laughter diminished, clean water sullied.

Arianna understood what these thoughts were showing her. They were showing her what once was, what used to be, and what could be again. The sea creatures were asking for help just as much as she was.

"Okay. Glad we're on the same page." Arianna knelt, this time not moving back when the woman of white came closer. The rain had let up some, but still sent hundreds of tiny ripples throughout the water. The cold didn't seem to bother the sea woman, who peered up at Arianna without blinking.

Arianna lowered her head, and when she spoke, her tone was

frighteningly serious. “Here’s what I need you to do.”

The Star Jumper

BY THE TIME she left the lagoon, night was upon The Never. Arianna flew undetected in the cloud-covered black sky, reflecting over her visit with the sea creatures. She wasn't entirely sure they were on her side, considering they flipped in the water and swam away just as soon as she'd finished outlining her plan. Either they were afraid, not willing to help, or didn't need to hear more in order to fulfill their part in her scheme.

She'd been counting on them to help further her plan of attack, which she didn't get to propose due to their swift departure. Without the mermaids, Arianna wasn't sure what would happen. But she couldn't let the feeling of the unknown hold her back.

She had work to do.

Arianna landed on the rooftop of an abandoned building on the outskirts of Pirate Port, watching the activity below her. It was quiet, most of the drunkards tucked away in the taverns or in alleyways with women dressed in two-sizes-too-small corsets. And on the edges of the port was her target, the pirate ship.

As a child, during her last visit to The Never, she'd promised herself she would never step foot on the ship again. Too many enemies, too many bad memories, were there to haunt her. Now she was willingly returning. Arianna felt like she was betraying her childhood self, and that sickened her. That self-loathing would drive her though, and so she used it to push away the fear and rebuild the confidence that had been chipped away over the years.

Adjusting her pack, which contained her brushes, a change of clothes, and a few pieces of food she'd picked up at the lagoon, Arianna lifted herself from the rooftop and headed straight for that ship. She didn't care who saw her, though she doubted many did—until her bare feet hit the deck with a heavy thud. The sound alone nearly made her sick, as did the feel of cold wood against her skin. She hadn't been on this ship since she was a child, and the years away did nothing to ease her anxiety.

Her eyes narrowed, refusing to show the tumultuous emotions clashing within her. Instead she waited for her presence to be known, and it didn't take long. She heard heavy boots pounding upstairs from below deck, and soon, they had formed a line in front of her.

Arianna eyed them all in turn, one side of her mouth curling into a sneer as she forced back the pain in her gut at the sight of them, greasy and filthy, unbrushed and unwashed. Only a few paces away, she could smell them just was easily as she could see them, a familiar stench she'd grown accustomed to as a child that didn't make her as nauseous as it did furious.

But she pushed back that rage as well and kept her stare even, head cocked slightly to the side. Her throat tightened only a bit, a slight quiver in her jaw, when a figure stepped through the line of suspicious pirates all clutching their favorite weapons. Arianna lifted her head ever so slightly and clamped her teeth together when X appeared.

He knew her as soon as he saw her, lips curling, tongue flicking. He placed a hand at his belt, fingers grazing the hilt of a sword. "Little Arianna, all grown up," he rasped, that dark, rough voice cutting through her. "Come back to us after all, did you?"

He took a step closer and she willed herself to keep her feet planted. Her toes curled in protest, hand moving to her own sword as she replied. "I have business with the captain."

X leered down at her, eyebrow lifting. His pitted face was cast in shadows, skin heavy over wide cheekbones, round eyes nearly black in the stormy night. He wore a blood- and dirt-stained gray vest open at the chest to reveal jagged and raised scars, and black pants that clung to muscular legs. Tattoos spread across his stomach, chest, and shoulders spoke of a life at sea. He was a wide man, full and strong, and altogether terrifying.

"My dear Star Jumper, whatever business you have with the captain, you can say right here."

She'd forgotten about her old nickname, and didn't appreciate hearing it now. "If it's all the same, I'd rather speak with him first."

X closed the distance between them, so close she could see her reflection in his eyes. Her hands threatened to shake but she held them tight at her hips. "Where is the Wild One?"

"Not here," she answered curtly. "Let's just say he didn't appreciate me taking charge."

"Mmm, times have changed."

The other pirates chuckled knowingly. X lifted a hand, but before he could touch her, Arianna stepped back, drawing the sword at her side as she did so. She held the blade evenly, level with his chest.

"The captain," she repeated, never taking her stare from X even as the men behind him all braced themselves.

X lifted a hand to ward them off, then drew his own sword. Its reach was easily twice the size of Arianna's, and twice as deadly. "Still thinking rashly, little Arianna. Perhaps times have not changed after all." She was outmatched and they both knew it. X seemed to think twice of the attack and lowered the sword just a bit. "Better not ugly up that pretty face before the captain gets a hold of you."

She scarcely breathed until he sheathed his sword, then mimicked his action. "Let's get on with it then."

X paused, turning his head slowly and grinning at her from beneath a head of greasy, dark hair. In that one look she relived everything that he was capable of, everything he'd done. She couldn't let it defeat her, and so she squared her shoulders and brushed past him when he gestured to a doorway that led below deck. The pirates parted for her, eager to know what would happen next.

In truth, she didn't know either; nor could she begin to guess where she was being led. Excitement mixed with dread as she walked down a set of creaky stairs, hearing water all around her, smelling rum and rot.

X brought her to a spacious room, entering into an alcove just off the main quarters. A quick glance around told Arianna that this room, with its evenly spaced lanterns on the wall and deep blue rugs stitched with light green patterns, served as both a bedroom and office, with sleeping arrangements tucked away in the back and the front area complete with elegant tapestries and an ornate wooden desk decorated with carvings of heavily armed pirates pillaging an unsuspecting town.

Behind that desk sat a man, who rose when they entered. He was a round, portly man with graphic tattoos of women and beasts covering nearly every patch of skin Arianna could see, save for his face. He was dressed neatly, albeit still dirty and sweaty, in a short-sleeved white shirt unbuttoned at the collar and a tall black hat topping his head.

Arianna eyed him, stopping in the center of the room, hand on the hilt of her sword. She briefly wondered why X hadn't taken her weapon, but certainly wasn't going to ask him. "You are the captain?"

"At your service, me lady." He offered her a mocking bow. "How may I be of assistance to ya?"

Arianna flicked a glance over her shoulder at X, then back at the man before her. "I have business to discuss with you. Alone."

He considered, then nodded at X. "Leave us be, matey. I can handle the little lass."

Arianna refrained from rolling her eyes, waiting until X left and closed the door behind him to continue. "Nice place," she commented, running a hand across the smooth oak desk, touching a finger to a globe. It wasn't an average globe with the world she was most familiar with, but a map of The Never and surrounding lands she hadn't explored.

Yet.

A small stone the color of the setting sun sat next to the globe in a velvet container, perfectly oval and smooth. She picked it up, marveling at the beautiful hue, able to feel the power of the land it hailed from.

A voice whispered through her thoughts, a voice not spoken aloud, but in a vision concerning this very treasure that once rested at the bottom of a lagoon. "*The Hunter stole something from us, red as the setting sun, smooth as the ocean floor. We know not how he got it, but we want it back.*"

That stone would be her salvation, or her downfall. But now was not the time to put her plan into action, and so she set it down and turned back to the pirate. "Looks different than the last time I was here."

"The Never is a different place now, lass. And so is the people in it."

"Perhaps." Arianna leaned against the desk and crossed her arms. "So. You can handle the little lass, huh?"

It took a moment for her question to register, and when it did, he smiled. "Aye, lass."

She lifted herself from the desk and turned, walking over to the window and peering out. In the night and rain, she saw not a thing. "Well then, get to handling."

She heard him approach from behind, slowly at first, then eagerly. When she sensed his hand out to touch her, Arianna spun around, her blade at his throat. The man gasped but remained still, arching his neck and succeeding only in having the point of the sword cut into his flesh. He didn't dare speak.

"You're all the same," she accused, sounding more bored than disgusted. "Now if you don't mind, take me to the captain. Your *real* captain."

His lips pulled back to reveal a set of yellowed teeth. "I *am* your captain, missy."

Arianna gave a quick, sarcastic laugh. "What kind of captain dresses like you, all filthy and grimy? What kind of captain lets his brute of a first mate talk better than him? You, sir, are not the captain." She didn't feel the need to also explain that she'd snooped around the ship before and saw the captain from behind, and this fat man certainly did not fit the frame of the hooded figure.

When the man only growled at her, Arianna shifted, making him turn with her. She wanted to force him into the chair behind the desk, give herself the advantage of looking down on him, but when she turned she saw what hung behind the desk.

"What…where did you get that?" Her voice rose as she looked at the painting, recognizing it instantly. Her painting, the one she'd tried so hard to recreate, the one she agonized over selling. "Where!"

"Tis just a trinket, lass. Nothing ta get excited about."

She pressed the tip closer against his throat. "Tell me what you know before I slit you from groin to gullet."

A slow clapping to her right broke Arianna's concentration. She looked over at the source of the sound, heart dropping when she saw who was emerging from behind a screen. "You," she breathed, strength faltering. Her arm holding the sword dropped, and she struggled to make sense of the figure before her.

Just when she decided upon what to say, movement burst behind her and she was struck, slumping into a deep sleep.

Twenty-Three

The Hunter Hunts

SHE AWOKE IN a fog, eyes heavy and forehead pounding. It took a moment for her head to clear, and another for her to rise to a sitting position. Arianna lifted a hand to her head almost immediately when a wave of dizziness passed through her.

"He really shouldn't have hit you that hard," that familiar accented voice said from somewhere far away, and yet, so close. "I do apologize for that, love."

Arianna blinked a few times and shifted, realizing she was lying on a fancy velvet couch, a blanket pulled up to her waist. Her sword was gone, as was her pack. Those were the least of her concerns though, considering the figure that sat directly across from her, one arm casually perched across the top of the chair.

At first she only stared, thinking that *this* was how a captain was supposed to look. His clothes were finely tailored—a crisp white shirt beneath a black jacket with gold buttons down the front, collar propped. His boots were worn but cared for, scarred with years of treks through forests and across wastelands of bone and body. His hands showed the spoils of many wars, rings of ruby and emerald decorating his fingers. The stories of those wars were written across his face, in the light wrinkles around his smirking mouth, in the set of his jaw, even in the neat yet careless way his dark hair was tied back at the nape of his neck.

He was smooth, suave, sultry. And staring at her with the brightest eyes she'd ever seen.

"You're him," she said, hands clutching the sofa edges. "You're the man from the gallery, who bought my painting. James."

He smiled. "Your memory serves you well, Star Jumper."

The nickname sounded sweet coming from him. "I don't…why? What the hell do you want from me?"

The man called James leaned forward. "You came to me, dear Arianna. I think the better question is, what do *you* want from *me*?"

As confused and frightened as she was, this was the moment Arianna had come for. She sat up straighter, ignoring the pounding behind her eyes as she stared at the captain, The Hunter. Her thoughts were confused as she let herself look him over, as though the very sight of him was enough to revert her back into a lovesick teenage girl. "I…I came to see you. I…came to join your crew."

The Hunter laughed. "Join my crew? You? The Wild One's partner?"

"We are no longer partners," she corrected him. "He thought he could control me. He thought wrong."

"And so you come to me. Why?"

"Why not?" Arianna took in a deep breath. "I was part of this ship once. Perhaps it's time I join it again."

"Perhaps, indeed."

His coy and indifferent attitude was starting to irritate her. "So…what do the men call you? The Hunter?"

He lifted a brow, bright eyes looking her over. "They call me Captain, naturally. I suppose you may call me Jim."

"I thought only your friends called you Jim."

He winked at Arianna, and despite herself, the gesture nearly made her smile. "No reason for us to be enemies. Yet." Jim rose from the chair and turned, heading for the door.

"Wait." Arianna jumped to her feet, and the sound of a chain clanking to the floor had her faltering. She looked down to see her ankle strapped in irons, which were attached to a post in the floor.

Her eyes were accusatory when she looked back up at Jim.

"Can't be too cautious, love."

Furious at the thought of being locked up, Arianna rushed at him. She got only a foot away before the chain jerked her back. "Take this off," she growled, grabbing him by the shirt.

"And they say the boy is wild," Jim retorted, not at all fazed by her weak attack. He placed a hand on her wrist, untangling her fingers from his shirt. "You must earn my trust, Star Jumper. And you can do that right here, chained to the floor." He grinned when Arianna only set her jaw and narrowed her eyes. "Such fire. You'll do well here, after you prove yourself."

Arianna jerked back when he lifted a hand to her face, but he only took her arm and held her in place. Even in her rage she found herself observing him curiously—the dark hair, the day's worth of stubble, the bright eyes she'd seen only twice before, once at her gallery show and once when she was a child.

"You look just like him, you know," she said before she could stop herself. "Just…younger."

Her words had an unexpected effect. Jim released her and stepped back, his expression hard. "I wouldn't know, now would I? Your little loverboy cut him down in cold blood."

Arianna scoffed. "Your father would have done the same if he'd been fast enough, or smart enough. It was their favorite game, trying to kill each other."

"The Wild One thinks he has won this game. Time will prove otherwise."

Jim turned on his heel and stalked out of the room, leaving Arianna behind.

HE LEFT HER there, alone, until the next morning. Arianna wasn't surprised by that until she realized that she was, in fact, chained in what appeared to be the captain's very own cabin. And as was her nature, she used her time alone to explore.

The room, despite being sparsely decorated, held an air of elegance to it that she found herself appreciating. On the walls hung deep blue tapestries that reminded her of the ocean at night, with lanterns hanging at even intervals that reflected off the blue with sparks of gold. The floor was solid wood and recently cleaned, lined with rugs made of a short fur she couldn't identify. It was not an animal of her world, or even of The Never, that she knew of.

In the center of the room was the globe, which held her fascination like no other. It glowed soft blues and greens, turning slowly to reveal patches of land among an expansive ocean. Their land, The Never, was outlined in gold. Others were marked by green outlines and more still in red. Places they'd been and planned to go, Arianna guessed. When she leaned in for a closer look, she could smell the sea and hear waves crashing against the shores. When she touched one of the smaller sections, it grew in front of her until she could see life on land in the form of mountain ranges, villages, and even tiny townsfolk going about their way, oblivious to the ever-watchful eye seeing their every move.

Set back from the globe was a section blocked off by blue curtains, which were worn with age. Through the holes she saw a gorgeous wood hutch and the edges of a bed. His bed, she assumed, and for a moment was annoyed that it was out of reach, leaving her to rest on an uncomfortable couch.

Rain splattered against the single round window against the far wall as she walked as far as her chains would allow. She'd already spent considerable time and energy trying to get them off, but her efforts merely left her fingers raw and achy. So instead she entertained herself by looking through maps left on the desk, pondering over places she'd never seen and lands she'd never heard of.

She'd never been good at reading maps, preferring to let others navigate, so she didn't understand much of what she saw. But she did understand one important thing—these were places the captain had personally visited or intended to explore, and part of her hoped she too would have the chance to see such places. The Never was all she'd ever known. She and Malachi never ventured too far out to sea, and never really cared much about what existed beyond the borders of The Never. They knew other places existed, but their world was here.

A slip of paper caught Arianna's eye, one that was different than the rest. Unlike the others, which were maps and coordinates, this one had writing scrolled across it in fancy penmanship. Curious, she slid the paper out from under a pile by the corner and had just read the date printed across the top when a voice from behind startled her.

"Caught red-handed, Star Jumper."

Arianna spun around to see Jim standing in the doorway holding a covered tray. Keeping his eyes on her, he shifted the tray to one hand and stalked over, leaning in close. Arianna took in a deep, nervous breath, backing up against the desk and considering punching him in the throat when he reached for her, around her.

She released the breath when he simply moved the piece of paper away, tucking it under a folder. He set the tray down on the table by the couch, her couch, then looked at her pointedly.

"What?"

"Eat," he ordered, gesturing to the tray after pulling off the cover.

She eyed the food, stomach growling as she fought to keep from salivating. Warm bread, steak and potatoes, and fresh corn stared back at her. "I'm not hungry," she lied.

Jim only lifted a brow. "You haven't eaten since you got here. Sit down and eat. It's not poisoned."

"Says the man keeping me in chains." But she moved a step closer. "Did you make it?"

He smirked. "Do you really think I did? It's from the tavern. Now eat. It will improve your mood, and I'd appreciate you letting up on all that." He waved at the window.

Arianna looked in that direction, frowning. "Letting up on what?"

"The rain. I'd like to set out to sea when it's not in the middle of the storm."

His back was turned, and she couldn't tell if he was making fun of her by tone alone. Arianna glanced out the window again, trying to make sense of his words. She'd always known that The Never responded to Malachi, his emotions, his desires. Did it also respond to her? It would explain the tumultuous storm that appeared during their fight, and why the rain still lingered. Perhaps in finally embracing her place in The Never, she considered, she had allowed herself to be connected to the land as he was.

A hunger pain in her stomach snapped her back to attention, and she realized that Jim was watching her, arms crossed, an unreadable expression on his face. She ignored him and sat on the couch, pulling the tray onto her lap and trusting in him enough to eat.

They both relaxed with each bite, her mood improving as she consumed the meal with hardly a break. Jim sat at his desk, staring down at his maps and papers and the mysterious letter. Arianna could hear the pirates as they moved throughout the ship, screaming curses at one another and banging around as they slumped into walls. Despite her chains, she was thankful that, for the moment, she wasn't in their company.

When her plate was nearly empty, Arianna looked at Jim out of the corner of her eye. He wasn't paying attention to her, absorbed in his own work. Even in her quick glance she could see that his brow was furrowed and he was deep in thought. The scruff along his jaw made his pensive expression even more intriguing.

She cleared her throat. "So…why am I in here? Why not the brig?"

"You're a young woman on a pirate ship, love," he answered without looking up. "This is the safest place for you."

"Why not feed me to the wolves?"

He did look up at that question. "Because I'm not quite sure what I'm going to do with you yet. And until I decide, I'd like to keep you in one piece."

Arianna shredded the remaining bread on her plate, taking the time to consider her predicament as he went back to his work. She'd known she would be taken captive at first, so being in chains wasn't surprising. How to get out of those chains, though, was an issue she hadn't yet resolved.

The ship lurched slightly in the waves, but the rain was letting up. Her mood really was improving, she thought, although she guessed Malachi, wherever he was, was still fuming. The thought of Malachi brought her back to the moment, remembering this ship, its former captain, the many battles they'd had with the terrifying yet gentlemanly swordfighter.

The pirate game had been her favorite, Arianna remembered. Sneaking around the port with Malachi, eagerly awaiting the ship's return from sea, daydreaming over the many adventures the ocean had to offer. When the ship was in port, they planned their mischievous tricks, loosening sails and dousing sleeping pirates with freezing water and taunting the captain with catcalls until finally he emerged, black curls blowing in the breeze, eyes shining in the moonlight, sword ready to battle the children who entertained themselves with his own misery.

"We didn't know about you, you know," Arianna said quietly, staring down at her plate. "Maybe things would have been different if we did. But…he never mentioned you."

"Well isn't that a pleasant bedtime story," Jim replied, condescension in his voice. "We killed the captain, sir, but we're sorry, he never cared enough to tell us he was your father."

"That's not what I meant," Arianna sighed. "I just meant, maybe we wouldn't have all hated one another, if we'd had someone else in common."

"Yes, how convenient of him to keep his only son a secret so he could battle with the wild children of The Never."

Arianna set down the bread, full. She stood, already tired of sitting on the couch. "Maybe he wanted to protect you—"

"Maybe you should not speak of things you know nothing of." He rose as well, walking around the desk to face her squarely.

"I spent a lot of time on this ship. I know more than you think."

"Yes, so I have heard."

She didn't know what he meant, but wouldn't give him the satisfaction of showing defeat. "Your father—"

"You will not speak of him."

"Look. Your father—"

Arianna was silenced by the hand that he slapped across her face. She stumbled back, holding her cheek and feeling like fire had just been pressed against her flesh. The throbbing raced from her chin to her temple, and she could do nothing but stare at him incredulously.

"It would appear violence is the only way to shut you up," Jim snarled, then pointed to the couch. "Get some sleep. Tomorrow you get to prove your worth."

The Cold Caverns

HER MIND REELED with thoughts of what tomorrow would bring, her thoughts keeping her up until late into the night. Arianna lay on the uncomfortable couch, listening to the light rain against the window, wondering what Jim would ask of her.

He'd stormed away after slapping her, although not far. He had disappeared to his sleeping quarters, where he remained the rest of the night. She could have followed as far as her chains would allow, demanding to be set free, but if she were honest with herself, she was a bit afraid. When she fought with Malachi, at most she feared a day or two of not speaking. When she fought with the captain, she feared for her physical safety. He really was the brute others claimed him to be, she mused.

But that didn't matter. She wasn't here to befriend him. She was here to rescue her land, and when she was done, she would leave him. Arianna knew her job was to charm him, earn his trust, figure out what he wanted from her, and save The Never. And saving The Never meant going along with whatever plans he had for tomorrow.

After hours of thought, she finally drifted into a restless sleep.

In sleep, she saw the ship through a child's eyes. Her eyes, when she first came to The Never. It was Malachi who found her that first night in her bedroom, but it was the captain she ended the evening with, having been captured during her return flight and later rescued by her new friend after a vicious yet playful swordfight.

That first night had been fun, running around the pirate ship, hiding in dark corners while the captain and his men searched for her. To Arianna, it had been a game of cat-and-mouse, and she hid her giggles behind her hand. To the pirates, it was a telling night that warned them of what was to come—playful albeit fierce battles with mischievous children. When the captain finally found her, and allowed her to leave, he ordered her to never return to his ship, for her own safety.

Arianna ignored that warning when she was a child, and paid the price.

She didn't realize she was thrashing about until a pair of hands shook her roughly. Arianna opened her eyes to see a shadowed figure looming over her, and on instinct she lashed out, only to have her fist caught by a strong hand.

"Relax, woman."

She recognized the voice, though it did little to slow her racing heart. Arianna pushed at the captain, nearly slapping away his hands as a shriek escaped from her throat. "Let me go. Let me go!"

Jim released her and stepped back. "Good, you're awake. Now you can stop all the yelling." He didn't ask why she was upset or what she dreamed of, but merely returned to his quarters.

Arianna watched him walk away, wishing Malachi was next to her. As kids, he'd always been able to keep her nightmares at bay, always knew what to say during those rare times when not even his games could distract her.

Instead of attempting sleep for the remainder of the early morning, Arianna prepared herself for the impending day. By the time Jim rose, dressed for a day at sea, she was as prepared as she possibly could be.

"Ready yourself, love. You've got a day's work ahead of you."

"So we're back to 'love' now, are we?" she retorted, refraining from kicking him squarely in the face when he leaned over to unchain her ankle. Finally free, she rubbed her sore skin and accepted the sword Jim handed her. It was her sword, taken from her earlier. "Trusting me with a weapon?"

"Would you rather I leave you defenseless?" The edge in his voice silenced her, as did the worry of another slap. Last night's sting still had half her face feeling raw. "This is for your protection, and for the job I have planned for you." Now she was interested, interested enough to also accept the clothing he handed her, though she snarled when he shoved her toward a dressing screen. "Put those on. Meet me outside the room."

She did as ordered, dressing in a pair of tight-fitting black pants, black boots that laced up mid-calf, a tailored white shirt clearly meant for a child but that fit her all the same, and a leather vest. With her hair tucked back in a braid and the sword secured at her hip, she looked quite the pirate, and felt just the same.

"Dashing, no?" she asked playfully as she stepped out of the room, giving Jim a mock pose. He merely scowled and turned her around, pushing her toward a set of stairs. Arianna shot him a dark look. "You best be keeping your hands off me, *Captain*. I'm not the kind of woman you can just push around."

Jim raised a hand and used it to point. "Go."

Arianna lifted a brow, but did as directed and ascended the stairs, nerves forming at what she may find on the other side of the door. Jim stopped her before she could place her hand on the doorknob and exited first. The bright morning sun stung her eyes, but she quickly adjusted, stepping out onto the deck to a flurry of activity.

Men bustled about, some hanging from netting as they hoisted the sails, others swabbing the deck, while others still tugged at ropes to keep on course. More pirates were up in the sails, dropping down to the deck to grab a rope or check their course. The perfectly choreographed movements nearly made her dizzy.

Arianna took in the sight through wide eyes, nearly having forgotten what it was like to be on the deck of a fully functioning pirate ship. These were not the men of Pirate Port, drunken and stumbling, but a well-oiled crew, gruff and determined. They looked and smelled of the sea, and faced their next adventure with lively spirit.

Jim took Arianna by the arm and pulled her halfway up a set of stairs that led to the helm. "Men!" he shouted, catching their attention. "Allow me to introduce the newest member of our crew, Arianna the Star Jumper!" He waited as the men responded with cheers and sneers. Arianna met their reactions with narrowed eyes and a scowl, hands on her hips.

"The Star Jumper will help us with our little…problem…at the Cold Caverns," he continued, and that news silenced the men, who now listened eagerly. "You will show her the respect you show me. The Star Jumper is brave. She is smart. And she is mine."

His last words had the men nodding uncomfortably, sparing one another curious looks. Arianna understood what Jim had just done, claiming her for himself so that no other would dare touch her. For that reason alone, she did not protest when he took her by the upper arm and dragged her into a room situated below the upper-deck helm. Along one wall was a row of wide portholes that overlooked the ocean, allowing sunlight to pour in and cast the suite in a golden glow. The other wall was covered in maps, with red and green pins marking several locations.

"Places you've been?" Arianna asked, touching the tip of a green pin. Jim confirmed with a nod. "So…where is this cavern?"

Jim walked over to the map and touched a speck of land in the middle of the ocean. "We have set course here. It is a small island, created by rock and sustained in stone. There is very little plant life, but the area is rich in fishing opportunities."

"Does anyone live there?"

"Yes." Jim turned away from the map and regarded Arianna carefully. Her arms were crossed, her stance wary. "A rather large clan inhabits the island. They keep to themselves, but do accept trades on occasion, though they rarely have anything of value to offer."

"Then what do you want from them?"

Jim moved to the table in the center of the room and showed her a drawing. Arianna peered down at the paper, taking in the image of a round blue sphere. Even in the crude drawing, she could tell that it emanated power. "What is it?"

"It is of no concern of yours," he replied. "I want it, and you will get it for me."

"Why me?"

"Because *you* are the only one who can step foot on the island. Men are not allowed on the island, and do not often make it more than a single pace."

"Why not?"

"No one knows. It seems the island is surrounded by a kind of magic we do not understand."

"What happens when men go on shore?"

Frustrated, Jim faced her. "You ask a lot of questions, love."

"Only way to learn."

"The only thing you need to learn is to do as you're told." Jim tapped a finger on the drawing. "This is your target. Obtain this, and maybe then I'll start to trust you."

Arianna crossed her arms. "And who says I've started to trust you?"

They stared at one another for a long moment before Jim relented and walked to the door. "It makes no matter whether or not you trust me. Until we reach the Cold Caverns, make yourself useful." He held out a mop, smirking in response to the look of dismay that crossed Arianna's face. "You want to be part of the crew, love, then you better start pulling your weight."

ARIANNA GRUMBLED TO herself as she shoved the mop into a bucket of soapy and now dirty water and pushed it across the deck. She shouldn't have been annoyed - every member of the crew had to earn his keep, after all - but she supposed it was the captain's delivery that had her back up.

"Pull my weight," she muttered, wringing out the mop. "You were the one looking for *me*, Captain Asshole."

It bothered her that he wasn't like his father, who had been evil to his core but also a gentleman. Jim had traces of gentlemanly mannerisms, but gave her the cold shoulder just as easily as he appeared to warm up to her. She'd expected him to enjoy her friendship as his father had, not to treat her like an enemy.

It troubled her even more that she *wanted* him to enjoy her friendship. Being back on the ship, she was reminded again of her daydreams as a child of being a pirate for just a day, pillaging and plundering, wondering what it was like to take what she wanted. More, she remembered how much she loved the sea. The smell of the salt air, the crystal blue water, the feel of freedom with every wave - this was home. This was right.

"Get ta swabbin', wench," a man growled to her right. Arianna snapped out of her daze, realizing she'd been leaning against the mop handle, staring out at the ocean. "You be the captain's alright, but you got a job to do!"

"Relax, Grouch," she replied, so naming the pirate as easily as she responded to him.

The pirate gripped a knife. "Don't you be tellin' me what to do, lass. I got seniority."

Arianna scoffed. "Seniority? Can you even spell that?" She held out the mop in defense when Grouch charged at her, then stared in surprise when the pirate was thrown into the side of the ship by another.

"Step aside, fool," X said to Grouch, who was curled against the railing. "This one's mine."

Arianna's grip on the handle tightened as she moved to her sword. "If you dare lay a hand on me, I promise you will lose it."

"Well now, that seems a bit overdone, don't you think?" X winked at her.

Arianna considered shouting for Jim, but was saved by his own call signifying land. When X's attention was diverted, she used the opportunity to escape his stare and find the captain.

"Your turn, love," Jim said when she appeared at his side. Quickly, he explained where she needed to go, what she needed to do. All the while, Arianna looked out over the ocean at the approaching island. From a distance, it didn't look intimidating, though it certainly did look cold. Stone mountains stared back at her, all sharp lines and shadowed caverns. The shore sparkled in the sunlight, though the rest of the land held but a gray, overcast fog.

It seemed too soon before the anchor was set and Arianna was being directed to a dinghy, which was lowered into the water with her on board, along with another pirate to row. She was silent for the next part of the journey, reflecting on her task, glancing back at the ship to see Jim watching her through a small telescope.

The boat scraped against sand, as far as it would be allowed to go. Arianna jumped out, booted feet splashing into the water, then pushed the dinghy out so the pirate could row back out to a safe distance. Alone now, and very aware of that fact, she faced the Cold Caverns.

It appeared empty, quiet with nary a sound to be heard but for the waves against the shore. Closer now, she realized why that shore sparkled against the sun, as the sand was mixed with what she guessed were thousands of crushed crystals that people from her world would have salivated over.

Never one much for flair, Arianna merely walked over them, barely hearing the crunch of her boots over such valuables. After a few steps she noted with horror that more than crystals were being crunched; bones of fallen pirates and traders also littered the shoreline as a warning to every man who may have entertained thoughts of trespassing.

From the shore led a gray wall, solid rock and icy to the touch. Arianna followed the wall a few yards, adhering to the map Jim had drawn so carefully in her mind. But he could only lead her so far, guiding her based on what he could see through a telescope from the safety of the ship—the sparkling shoreline, the stone barrier that rose up so high she couldn't see the top, the thin and rigid trees that dotted the landscape and provided little shade as she slowly made her way. Finally she reached a crevice so narrow that she barely fit through. Taking in a deep breath, she slipped through.

Now, she was on her own.

There were only legends of this place, Jim had told her, stories told by sailors half mad with drink or disease. They spoke of an island of stone, where ghosts haunted the mountains and hid in the shadows of the rocks. Should any man step foot on the shore, he met his maker in the eyes of the forsaken. Should any woman dare enter the caverns, she was taken in and welcomed, only to never return.

Arianna would be the one who returned, the only person, man or woman, to leave the island alive.

She peered into the darkness, feeling her way until she could no longer follow the path without light. Lifting the torch the captain had given her, she lit the end and allowed the fire to light the way.

Stone lit up in gold, flickers of orange and red reflecting back at her as she walked through the narrow passageway, convincing herself that the walls weren't closing in, that the air wasn't getting lighter. It was as eerie as it was deceptive, her footsteps reverberating all around her, the sound of her breath magnified, the flames singing as they burned.

She turned right, then left, going the only way the maze would allow. When she finally came to a crossroads, she made a blind decision and turned right, her hand trailing along the cold stone, body shivering in the chilly air. The cavern got smaller with the next turn, nearly forcing her sideways. Just when she thought she couldn't handle the maze of rock any longer, Arianna saw a soft blue glow just ahead. She kept her eyes trained on that spot, letting it guide her. One more step after the next, and finally she entered a spacious cavern.

Tiny crystals sparkled from every angle, from the smooth and even floor to the cathedral ceiling with rounded stalactites to the pitted and jagged walls. The air was fresh here, with the slightest hint of citrus. The air was so chilled that her breath clouded in front of her and icicles began to form on the tips of her hair, which was wet from the spray of the ocean during the row to shore.

Shivering, Arianna walked further into the cavern. In the center of the sparkling cave sat a podium surrounded by an enchanting azure haze. Arianna stared at it, letting the color fill her eyes, letting it draw her closer to that perfectly round, perfectly blue sphere. When she was mere inches from it, her hand lifted closer, closer.

"*Enough.*"

The gravel voice startled Arianna into dropping the torch. It landed at her feet and rolled toward the podium. She turned about, seeing only rock walls. "Who…who's there?" she asked, slowly turning another circle. Even knowing she had company, she still felt alone, cold. "Hello?"

"*You will not touch the crystal.*"

Arianna looked over her shoulder at the sphere. She'd thought it was some kind of stone, like the rest of the caverns. "I don't…who are you?"

"*We are the keepers of the crystal, the keepers of the isle.*"

Arianna cast another look around, gray stone meeting her eyes. "We?" She bit back a gasp when that gray stone began to move, and from the walls stepped camouflaged figures.

Dust fell from their shoulders as they moved away from their hiding places, opening bright gray eyes and locking them onto her. Every part of them was made of rock, which shifted and grated with each surprisingly smooth movement. The women weren't tall, but they were lean, lines of muscle revealed in crisp stone lines. Their bodies, though nude, weren't fully defined, and so Arianna saw only curves and indentations in all the right places to tell her that these strangers were, in fact, female.

She wanted to ask who they were, how they lived in the stone, wanted to lie about taking the crystal, but couldn't form the words.

She merely watched as they approached her.

"*A woman comes willingly to our shores*," one of them whispered, so close they were nearly touching. Arianna stood frozen, eyes wide as a hard finger grazed her shoulder. Her skin burned at the ice-cold touch. "*Perhaps you have come to join us*."

She found her voice. "No," Arianna answered, taking count of the five figures. "I'm just here for a visit and really should be going."

"*Oh, but young Star Jumper, none who visit our island leave to tell the tale*."

"No? Then how do people get their legends?"

Her question gave them reason to pause, glancing at one another for the answer, and she used that hesitation to her advantage. Arianna shook off the hand that gripped her shoulder and grabbed the blue crystal, teeth gritting when the cold sphere burned her hands.

Five simultaneous screams pierced her ears, so high pitched that even their own ears threatened to rupture. Arianna felt blood tricking down her neck as she ran, leaving the torch behind and racing for the narrow crevice that would lead her out of this trap.

The stone women clawed at her back, ripping through fabric and flesh, pulling at her hair. Arianna cried out when one of them got hold of her ankle and sent her tumbling to the ground, her knees striking stone. Something sharp was sent through her side, straight through from back to stomach. She picked herself up quickly, kicking at the figures and for once thankful that the space only allowed for one at a time to pass through.

"Let me go!" she yelled at them, her voice coming back at her. "I have to do this!"

"*You take what is ours. You take what does not belong to you*."

"I'll bring it back!" She wasn't lying, as she did intend to return what she was stealing, but her promise went unheard. The chase continued, only the blue glow giving direction. Arianna breathed heavily, suffocating in the confined space, terror eating at her insides. Her hands burned; there was no time to wrap the ice-cold sphere in her shirt, and so she suffered as she ran, determined to overcome this death sentence.

When she was but steps from freedom, one of the women raked a hand down her shoulder, nails digging in deep. Arianna tripped, the crystal slipping from her grasp and sliding just outside the cavern opening. She stumbled out after it, letting out a frustrated cry when a hand grabbed her ankle.

"I'm trying to save you!" she shouted at the stone woman, kicking to get free. "This is the only way!" There was no time to explain the truth, and the keepers of the isle would not have it anyway.

"*Give it back*," she rasped, crawling out of the cavern after Arianna. "*You cannot take our hope, our power, our life*."

"I need it," Arianna growled, her pain and blood loss sending her into a fury. "You will not stop me from what I have to do!"

The two rose to their feet, breathing hard, sounds of the others still making their way through the cavern echoing out at them. Arianna squared off with the alpha, one burned hand on the hilt of her sword.

"*Give…it…back*."

"Come…and…take it." Arianna drew her sword, swiping an arc in front of her when the stone woman charged. Sparks flew as the blade drew across stone, and again when Arianna brought the sword down, shoving the tip against the creature's chest. Her hard skin popped, a crack forming from sternum to navel. Focusing on that crack, Arianna sent the blade directly into its center, screaming at the woman, her fury spread across her face.

The stone woman's eyes widened as she slid to her knees, clutching her cracking and crumbling chest. Arianna stared at the figure, lips parting in realization of what she'd just done. Only the sounds of the creatures' wailing at the discovery of their fallen sister could break her of her shock.

"I…I'm sorry," she whispered, a single tear slipping down her cheek. It was the only parting words she offered before she picked up the crystal and raced back to the boat waiting for her.

Twenty-Five

A Dark Scent

HER FEET HAD barely touched the deck before she collapsed, weakened by her wounds. She was vaguely aware of someone picking her up, that same someone barking orders to bring the crystal to his quarters. It wasn't until she was back in the captain's room, on the floor in front of her couch with something pressed against her forehead, that her head started to clear.

"What…" Arianna pushed at a pair of hands that were touching her back, surprised to see that her own were already wrapped in blood-stained bandages. She tried to turn but was held in place. "Hey. Get off." She struggled again, weak but determined.

"Sit still," came the curt order in Jim's voice.

"Get off," she said again, tugging at her torn shirt, her mind still hazy. She shoved him, but he only kept pulling at her shirt so she attempted to strike.

With a sigh, Jim grabbed her wrists and pressed her against the edge of the couch, leaning in close. "You can let me do this, or I can let one of the men clean your wounds. Would you rather have their hands all over you?"

She wanted to spit at him, but with his face so near hers, she could tell he was being sincere. His eyes were soft, concerned, and she realized then that she must be more injured than she'd thought for him to show any amount of tenderness. So she relaxed, let him take care of her, enjoyed the warmth that radiated from his touch and enveloped every part of her.

"You shouldn't be so tense, love," Jim said as she laid on her stomach. He moved to her shoulder, pulling away torn bits of fabric to reveal jagged scratch marks. "Women have fallen in love with me over my massages."

"I would never love you."

"Well, now you're just hurting my feelings." There was humor in his voice, his fingers gentle as he wiped away blood.

Arianna looked at the wall, biting her teeth together to combat the pain. She could feel him cleaning the wounds and placing bandages at her back. "You knew what would happen sending me in there," she whispered. "You knew I would get hurt. I think I get to hurt your feelings a little bit."

He finished her back and shoulder, then spent time cleaning the wound that went through her side. She knew she'd been lucky with the attack, as the stone dagger had gone through flesh alone, and needed only a few painful stitches as reminders of the fight. Arianna grit her teeth together with each pierce of the needle but refused to show weakness, silently grateful when Jim placed a bandage to her skin.

At long last, he directed her to sit up. She did so, moving slowly and with his help. "You did well."

She kept her stare even when he moved in front of her, wiping a wet cloth across her brow. "I hope it was worth it."

He grinned that malicious, wanting grin. "Oh, it will be."

"I don't suppose you'll tell me why."

"I don't suppose I will." He winked at Arianna, who merely rolled her eyes and decided not to tell him what the stone women had said to her in the caverns. "Close your eyes." He sighed again when Arianna purposely kept them open, unblinking. "Fine, have it your way." Jim dipped the cloth in a basin and brushed it over her forehead. The medicated water dripped down, stinging the corners of her eyes. "I warned you," he said unsympathetically when she cried out and tossed a clean rag at her so she could wipe away the mixture.

Arianna waited for the pain to pass, holding the rag tight against her face. She hurt all over, the worst of it on her back. She'd paid the price for the captain's greed and was still none the wiser. Something would have to change.

"Are we done, then?" she asked, still holding the cloth to her eyes.

"For the night," Jim answered, standing. He drew Arianna to her feet, lifting a hand to her chin and peering at her through narrowed eyes. "You are alright?"

Her response stuck in her throat when he leaned closer. She took in the scent of him, felt gentle fingers brushing her cheek, and shook off the feelings of want and need that surged through her. "I'm fine," Arianna answered, lowering her gaze to the floor.

"Good. Come."

She looked up, wondering if her eyes were as red and puffy as they felt. "Come where?"

He guided her toward his sleeping quarters, Arianna backpedaling when she caught on. Jim held firm to her upper arm. "You need to sleep on your stomach, and you can't do that on the couch. I will sleep there. I need you functional, so get in there and go to sleep."

She sat on the edge of the bed, nervous. Nightclothes had been set out for her and she wondered if he expected her to undress with him standing there. To avoid that awkward question, she glanced around nonchalantly, her gaze resting on a wood-stained dresser with a rust-spotted mirror. Not much sat on the dresser except for a candleholder, three stacked books, and a ring. From beneath the books she saw a piece of parchment and guessed it was the same one she'd barely seen on his desk tucked under a map.

Jim saw her staring and moved in front of the dresser. "That," he said plainly, removing the parchment and placing it in his pocket, "is none of your concern. Get some sleep."

Arianna stared through the curtains after he'd shut them behind her, seeing his shadow moving about the cabin. It was only mid-day, but she was exhausted. She turned to the bed, letting its inviting comforters and plush pillows draw her down.

It was hard to find a comfortable position, but eventually she settled down, surrounded by a small island of luxury, lulled to sleep by the captain's dark scent.

FOR TWO DAYS she slept, rising only to relieve herself and attempt to eat. On the third morning Arianna opened eyes to dawn's early light welcoming her back to consciousness. She lay on her stomach while she woke, feeling tender skin on her back, healing ointment on her hands, a sharp pain in her side, and a dull headache behind her eyes.

But, at least she didn't feel like she was dying anymore.

Arianna shifted so that her head faced the cabin, seeing a dim orange glow from the lantern. A shadow passed in front of that lantern and she latched her eyes onto it, peering through the holes, unable to look away as she watched the captain dress for the day.

He wore only his undergarments, sun-tanned skin dark in the lantern's light. His back faced her, and she saw a large tattoo of a skull above two crossbones, the symbol of his father's reign, above three lines of words she was too far away to read. His shoulders and arms were lithe, muscles well used but not overly so. When he turned, she saw a smooth belly and strong hips. He wasn't as tall as other men, but he carried himself well, like a gentleman, she considered.

As she watched through unblinking eyes, Arianna found herself comparing him to the other man she'd recently admired. Jim was lean where Malachi was full, softly featured where Malachi was hard. Jim proudly displayed a runner's build, Malachi that of a trained boxer. Both were well lined, very different in their builds but admirable in their own rights.

Jim pulled on his pants, weapons belt and buckle jingling. His shirt came next, though he left it unbuttoned as he began to lace up his boots. "It's not polite to stare, Star Jumper."

Arianna silently cursed, squeezing her eyes shut for only a second's time to ridicule herself. When she looked back out, Jim was staring at her, one brow lifted. Knowing she was caught, she rose, biting back a wince when her back felt as though it could tear itself apart.

"I wasn't staring," she replied, a weak defense. "I was… assessing my wounds before rising."

"Of course you were." He wasn't smiling, so she couldn't decipher his words. Jim drew back the curtains and entered his chambers, taking advantage of her hesitation by reaching up and tucking her hair back behind her ears. The gesture was so gentle that Arianna faltered, momentarily baffled and unable to move, even when he lowered his head against hers.

"Well then, you've seen me in my undergarments," Jim commented, voice steady and nearly demanding. "It's only fair that I see you in yours."

Arianna huffed, the remark snapping her out of the moment. She pushed him away. "You must still be sleeping, Captain. Only in your dreams will that ever happen."

"Are you flirting with me, Star Jumper?"

"I don't flirt with pirates."

His face darkened. "No, you only allow them to seduce you."

Arianna frowned. "What's that supposed to mean?"

Jim waved her off, buttoning up his shirt and tying back his shoulder-length black hair, looking the part of the dark and dangerous pirate. "Get ready. The day is upon us and we have work to do."

Arianna stared after him, fuming over his accusation. She'd never seduced a pirate a day in her life, and wondered what lies had been told to him to make him believe such a thing. She had an idea of who was feeding him such untruths, and told herself that the next time he attempted to get that close, she'd set the record straight and make sure he knew where they stood with one another.

She dressed quickly and was about to head out when a tapping at the porthole had her pausing. They were in the middle of the ocean. No one could be outside the window except…

"Malachi."

Arianna rushed to the window, shoving it open and gripping the sill. He hovered just out of reach, his green eyes narrowed. She smiled wide, genuine happiness flooding through her. At her smile, he too came forward, placing his hands on top of hers.

He started to speak, but clenched his jaw when Arianna pulled her hands back, grimacing. He took her by the wrists. "You are injured," he stated, then saw the bruises on her face, the bandage showing on her shoulder. "Today, The Hunter becomes the prey."

"No. Malachi!" Arianna reached through the window and grabbed his shirt, speaking as loudly as she dared. "It wasn't the captain or his crew." She could tell he didn't believe her, and so quickly, quietly, she explained what happened to her. "I don't understand it, though. He seems to be collecting these…these trinkets. Crystals and rocks and things I can't even identify, but I don't know why. He's got all these maps, but doesn't tell me anything. He's—"

She stopped when she looked at Malachi, really looked at him. "Malachi, you're exhausted."

"It's a long way out, my Arianna." Malachi rested his arms on the sill and leaned against the side of the ship, taking a moment's break. "Far enough for you, it seems."

"What's that supposed to mean?"

He gestured to her, his green eyes full of resentment despite the shadows beneath them. "You look like a pirate. You smell like a pirate. Are you also living like a pirate?"

She knew what he was insinuating, and was insulted. He saw that insult on her face. "I came to see for myself what you have been doing, and bring you back, if I must. The darkness has spread since you left. The boys are out of control, fighting with each other and the natives, who have become more and more courageous in their attacks. The Fae Forest no longer sees the sunlight, and has begun to perish in rot and decay."

Arianna listened in horror, swallowing hard when he was finished. "How is that possible? I haven't been gone that long."

"Long enough," Malachi answered, running a hand through his wind-strewn hair. "The Never needs you to survive, and perishes in your absence, in your betrayal."

"Betrayal?"

"There are rumors of your actions, rumors that the Star Jumper has turned her back on The Never and killed one of the keepers of the stone isle."

Arianna hesitated. "Well, I did, but I didn't have a choice. I didn't!" she insisted when Malachi cocked his head to the side. "They were attacking me. I kept promising to bring the crystal back, but they wouldn't listen. I didn't know what else to do. Malachi, I've never killed anyone before." Her eyes filled with tears at the memory, softening the look of disbelief on Malachi's face.

"It is never easy to take a life, Arianna of the Stars. Even to save your own."

"I have to get him to trust me. If he doesn't, then this is all for nothing. Killing the keeper was all for nothing…Do you trust me?"

Malachi lifted a hand to her cheek, thumb grazing over her lips. "Of course, my Arianna. I would not be here if I didn't. I…I miss you. I reacted like a child to you leaving, and I cannot do that. We are no longer children."

"No, we most certainly are not." Her sly tone had them both grinning. "I miss you too, Malachi…But I can't come back. Not yet. Not until I figure this out." She saw the flash of anger that he quickly tried to suppress. "I'm close, I know it. I just have to earn his trust and he'll tell me what he wants. I have to know why he has my painting and what he knows about me. It's the only way to save The Never. It's the only way to keep the boys safe, and the natives, and the fae, and everyone else."

Malachi didn't answer for a long moment. His hands still gripped hers, tightening their hold. Finally he leaned through the window and kissed her hard. She cherished the feel of his lips, the taste of his kiss, sadness filling her at the knowledge that she had to stay behind.

With that thought in mind, she broke away. "Dawn's almost here. You're going to lose the cover of fog. You need to go before they see you." Arianna almost giggled when he came in for another quick kiss.

"Don't kill any pirates without me," he said with a wink.

"Never," she replied, and offered a single wave as he departed, disappearing into the horizon.

The Golden Vine

A TRACE OF her smile still existed when she bounded up the stairs and out into the morning air. Pirates were bustling around her, keeping the ship sailing east, with the captain at the wheel. She joined him there, taking the telescope he handed her, noting the cloudless sky slowing turning from dawn's pink to morning's blue, the smooth ocean waves.

"We set sail for that island while you wasted time on sleep," he told her, getting a side-eyed glare in response. "We will find our next treasure there." Jim spared her a glance, seeing the soft curve of her mouth. "Someone seems to be in a good mood. If I'd known what pleased you, I'd have stripped down sooner."

Arianna lowered the telescope after taking in the island they were rapidly approaching. "You think far too highly of yourself, Captain."

"Now now, don't be a tease." Jim turned the wheel a degree, focusing on the island. "I am taking a crew on this trip, yourself included. It will be simple, quick."

"I take it men can risk their own lives this time?"

He ignored her. "Most of the natives have been…dealt with. There should be no trouble."

"What are we looking for?"

"You will know when I tell you."

Arianna sighed and closed the telescope, handing it back to him. She'd rather work than talk to him, and so she joined two of the pirates - Tats, whose skin was pure as could be, and Glasseye, whose name was but a reflection of his face - as they directed the sails with the wind. Her back stung with each movement, but she refused to let her injuries slow her down.

While she worked, she thought about Malachi. His visit, quick as it had been, had lifted her spirits. She'd missed him more than she realized and was happy to know that he'd flown all the way out at sea just to check on her. Check up on her, Arianna corrected herself, but she couldn't blame him. If she'd heard rumors of Malachi killing innocents, she'd make a checkup visit as well.

But even knowing he was suspicious didn't dampen her spirits. Doubtful or not, he still came for her and apologized for his past behavior. In hindsight, Arianna figured she should have also apologized for running off like she did, and vowed to do just that the next time she saw him. For now she would be happy with the memory of his visit, and the feel of his kiss.

"Hold tight ta that there rope, lass!" Tats called to her. "The wind picks up at the shore!"

Arianna tightened her grip on the rope, thankful for the bandages that protected her still-tender palms. Tats was right; the wind did blow stronger as they approached, forcing them to set anchor as close as the captain dared.

The crew—Jim, Arianna, Glasseye, X, and three other pirates she had yet to meet—assembled in the rowboat and was lowered to the water. The ocean was calm despite the wind, the air warm. Arianna observed the island, appreciating its beauty. Unlike the Cold Caverns, this isle was green, with towering trees that reached up toward the sky and mountains covered in colorful fauna. She could see a waterfall off in the background, could hear birds singing even from this distance, could smell flowers in the air.

The boat slid onto shore, the crew stepping out onto pearly sand that gleamed in the sunlight. A dense jungle wall was only a few feet away, denying them entry.

After securing the boat, X pushed to the front of the group, machete in hand. "Follow me, lads," he ordered, leading them down the beach. Arianna followed, surmising that the crew had been here before and knew something she didn't about how to enter the forest.

As she suspected, X turned sharply when they reached a narrow trail. They followed single file, X at the lead, Glasseye next, Arianna pulling up the rear. Jim marched in front of her, sword grasped in his right hand. She wondered why he had a weapon out when he'd already claimed most of the natives had been taken care of, but decided one couldn't be too careful and drew her own sword as well.

Arianna looked around as they walked and couldn't help but smile at the sights. Flowers she'd never seen before rose as high as her shoulders, bright pinks and purples contrasting against dark green stalks. The ground was soft, even bouncy in some areas, covered with leaves that fell from wide-trunked trees. She saw animals in those trees, furry little creatures that resembled squirrels, others like monkeys with their long tales and round faces. The animals chirped at them as they passed beneath their branches, either welcoming or warning them, Arianna didn't know.

When they came upon a fallen tree, the pirates leapt over it with ease. Arianna climbed over, careful of her wounds, pausing just before jumping off and observing what appeared to her as strange white mushrooms growing on the bark. They were thick and bulbous, with a sweet smell emanating from them, but what caught her attention was the fact that they were moving. Thin spines moved in and out of the bulbous parts, and retracted quickly at her touch.

Arianna jumped when Jim shouted at her to get moving and slid off the log, forgetting the spiny mushrooms. She fell into step behind him and followed dutifully through the dense jungle, swatting away rogue insects and pretending the humidity wasn't as suffocating as it felt. The air and trees pressed against them, trying to push them out and away. It got hotter the further into the jungle they marched, and just when she thought she couldn't bear it any longer, X stopped.

They were on the edge of a cliff, so high up that they couldn't see the ground below. Arianna stared down the edge, at the mist and clouds that filled the open air before them, and was puzzled. They'd started at sea level, and marched at only a slight incline for no longer than two hours. Now they appeared to be at the top of a mountain.

"The people here have a strange, strong magic," Jim said at her side, seeming to read her thoughts. "None can explain the sight you see."

Arianna swallowed hard, a bit unsettled by such a magic. She could accept it—The Never was a place where the unexplainable thrived—but it unnerved her nonetheless. "So we're on the edge of a magic cliff. What next?"

Jim used the sword to point directly out in front of him, and slightly higher. Arianna followed the sword, peering through the mist at a tree, larger than had ever met her eyes before. Its trunk branched out from a mountainside in the distance, defying the laws of gravity. Limbs arched this way and that, covered with wide yellow leaves.

"What? The tree? What about it?" she asked.

"As I said, the natives have a strong magic, though unfortunately for them, that magic doesn't extend to their defenses. Just the land. No one can find the mountain where that tree resides, just as no one can find a way around this cliff."

"What's so special about the tree?"

"The tree? Nothing. It's what's *on* the tree that I want." Jim opened the telescope and gestured for her to look through it. "At the top, wrapped around the narrowest branch."

Arianna searched, scanning the tree up to the top, looking from branch to branch until finally she saw one no wider than her arm. She traced it down to its base, where a vine was wrapped around it twice. But not an average vine, she realized. This one was gold, shimmering in what little sunlight managed to burn through the mist.

"You want the vine? What's stopping—oh." The truth dawned on her then and she lowered the scope. "You need me to fly out there and get it."

Jim handed her a small saw. "Happy flight, Star Jumper."

Her lip curled in annoyance, more so at yet again being the only one to risk her life than actually at having to retrieve the item. She stepped to the edge, nervous. Flying was as simple as a single thought, but it frightened her a little to leap off a mountainside with only the hope that she would float on the air.

"No guts, no glory," she muttered, and took off for the tree. It boosted her pride that she didn't falter and she grinned as she left the pirates behind, knowing she could do what they couldn't and look good doing it.

Having improved her speed, she reached the tree rather quickly, landing on the base and walking her way to the top. The bark cracked beneath her boots and she found it difficult to step carefully, being so used to trekking barefoot through tree and wood.

Arianna ducked around branches, pushing leaves out of her way until she came to the golden vine. Up close it was even more luminescent, full of life and beauty, even though it was no thicker than an average necklace chain. Squatting, Arianna looked it over, seeing that the vine had attached itself to the trunk with two thick barbs.

Not wanting to waste time, Arianna unwrapped the vine from the trunk, surprised at the simplicity of the job. The vine was sticky and no longer than her forearm, and so she wrapped it around her wrist like a bracelet, from wrist to elbow, as she took it from the branch. When she reached the base, she used the saw Jim had given her to cut through the barbs, detaching vine from tree.

Finished, Arianna sat back on her heels. "Well, that was strangely easy."

The words had no sooner left her mouth when the tree shifted, groaning and shuddering. Arianna stumbled and gripped a branch, the saw falling from her free hand and into the abyss below. Turning her head, she peered through the branches to see that the tree was cracking from its mountain base, and the mountain itself was crumbling along the edge. The sky darkened, gales of wind pushing against her, the sound of wails and indiscernible curses meeting her ears.

Before she could move, the tree fell, taking her down with it.

Arianna was tossed about, back and stomach hitting branches as the tree tumbled. Desperate, she kicked at the trunk and struggled to find an opening in the leaves, branches scraping at her arms and cheeks. She was dizzy, thrown head over heels and back again, her breath raspy and her eyes wide. How far down she'd fallen, she didn't know, and feared that too soon the ground would come up to meet her as she struggled in this cage of limb and bark.

The vine around her wrist tightened, as though it too were frightened and needed something, someone, to hold on to. With a final burst of energy, Arianna shot through the branches, keeping her eyes on the sky, gritting her teeth together at the feel of thorn and limb tearing at her face and neck. When she was finally free of the tree, she took a moment to get her bearings. She was still high above the ground, barely able to make out the rocky terrain below. Ahead of her was the cliffside, where waited the pirates.

She took her time getting back to them, not wanting to appear frazzled when she returned. "Piece of cake," she said when she landed, voice wavering only once.

The pirates stuttered out their approvals, but Jim's expression was hard as stone, though the slightest of hitches in his tone defied his face. "The vine. Give it to me."

Arianna held out her arm, but just as Jim touched the gold, an arrow shot over his shoulder.

"Natives!" Glasseye shouted, drawing his sword.

"I thought you took care of them!" Arianna accused as they ducked into the protection of the woods.

"I did," Jim answered. "Most of them."

There were no more words to be said as they ran, arrows sailing over their heads, next to their bodies, one of them finding its home in a pirate's throat. Arianna leapt over the fallen man, not giving him a moment's thought. She never saw who she was running from, but she could hear them shouting at her in a foreign tongue, footsteps loud and frantic behind her. The jungle didn't look so beautiful to her now, only dark and deadly.

They reached the fallen log, Arianna leaping over it easily this time. A man's irritated cry had her stopping, booted feet sliding against black dirt. She looked back to see Jim on the ground, white mushroom spines wrapped around his ankle. He was clawing at them with his sword, two spines shooting from the log for every one he severed.

Arianna moved to help him, and just as she did, saw one of the natives approaching from the forest. Jim, so focused on freeing himself as he was, didn't see the impending attack. The native, a small, pudgy, completely naked man with scaly green skin and oval-shaped yellow eyes, lifted his spear and prepared to throw.

She didn't think, didn't bat an eye. Her blade met the center of his chest almost as soon as it left her hand, and it was only when the man fell to his knees, green blood seeping from the lethal wound, that Jim noticed he was under attack. He looked at the native and over at Arianna, whose arm was still in its throwing position.

"You're welcome," she said, straightening. "Now quit messing around and let's get on with it."

With a snarl, Jim pulled her knife from the native and sliced through the spines in one swipe, rolling out of the way before more could grab hold. He took Arianna by the arm and ran at her side the rest of the way to the shore.

THEY HURRIED BACK to the ship and set sail instantly, eager to get away from the island and what was left of its native inhabitants. Only when they were a safe distance away did the men start to question what had happened.

The captain regaled them with the tale, playing up the most dramatic parts. Arianna was surprised when he took hold of her wrist, lifting her arm. "Men, we have here a true captain's hero!

Give the Star Jumper her proper dues for saving my life!"

She grinned when the pirates burst into applause and cheers, some offering her bottles of rum, which she politely declined. Out of the corner of her eye she saw X leaning against the railing, arms crossed and a frown on his face, but she refused to give him attention. Instead she allowed Jim to pull her into the gathering room below the helm, where he held out a hand after closing the door behind them.

"Give it to me."

"Give what to you?"

Jim sighed. "The vine. Give me the vine."

"Oh." Arianna pushed up her sleeve. "Here." Moving to her side, Jim took her hand and went to unwrap the vine, which was still wrapped from wrist to elbow. His brow furrowed when it didn't budge, sticking to her skin instead. Arianna chuckled. "He must not like you."

Frustrated, Jim picked at the vine and let out an annoyed huff when it only stuck closer against her arm, nearly melding into her skin. "What did you do?"

"I didn't do anything. He just likes me more."

"He?"

"Naturally." She touched the thin vine, amazed at how it had flattened against her arm. "He is drawn to my feminine scent."

Anger flashed in the captain's eyes. "This isn't a joke, Star Jumper."

"Relax, Captain. It's just pretend."

"There is no pretend on this ship. You do things *my* way."

Arianna scoffed. "Tell that to him," she challenged, holding out her vine-wrapped arm. "Maybe if you weren't such a grouch he'd warm up to you." Her attempt to appease his inner child failed, and she grimaced when Jim charged, slamming her against the wall. A cry escaped at the pain that radiated throughout her back when she hit a hook drilled into the wood.

"If this is the game you wish to play," he growled, his fury surrounding him in a gray shadow that Arianna felt as much as she sensed, "then so be it."

Yanking open the door, Jim called for X. "Take her to my cabin and put her back in chains," he ordered. "I'll be there in a few minutes."

"With pleasure, Captain." X leered at Arianna, who had shrunk back against the wall. She nearly spit at him when he touched her, dragging her from the room and down to the captain's quarters.

There, he brought her to the couch and clamped the chain, this one shorter than the last, around her ankle. After securing the lock his hands lingered, traveling slowly up her leg until she kicked out.

"Behave, little Star Jumper," X warned, rising so that he towered over her. He delighted in the look of disgust and terror that crossed her face when he pressed against her, fingers brushing the back of her neck. She tried to pull away but he only held on tighter until she gasped out in pain.

"Our time will come. Soon," he promised, and slipped out the door, leaving Arianna trembling.

SHE SLEPT POORLY that night, chained in place with memories of the past haunting her. Arianna could only watch as the child version of herself relived the past in dreams.

Little Arianna stared up at the captain, wondering if she was fast enough to reach up and tug those black curls before he could catch her. The captain was quick, but not as much as she.

"You're a mischievous little bugger, aren't you?" the captain asked, then sighed. "I told you not to come back to this ship. Now what am I going to do with you?"

"Play a game," the girl suggested eagerly. "Walk the Plank!"

The captain hid a grin behind that long-handled mustache. "No games tonight, little Star Jumper. You've been naughty sneaking around the ship. Naughty children must be punished."

Arianna wasn't afraid of him. She liked the captain, and took his threats as challenges to soften him up. She rose at his feet, bounding just out of reach. "Come and get me, Mr. Codfish!" She laughed as she jumped back, but her giggle was cut short when he didn't follow. "Don't you want to play?"

"Not tonight, child. X, take her away." The captain waved a tired hand in her direction.

Arianna frowned when the man called X picked her up. "Let me go," she ordered. "I don't like you."

"That's quite alright, little lady. You don't have to," he responded, carrying her through the hall, down a flight of stairs. X brought her to a small room with a single bunk. The girl could tell it hadn't been used recently, as even the pillow was covered in a layer of dust.

Arianna spun around when she heard the door slam shut. Her brow furrowed when X locked it—locked them in, together. "What are you doing?"

"Just you and me now, lass."

When he smiled, Arianna knew something bad was going to happen. Her mother told her never to get into cars with strangers, never talk to strangers, always beware of bad men who want to do bad things. X was a bad man. She'd seen him kill, maim, torture—all within just two trips to The Never and the pirate ship.

"You can't do anything," she said quickly, backing up against the wall. "I'll tell. He'll punish you."

"Little Star Jumper, he doesn't care. He gave you to me, remember?" X crossed the tiny room in two strides, leaning over until he was face to face with the girl. "Naughty children must be punished."

Her cry of protest caught in her throat as X covered her mouth with a hand that reeked of fish guts and sweat. In the dim lighting she could only see shadows against the wall that told the tale of what would happen—her clothes violently ripped away, his belt removed, the buckle striking the back of her legs when she attempted to get away.

Tears streamed down her cheeks, her lips quivering beneath the hand that he re-clamped over her mouth. She saw parts of him she didn't want to see, felt parts of him that shouldn't be touching her, heard his grating laugh when she whimpered.

Unable to escape, painfully pinned in place, biting her bottom lip when the hand on her mouth slipped away, the child did the only thing she could think of to free herself from his clutches—she screamed.

Arianna expected X to slap her, hit her, to yell at her to be silent. But this time, in this altered memory, he said her name. Gently at first, then with force. Louder, louder, in a voice not his own. His hands took her shoulders, shaking her, and she struck back, fighting for her freedom, desperation sounding in her throat.

"No!" she screamed, thrashing about. Those hands tightened, but the voice softened. "Please, no!"

"Arianna. Arianna, wake up! *Now.*"

The last command snapped Arianna into consciousness. Through wide, glazed eyes she saw Jim kneeling next to her, his face a portrait of genuine concern. His disheveled hair and rumpled clothes told her he hadn't been awake long. Some part of her, though, was still afraid, unable to relax with his hands on her, and so again she struggled, tears falling down her cheeks.

"Calm down, Star Jumper. You're safe."

To Arianna's surprise, Jim pulled her against him and wrapped his arms around her. To her dismay, she let him, fingers grasping his nightshirt as her breath came out in sobbing heaves. Her head buried in his shoulder; she could do nothing but wait for the fear to pass and was comforted by his gentle caresses against her hair.

Jim shifted, moving to the couch and drawing Arianna closer. "What did he do to you?" he whispered.

Arianna fought to keep the memories from returning. "What didn't he do?" she whispered back.

Twenty-Seven

Battle and Bloodshed

SHE SLEPT PEACEFULLY the rest of the night, and awoke to find herself laying against Jim, one arm draped across his chest. Arianna sat up quickly, feeling his hand on the small of her back, and pushed herself away.

Jim stirred at the movement, smiling groggily when he saw her. "Good morning, Star Jumper. I trust your dreams were better?" His smile disappeared at her glower. "Don't look so startled, love. You fell asleep on top of *me*."

She couldn't help but make a face at his smugness, and at the way he leaned back, hands behind his head as though thoroughly satisfied with himself. Guilt flushed through her when she realized that she'd actually enjoyed sleeping so close to him. "In the future, keep to your own bed."

Jim frowned, untangling his legs from around her and standing, walking away from the couch. "For a woman so concerned with me trusting her, you certainly have no problem not trusting me."

"Why would I?" Arianna shot back, all traces of sleep gone from her body and mind. "You've chained me up yet again for something I can't even help and refuse to tell me why you wanted me here in the first place." She recoiled when she heard the words spoken, knowing it was too late to take them back.

Jim heard them as well. He turned around slowly, eyeing the

woman in chains. "Why I wanted you?" he repeated. "And what makes you think I wanted you?"

A dozen thoughts swarmed her mind, a dozen excuses, a dozen lies. But she was tired of lying and deceiving, at least for now. If she wanted to earn his trust, and do so quickly, then she had to be honest.

"I heard you say so to X," she admitted, clasping her hands in front of her and feeling the golden vine warm against her skin, responding to her nerves. "When I came back to The Never, I was curious about the ship and...and wanted to see if any of the old faces were still here. So I flew out here and looked in a few windows."

"And what did you see?" His question was quiet, deadly serious.

"I don't know. I don't!" she insisted when his eyes narrowed. "It was just a room with red walls, and you, making a canvas. That's how I knew you meant me. Why else would you be making a canvas? So I went back and gathered some brushes, thinking maybe I could be of use."

"Of use to what?"

"I don't know. You won't tell me." She crossed her arms and stared at him pointedly, hoping she was taking the heat off herself for spying. Uneasiness welled in her gut when he only stood in front of her, considering her statement.

"Alright," he decided. "Get dressed, and I'll show you what you think you saw."

After tossing on her clothes, Arianna followed Jim out the door. It was early yet, half the men still asleep, the other half stumbling about the deck looking for breakfast. Dim light seeped in the cracks and through windows, lighting their path deeper into the heart of the ship.

At long last they reached a closed door, a solid wood door with a heavy lock. Jim took a chain from around his neck and used the key, pushing open the heavy door and gesturing for her to enter.

Stepping inside and squinting through the shadows, Arianna saw that they were, indeed, in the room with the red walls. The worktable was still in the center, topped with a finished canvas and, she saw with surprise, her brushes. She'd completely forgotten that she arrived on the ship with a pack, which contained her brushes and clothing.

"So, you want me to what? Paint you something?" Arianna walked to the table, running her fingers over the canvas. It was finely crafted, with perfect corners and tight material that she couldn't quite identify.

From the doorway, Jim answered softly, "The thought had crossed my mind."

"But why?" Picking up one of her brushes, Arianna cherished the feel of the wood and bristles against her skin. It had been so long, too long, since she'd last held it and she missed painting. In that moment she would have painted anything he asked of her simply for the chance to actually be an artist again.

As she reflected on her love for paint and canvas, her eyes drifted over the red walls. Not quite walls, she noted, but curtains, curtains covering something all the way around. She could just make out the shapes beneath them, squares and rectangles, and a few ovals. Brow furrowing, Arianna glanced over at Jim, who was watching her steadily, then slowly padded up to the wall directly in front of her.

Almost hesitantly, she lifted the edge of one of the curtains, then ripped it off the wall in shock when she recognized the painting beneath it. It was her own, one she'd painted many years ago of a lake rippling with the threat of an approaching enemy. Wordlessly she moved to the next curtain, yanking it from its holdings. Another of her pieces stared back at her, a mother in a graveyard crying over her departed child.

Curtain after curtain she pulled down until none were left and she was surrounded by her own artwork. They were seemingly random paintings from different stages in her life, save for one connection - they were the pieces she'd often been told were dark and dreary, or downright frightening.

Though they fit perfectly on a pirate ship.

Arianna swallowed hard, shaking her head slowly. "I...I don't understand. Why...what is this?"

Jim entered the room, taking in each painting in turn before answering. "I suppose I am one of your biggest fans, Star Jumper. You've sold many pieces over the years. Did you never question who purchased them?"

"No. I never really cared." Setting the brush down, Arianna lowered herself onto the chair. "So you've been collecting my art. I thought I saw you at the gallery but everyone acted like I made you up."

"People see only what they wish to see, and that is usually not anything out of the ordinary."

"Why didn't you just tell me this when I first arrived?"

Why did you not tell me about your spying?"

It was a fair question, and not one she had the answer to. But she did know how to respond to such a display of admiration all around her, a display that renewed her childhood longing to experience pirate life, even if just for a day. "I'll paint you a piece worthy of your ship. But the inspiration has to be there."

Running a finger over the painting closest to him, Jim lifted a brow. "And what, dear Star Jumper, will give you such inspiration?"

A grin crossed her face, one filled with sinister intentions. She wouldn't have this opportunity ever again, and decided to embrace it wholly. "Battle and bloodshed, Captain. And nothing less."

FOR FIVE DAYS they did just that, fighting back to back, side by side, one island after the next. The ship sailed to lands she'd never known before, with people she'd never met before, and it was all the same to her whether they lived or died. Something had changed in her since seeing those paintings on the wall, since learning of the captain's fondness for her work and desire for a piece to call his own. Arianna wanted to give him that, wanted to please him, and most of all, wanted to remember what it felt like to be free and embrace every part of who she was regardless of the consequences. And she was wild. She was savage.

She was free.

Together with her pirate crew, Arianna sailed the seas, clinging to the ropes high above the deck in anticipation of their next adventure, leading the pack on ground trips, drawing her sword whenever necessary. She saved the lives of her crewmates, had them save her own, finally feeling as though she were part of a group that truly understood her. She could be chaotic, mean, ferocious, but also kick back and relax, crack a joke, all with the scent of blood beneath her fingernails.

At each village, they pillaged. At every town, they plundered. Arianna and Jim were the first to march off the ship and onto shore. When they visited the small port town of Seascape Haven, they feasted on the season's harvest, taking as much as their stomachs would hold—and then more for the ship. Their next voyage took them to a sprawling city nestled along the coast, and it was there that Jim set his sights on a vault, threatening to behead the governor's daughter and nearly doing so before the old man agreed to reveal its single content—an ornate gold necklace with the biggest ruby Arianna had ever seen set in its center.

She remembered Forest Friar with the fondest of memories, basking in the sight of delightful little treehouses and enjoying the company of the villagers. The pirates were welcome here, in this little home away from home. The men spent the night in the company of women, Arianna resting beneath the stars after a confusing interaction with the captain. She'd watched him be led away from the night's feast by a gorgeous young villager, a knowing grin on his weather-worn face, but there had been a moment of hesitation when his eyes met Arianna's, as though he would have released the woman's hand had Arianna of only asked. Instead she turned away and he disappeared behind a dark curtain.

Now she replayed the scene in her mind while watching the stars. She wondered what his hesitation meant, what he'd been about to say just before the woman leaned into him and whispered something charming and seductive. But most of all, she was disappointed that soon the days and nights of taking what she wanted would soon be over. She justified her actions by thinking that they were away from The Never at foreign lands, and so she wasn't harming her homeland. She was simply temporarily giving in to the side of her that hated following the rules all the time.

Despite her better judgment, she enjoyed freedom from responsibility and got a thrill in finding each new treasure The Hunter sought out. Part of that thrill was in the way villagers spoke his name in hushed, almost revered tones, and knowing that she was safe from his wrath.

It was on the sixth day of pillaging and plundering that Arianna and the crew walked off a battlefield—what was once a town now left burning—and decided it was time to sail back to Pirate Port. They'd been at sea for weeks now and craved a bit of what home would bring. Arianna celebrated with them, ale in hand, rejoicing in their victory. The men looked much like her, disheveled, dirt and blood stained, with wild glints in their eyes that spoke of a thirst for more.

Arianna left them like that, downing the rest of her drink and retreating to the captain's cabin. He no longer chained her at night, but they kept their distance in close quarters, regarding one another silently, suspiciously. Jim hated that the golden vine still clung to her; Arianna despised being treated like just a member of the crew, even when she wanted nothing more.

She stumbled into the cabin, dizzy from the ale. Her back was to the door when she removed her vest, taking in the sight of what was once a white shirt now stained red. That same color coated her hands and dripped down her face from a shallow gash on the side of her forehead, courtesy of a soldier who'd fallen only seconds after his attack.

Arianna heard the door open, and refrained from laughing. "The celebration doesn't continue here, Captain."

"Oh, but we have much to celebrate."

She froze at the sound of that voice, so frozen that she could scarcely move when the figure approached from behind. X took advantage of her fear, moving his hands to her hips. Arianna looked down, seeing his grimy and tattooed fingers gripping her waist.

"You've been avoiding me, little Star Jumper."

There were so many things she wanted to say, curses to shout, names to call him, but her throat closed up. She didn't understand why, after so many years, she was still afraid of him, why she became that child in the dark room. She *wasn't* that little girl, wasn't weak. She was powerful. She had killed people.

So why not X?

His hand moved to her stomach, another on her back. Arianna cried out when he slammed her down, chest against the desk. Fury replaced fear. Through narrowed eyes she saw the half-empty bottle of rum only inches from her face and grabbed it before he could stop her. In one swift movement she spun, sending the bottle crashing down on his head and kicking him square in the chest when he stumbled.

X fell to one knee, gripping a deep laceration just above his left eye, and Arianna used his faltering to her advantage and fled. She ran to the only room she knew would protect her—her gallery. Jim had given her the key and she used it now, rushing into the room and locking the heavy door behind her. X couldn't get through the door without an ax and a lot of noise, and so she knew, hoped, she was safe.

Collapsing against the door, Arianna sunk down to the floor, drawing her knees up to her chest and burying her head in her knees, taking what seemed like an eternity to slow her racing heart. She was ashamed of the way she reacted, letting childish fear overcome her senses. But then, she was also proud of herself for finally taking a stand and protecting herself. That stand came too late to save her childhood self, but as an adult, she could find the strength to fight back.

As her heartbeat slowed, Arianna started to worry about the repercussions of her actions. She had attacked the first mate, but more than that, her enemy. He wouldn't take her actions lightly, but would find a way to get her alone and make her pay for what she'd done.

To her surprise, X didn't seek her out.

But The Hunter did.

He called to her through the door, foot tapping impatiently until she dragged herself off the floor and unlocked the latch. Arianna paced the room as he entered.

"Figured I'd find you down here," he said. "What are you doing?"

Arianna stopped pacing and all but gaped at him. It took her a moment to accept the fact that he must not have known what X tried to do and had come to find her of his own volition. "Um, nothing. Just thinking. Planning out a painting. It's part of my process." It was partly true, she told herself.

"So then it would seem you were correct. Battle and bloodshed really do inspire you." Jim reached out and wiped at a speck of blood on her chin, bothered when she turned her head away. "Do I not suit you, Arianna? Does charm not work on the Star Jumper?"

When she didn't respond, he moved closer, taking a tight hold on her arm. "Or perhaps it is violence that earns your affection. I had hoped it not to be true, but it would appear my father was right."

Now she did speak. "Your father? What does he have to do with anything?"

His confusion was as clear as her own. "I know what he did to you, Star Jumper."

Arianna held out a hand. "Your father was kind to me. He never laid a hand on me, and hardly ever even raised his voice, even when I was being a complete brat. He was a gentleman through and through. Unlike *some*," she said pointedly, shaming him into releasing her and stepping back.

Shaking his head, Jim reached into his pocket and pulled out a piece of parchment, the same one he'd caught her peeking at when she was first chained in his office. "I believe this states otherwise."

"What is it?"

"It's an entry from one of my father's journals." He held the parchment as though afraid it would burst into flames. "Would you like to know what it says?"

"Sure."

He barely needed to read from the journal; he'd read it so many times before. But still the captain hesitated, eyeing the parchment for a long while. Arianna stood back, arms crossed, expression wary yet curious.

"Our little Star Jumper went home today, for good this time, I suspect," Jim began, eyes cast downward. "Of all the things I've done in this lifetime, of all the wrongs I've committed, she is the one I regret the most. She came to The Never an innocent child, exploring the land with the boy, that wretch of a lad, so full of life and laughter. I took her on board thinking to make a good pirate out of her, but she succumbed to the evil that lives in those of us who have chosen this life. She left without that spark in her eyes, nary a laugh in her voice."

"Jim," Arianna whispered, not wanting to hear more. But he wasn't finished.

"What kind of captain have I become, fighting with children, betraying the trust of the one who saw what good was left in me? Many achievements I have made in this life, but my biggest failure has been in caring for the little Star Jumper, and letting happen what took place in the bowels of this ship."

"Jim," she said again, plea in her voice.

"And now, now I leave her alone," the captain continued on, jaw clenching between sentences, "in the hopes that she may forget the innocence stolen from her and live the life that she deserves, even if that life is with the crude little cuss that to this day challenges and vexes me. Perhaps the children were right in their taunts. A codfish captains this ship, a shell of a gentleman who will forever live with the regret of letting the brightest star in the sky burn out."

Tears filled Arianna's eyes, and she was silent for long after Jim finished reading. So many memories, too many, filled her mind. Despite what happened on this ship, she had loved that captain. Never having known that Jim existed, she even suspected that he loved her as well, maybe even as the child he'd never known. When she last left The Never, Arianna had taken one final visit to the ship.

She remembered that trip now. Night had fallen, as it always did when she returned to her homeland, and Pirate Port was quiet. Her skinny child's form slipped undetected around the port, to the side of the ship where the captain's quarters, now Jim's cabin, were located. Into the window she peered, seeing the captain sitting at his desk, glass of brandy in hand, cigar smoking between his lips. He'd removed his regal black hat and fancy black coat, for once looking the part of a mere gentleman at rest than the most feared pirate to ever sail the open sea.

He'd sensed her presence and turned, catching sight of the tiny face staring back at him through the window. He didn't move to rise, though he did take the cigar from his mouth and set it on the desk. Arianna had lifted a hand, offering a single solitary wave, and he nodded once, both their eyes filled with all the words they'd never said and would never get to say. They knew this was their final good-bye, and it would have to do, for too much had happened for their last union to be one of pleasantries and friendly farewells. She cried the entire flight back, for the loss of the captain, for Malachi, for herself.

Seeing that Arianna was lost in her memories, Jim spoke first, clearing his throat almost nervously and rolling the parchment. "So, you see, I know what he did."

There were so many issues she wanted to address, but one stood out the most. "So you…what…thought your father did all these awful things to me and…thought you'd try your hand too?"

Insult filled his face. "No. How could you think that? He has so many journal entries about you. The games you played. The way you made him laugh. How much he missed you when you were gone and looked forward to your return. At first I thought he thought of you like a daughter, but then I read *this* and it all made sense. He was sick, twisted, vile. I wanted to make up for what he'd done. I wanted to prove to you that I am *not* my father." His hand fisted, crumpling the parchment.

Arianna saw the pain on his face and it touched her. He may have been a pirate, may have killed for the fun of it, may have slapped her across the face and chained her to a couch, but he was still the son of one of the best men she'd ever known.

"No, you're not your father," she replied, softening. "You have his eyes, his ambition, his style. But you rise above everything that he was."

When he lifted his eyes to hers, she saw sadness in them. "How can you trust me, with what he did to you?"

"I told you, Jim. Your father was kind to me. He never touched me."

"Then what is he referring to?"

"Exactly what you think he's referring to."

"How…how many times did it happen?"

"Does it matter?" Arianna sighed, fighting to push back the awful memories that still nearly made her sick to her stomach. He didn't need to know the details, and she wasn't willing to voice them. The memories were bad enough in her head. Saying them aloud made them too real, too unbearable. "But…it wasn't by his hand. He knew it happened though, so I suppose that's the regret he was talking about. But he never touched me."

"Then who did?"

It was the moment of truth, the one that she had feared. What if he didn't believe her? What if he sided with the enemy and shut her out? What if he blamed her, the child who never stood a chance?

"X."

It was but a single letter, and it was all Jim needed to hear. The parchment fell to the floor, a heavy boot landing atop it as the captain stalked from the gallery. Arianna stared after him, unsure if she should follow or stay put. For the moment she stayed, listening to the sounds of the ship and stumbling back when creaking wood and lapping waves gave way to heavy bootsteps - two pairs.

She didn't have to wonder long what Jim was doing. It was only moments after his departure that the captain returned, hauling X into the gallery by his shirt collar. Neither man said a word, though X's bloody mouth told Arianna he'd tried to speak at some point.

Jim only gestured to the hulking man that had stolen the Star Jumper's innocence, asking her the silent question, needing the confirmation. Arianna barely spared X a glance before she nodded, and that nod was all Jim required to drive his sword deep into the other man's gut.

Arianna jumped, shocked by the easiness in which the captain murdered his first mate. That same shock was spread across X's face as he slid to the floor, knees hitting first, then falling over onto his side as gargling sounds escaped his throat. The sword still protruded from his stomach, blood pumping from the wound.

Could it be that simple? Arianna wondered, lowering herself to her knees. Could her fear leave her just like that, so many years of torment lifting from her shoulders at the sight of that once-hulking figure now curled into quivering ball of blood? Could it, finally, be over?

As if in a trance, Arianna reached out and touched the blade. X's glazed eyes followed her finger, his face pale and his body shuddering in its last moment of life. She traced the metal down to where it met his flesh, wetting the tips of her fingers with his blood just as his final breath was expelled.

She rubbed her fingers together, for once knowing the feel of his blood instead of her own being spilt. "No, you're not your father," she whispered. "You're…you're what your father never could be."

Straightening, Arianna swallowed and faced the captain. “You still want that painting?”

Death of an Enemy

JIM LEFT HER alone, at her request, with the body of her tormenter still slumped against the floor.

Canvas in one hand, brush in the other, Arianna sat cross-legged in front of the body. She pulled the tray of oils next to her, and then simply sat, staring at X.

A mix of emotions tore at her, some that forced her to swallow back bile that rose in her throat and others that nearly made her giddy. She'd left The Never because of X, never able to return after her nightmares worsened and her mother forced medication into her as a result. She'd returned despite him, hoping he was gone from this world, knowing she wouldn't be so lucky.

And now he was gone, dead, cut down by his own captain. X never knew it was coming, or why he was murdered. Arianna didn't feel sorry for him. She didn't feel anything for him, not anymore. But for Jim, for Jim she felt gratitude. He had, quite literally, destroyed her worst nightmare. Perhaps the memories would last forever, but the physical reminder, she would never have to face again.

Snapping out of her reverie, Arianna leaned forward slightly with brush in hand, touching the bristles to blood, marveling at the deep red that soaked into the brush. With one smooth stroke, Arianna brought the bristles to canvas, and painted the death of an enemy.

The painting took two days to complete, days in which she

scarcely ate and spoke to none, not even the captain when he arrived with food. Arianna hid the piece from his eyes when he came, allowing him only to remove the body when it started to reek and dispose of it in the sea. No longer did she have use of it, the shell of a formerly terrifying man, the corpse of an enemy destroyed right before her own two eyes.

The dim lantern light flickered, reminding her to replace the oil. Her back ached when she shifted, having been hunched over the painting for so long. Arianna stretched, tired arms and sore hands over her head, stiff legs relieved by the movement, then refilled the lantern for fresh light.

The corners of her mouth turned upwards into a smirk when the bright light flooded over her painting—complete. It was finished, set against the wall proudly in all its dark glory. It was the most sinister piece she'd ever created, and yet, beautiful at the same time.

In the foreground lay a man, death surrounding him with his own blood—real blood from a real enemy. He reached out to another figure that stood barefoot in the dirt with her arms crossed, a satisfied glower on her face as she watched the enemy perish. She wore a strange outfit, a combination of forest frock mixed with pirate style that gave her a look that told all she was native to this world.

Just behind the woman was another figure, a finely dressed man with his hand on the hilt of a sword, watching her as she watched death in progress. His expression was seductive, malicious; hers was wicked, malevolent. The ground was stained red, what parts of it wasn't cracked and threatening to swallow the fallen figure whole.

In the background was a forest on fire, casting the two figures in an orange glow with gray smoke and sparking ashes curling around them. Trees burned, some already fallen to reveal mountains in the distance. A black mist surrounded the peaks of those mountains, the same mist that invaded the sky, the earth, the fire.

This was death. This was revenge. This was a lifetime of unhappy dreams burned to the ground.

Arianna finally felt the chains of lost innocence release her.

There was something cathartic in her painting, which was dark even for her. There was something oddly comforting about using her enemy's blood to create a piece she considered just as beautiful as she did disturbing. Some part of her was able to relax, no longer on guard, no longer afraid, and she realized then just how much of her life she had lost to fear. Never being herself, relying on those who knew better, too cowardly to accept who and what she was.

But now she knew what she wanted. She knew who she was, and she was brave enough to admit it.

Her attention was disrupted when the gallery door opened. She smiled at Jim and gestured to the painting. "It's finished." He came to her side, peering down at the still-wet canvas. For a long moment he was silent, taking in every bit of the piece so closely that she started to worry he hated it.

"Out of nothing, we create something." His reflection was quiet, personal. "It's perfect," Jim announced, earning another smile from her. "A painting fit for a pirate ship." Picking it up from its edges, the captain carefully hung the painting on the wall then stepped back to admire it. "This calls for a celebration," he announced. "Get cleaned up."

"WELL, THAT'S ATTRACTIVE."

Arianna couldn't help but scoff at her appearance. Standing in the captain's washroom, she observed herself in the rusty mirror and shook her head. As was known to happen when she went into her painting trances, she'd lost track of time, and with it, regular bathing habits.

Days' old blood was scabbed on her face, down her neck, across her shoulders. Not her blood, she remembered, but the blood of those she fought, the life-force of people she never knew, and would never know.

Their life-force, she thought with a sneer. *It belongs to me now.*

Underneath the blood were traces of her previous injuries. Parts of her skin were yellowed with old bruises, around her eyes and chin and shoulders. Her back was scarred from the stone keeper's nails and a scab along the edge of her ear had her wondering when she was struck there. Dirt was caked in her long hair and along the edges of each lesion, coating the undersides of her nails. Her bottom lip was slightly puffy, but she couldn't be certain that it was a battle wound or from chewing on it in concentration during days of painting.

Stripping off her soiled and stained clothes, Arianna allowed herself a hot bath, washing away war, bad memories, fear, soaking in warmth and tranquility. Jim had set out soaps and shampoos for her and she used them liberally, enjoying the exotic scents. Only when the water turned cold did she stir, her muscles rejuvenated, her soul restored.

A set of fresh clothing had been laid out for her. Clothes for a woman, Arianna noted wryly, picking up the fitted button-down black shirt that matched equally fitted black pants. The shirt was short sleeved, ending just above her elbows and contrasting nicely with her tanned skin as well as the golden vine that still insisted on wrapping itself around her forearm. There were no shoes, so she padded into the cabin barefoot.

The captain was waiting for her, standing next to his cloth-covered desk wearing a smug expression and not much else compared to his usual dress. *To be fair, though,* Arianna considered, *he usually wears far more clothes than most normal people*. Like her, he was barefoot, which surprised her just a bit. He'd removed his belt, which held his sword and dagger, both of which were tossed carelessly on the couch. His shirt was slightly rumpled and tucked into the waistband of his pants, unbuttoned down to his navel. His hair, normally tied back, was loose, touching the tops of his shoulders in black waves.

She'd heard talk of the captain's dark aura, the way The Hunter could seduce a woman just with a single gaze, but until this moment Arianna hadn't realized the power of that draw. He was an enchanter in his own right, handsome and debonair, indifferent yet full of desire. And right now, his eyes were on her.

Arianna sauntered over to him, stopping just out of reach and ignoring the tendrils of seduction sneaking their way across her mind. "So, how are we celebrating?"

His gaze never leaving hers, Jim reached over and removed the cloth from the desk to reveal an impressive spread of cheeses and caviar, fruits and crackers, more foods she didn't know the names of, and next to the tray, a bottle of red wine. Two glasses waited to be filled, and he topped them off, handing one to Arianna and clicking his glass against hers.

"To a job well done."

"To freedom," she replied, taking a sip.

They dined alone together for the first time that night, sharing stories of various adventures, laughing over their mishaps, making plans for future battles. The cabin was warm, homey, by the time the tray was empty and their bellies filled.

When Arianna sat back, wine glass empty and eyes sleepy, Jim rose and walked to a hutch, opening one of the cabinets where rested a music box. While she waited for him to select a song, Arianna grazed a glance across the desk, her eyes landing on the curious red stone that sat atop a velvet stand, the same stone she'd admired during her first visit to the captain's cabin. She reached out and picked it up, turning it in her hand, marveling over the way it felt wet and cold yet was completely dry. When the music started, she shifted ever so slightly, pocketing the rock discreetly.

A slow, harmonious tune sung its way through the cabin, a song of violins and flutes that spoke of tragedy. Jim walked back to his dining companion and gently took the wine glass from Arianna's hand, setting it down onto the desk.

"May I have this dance, Star Jumper?"

The song called to her, inspired her. Arianna took the hand that he offered. "But of course, Captain." She laughed when he swung her into his arms, bodies joining, hands clasped. She wrapped one arm around his neck, his around her back as they spun about, dizzy from the wine but graceful nonetheless. Their feet moved in tune with the music, eyes drawn to one another, desire woven around them in an almost tangible scent.

When the song shifted to an instrumental story of love, Jim swung Arianna out, twirling her in so that her back pressed against his chest. She molded against him, head falling back against his shoulder as they swayed. His hand moved from hers to her stomach, and up, grazing her breasts, resting at her throat, gripping her neck with just the hint of force. In her trance, Arianna allowed him to hold her, a willing prisoner in his arms, eyes closed as his lips traced her throat, tasted delicate skin, his breath warm against her collarbone.

Images of lust played unexpectedly in her mind when the fingers on her neck slid against her chest, opening buttons, sliding beneath the edges of her shirt. His other hand rested on her belly; she longed for more, her wanting rewarded by his teasing explorations. Arianna arched against him, gripping his arms, his hair, whatever she could find. Her breath was nearly stolen from her when he pulled back, but only to move in front of her.

She saw the desire in his eyes, felt it radiating from him as he touched her collar, moving the shirt away from her flesh. The soft fabric fell to her waist when he pushed the edges back to reveal her bare breasts, caressing delicate skin and taking in a shallow breath when she mimicked his actions, sliding his own shirt down before he lowered his mouth to hers.

The kiss was gentle but desperate, inviting but dangerous, familiar but filled with the threat of the forbidden.

Forbidden. Why was it forbidden? Arianna struggled to clear her mind even as she gave into the warm body so very much like Malachi's, and yet, so very different.

Malachi.

Pressing a hand to Jim's chest, Arianna broke the kiss. She wanted to tell him enough, that she couldn't do this, but he only took her mouth again, urgently this time, lifting her so that she sat on the edge of the desk. Her mind clouded as he pressed her onto her back, her legs straddling his hips while he kissed her neck, her collarbone, her breasts, tongue sliding down the center of her stomach.

She wanted this. She wanted him, all of him, in and around her, consuming her. It wasn't seduction driving her lust, but desire for everything he stood for that she craved the most. And yet, when his lips reached her navel, she knew her wanting was wrong.

"Stop." Her command was breathless. "Jim, I can't." Arianna rose, quickly pulling on her shirt. "I…I'm sorry."

It took him a moment to return to reality, and he braced his hands on either side of Arianna, head buried in her shoulder. "Did I hurt you?" he asked, sounding nearly ashamed of himself.

"No, of course not." She drew back, taking his face in her hands. She blinked a few times to clear her mind, though fingers of wanting still clutched her thoughts. "I just…we can't do this."

His worry turned to confusion, then suspicion. "You want me, Star Jumper. I can see it. I can *feel* it."

"I do want you." That wanting worried her, made her wonder where it came from and why she was having such a hard time shaking it off. She slid off the desk, buttoning up her shirt with trembling fingers though he made no move to reassemble his own attire. "But I can't have you."

"You already have me."

"It isn't right."

"*What* isn't right?" His annoyance rose to the surface. "You are free, Star Jumper. You decide what is right. *This* is right. *We* are right."

She shook her head, surprised by the tears that formed and the burning in the back of her throat. "No. Jim, I…"

"I see," the captain said softly, seeing deep into her thoughts. "This is about the Wild One. You think of him, even when with me."

"…I love him."

"Do you even know the meaning of the word?"

"Of course I do."

"Do you? You say you love this fool of a man, but will you willingly give up your life for him?" Jim's eyes narrowed in challenge.

"I would risk everything that I am for him."

"So confident you are." His sneer spoke of his disbelief. "And are you ready to be a mother to the boys whose own parents didn't want them?"

"Don't speak of them like that," Arianna shot back. "They are good boys, and they are loved."

"So says the woman who has already left them twice."

The mood of lust and desire faded, replaced by coldness. The music betrayed their hearts, until Jim stalked to the box and slammed it shut. "You are quite the trickster, Star Jumper," he said, his back to her. "And you are cruel, playing with hearts as you do."

It hurt that he was right. "I never wanted to hurt you. This place…it changes you. It makes you forget. It confuses you, until it's almost too late."

Jim turned, eyes piercing through her. "A convenient excuse, no? And a clever one likely learned from the Wild One."

"What is this hatred you have for him?"

"He took everything from me!" Jim shouted, hands fisting as he fought for control. "Everything I want. Everything I need. Everything I love. And now I want it back."

Arianna dared a step closer to him, hoping to soothe the feelings she had so carelessly injured. "It's easy to want the things that someone else has. The real challenge is in being okay with what you do have all around you."

His hand gently caressed her neck. "So you have made your choice?" The sadness in her eyes, the pity for him, affirmed his question. Arianna gasped when his grip tightened. "If I can't have you, then neither will he."

Arianna protested, but her cries went unheard, her struggling ignored, as he bound her wrists and ankles in chains so heavy that she could not fly. He left only enough slack so that she could scuffle in front of him as he pushed her from the cabin, up the stairs, onto the deck. It was dark, chilly in the night air. Most of the crew was still out, seeing to the ship, drinking the last of the rum, looking out at the lights of Pirate Port that beckoned in the distance.

They were close, Arianna saw, so close to home. And yet, too far away to save her now.

Jim brought her to the deck, holding her from behind. The men crowded around, eager to know what was happening. "It's easy to want the things that someone else has," he whispered in her ear, then shouted at the pirates. "Men! She's all yours."

He released her with a shove, sending her stumbling to her knees. Arianna rose quickly, eyeing the men as they glanced at one another with malicious and greedy grins. A look to her left showed the railing, and just beyond it, a tumultuous ocean. A look to her right showed Jim standing with his arms crossed and expression full of regret.

"Maybe you're just like you're father after all." Her words had the desired effect, and she knew she hurt him when Jim uncrossed his arms and shifted uncomfortably. But the time for regret was over. "Bad form, Captain. Bad form."

Moving as fast as the shackles would allow, Arianna raced for the railing and leapt over the edge.

Twenty-Nine

Anything Is Possible

IT WASN'T A long jump, but it was far enough for chaos to explode in a matter of seconds. The pirates reacted quickly, drawing their weapons and firing at her falling body. A bullet found her side just as the captain shouted, "Don't shoot her, you idiots! Get her back! She still has the golden vine!"

She hit the water hard and sunk fast. The sea hugged her in a cold embrace, as black as the night itself, pressing against her chest as she struggled. But the irons were strapped tight to her wrists and ankles, pulling her down despite her desperate attempts to swim for the surface. Pain escalated in her hip, blood mixing with water, weakening her.

The sounds of gunfire and shouting pirates faded as Arianna sunk deeper. Her struggles ceased, mind foggy, chest aching when the last of the air escaped. Despair replaced oxygen. She'd hoped the ship was close enough to Pirate Port to be detected by those who knew any and all that entered their waters. She'd hoped they would stick to their part of the deal, the one she made when she told them she planned on making this same leap off the deck and into the cold sea, taking with her whatever she could from the captain's quarters to thwart his plans. And she had—the vine wrapped around her wrist held great importance to him, though she did not know why, as did the red stone she'd slipped in her pocket when he turned his back for the music box. They were mere trinkets to her, but to the pirates, they meant something far more.

It doesn't matter now, she thought. She wouldn't have the chance to discover their meaning. The chains had trapped her beneath the ocean's surface no matter her attempts to fly, and though the merfolk were supposed to be on the lookout for her return, she was alone now.

A light in the distance revived her as much as her body would allow. Arianna's feet touched the ocean floor, ears burning, eyes watching. That light came closer at a rapid pace, splitting into four orbs - one white, one blue, another pale pink, and the last a beautiful forest green.

When her eyes adjusted to the brightness, Arianna saw the creatures who had kept to the agreement after all. The woman of white smiled at her, as much as she could with her razor-sharp teeth. The woman of green swam to her, pressing her lips against Arianna's, offering a much-needed breath of air.

Arianna accepted the life-saving kiss from her, then from the woman of pink, and finally, the last of the group, one of the few male sea creatures in the lagoon. The man of blue gently took hold of her, chains and all, his light and that of the others wrapping around her. Together, the five raced away from the pirate ship to the safety of Misty Marsh.

ARIANNA DIDN'T REMEMBER much of the trip to the lagoon, save for the feel of cold water rushing against her skin and the strange sensation of air blown into her lungs by the creatures' kisses.

She recalled being slid onto a smooth rock, shivering as water beaded off her body. Something heavy was draped over her legs and her shirt was removed. In her state of near delirium, she didn't have the thought to be self-conscious, though she was very aware of the fingers probing at her hip and sharp nails cutting into her flesh to remove the bullet.

Teeth grit, jaw clenched, hands fisted, Arianna could do nothing but wait as they worked. The bullet was pulled from her body and the wound cleaned, then stitched up. It was with horror that she realized she had other injuries as well, for those healing hands moved to her thigh, then to her right wrist, and finally to the spot where her neck met shoulder. Luckily—if she could consider herself lucky—they were only flesh wounds, though the lesions did require cleaning and bandaging.

She drifted in and out of consciousness, seeing blurry faces, hearing soothing murmurs, and for a short while that cold hard rock felt as soft as feathered pillows beneath her healing body. Finally, she was left alone to heal, to let her body do its work and her mind clear now that she was away from the one they called The Hunter.

Arianna rested in the cavern of the lagoon, somewhat aware of the rain pattering against stone and water lapping against the shore. At some point, food and drink were held to her lips and she feasted as much as her body would allow, which wasn't much. At long last, the fog behind her eyes lifted and she realized exactly where she was.

The lagoon was quiet when she stirred, struggling to a sitting position.

"You're alive."

Arianna jumped, startled at the sound of the familiar voice. She rose to her knees, peering at the woman sitting next to her so casually. At first she could only stare incredulously. "...Mom?"

Georgia smiled at her daughter, though it was a smile masking pity. Her short hair framed a tired face, her long body clad in a skin-tight white dress that trailed down to her bare feet. The older woman mirrored Arianna in so many ways, and yet differed in so many more. "I was worried about you."

"How did you get here?" Arianna scooted closer to her mother, wary but pleased.

"You are my daughter, Arianna. I'll always find you."

She stood, not at all bothered by the healing injury in her thigh. "You never came here before."

"I never needed to."

"Right," Arianna shot back as Georgia also rose, straightening her slender form. "You just medicated me, made me forget everything."

Georgia sighed. "I cannot make you forget what isn't real, sweetheart."

"But it *is* real!" Her cry echoed around the cavern, desperate and offended. Arms out at her sides, Arianna turned slowly. "Look at this. Look out there. Look at everything The Never is, and try to tell me it isn't real."

Georgia's eyes never left Arianna. "Honey, I am looking at you. I'm looking at *you*, and everything I dream of for your future. I'm looking at a woman who has a man who loves her, and who is heartbroken that she won't come home."

"I am home," Arianna whispered.

"This isn't home." Georgia reached out and rubbed Arianna's arms, kissing her forehead. "This isn't real. It's not possible."

Arianna stepped back, out of reach. "*Anything* is possible, if you believe it to be."

If her mother heard, she made no note of her claim. "What about John? It was one thing to have these little dreams of yours as a child, Arianna, when they hurt no one but yourself. But can you do this to John?"

She pictured him in her mind. John, so loyal and loving, so sure of their bond. "I'm…I'm not doing anything to him, Mom. I'm just being me. Letting myself believe in what no one else can see. Why is that wrong?"

"You know why," Georgia pushed back. "You are a smart woman, Arianna, but this place you go to, it's merely a hideout, allowing you to avoid everything you don't want to face in reality."

"Oh really," Arianna said quietly, anger building. "Then where is your hideout? Where do you go to avoid everything *you* don't want to face?"

"That isn't fair–"

But Arianna was done listening. "No, it isn't fair. It isn't fair that I have medicine forced down my throat. It isn't fair that you have a daughter who can't live in your perfect little world. It isn't fair to John to be trapped with a woman he will always have to babysit. It isn't fair." She turned away from her mother. "The Never welcomes me, Mom. Every time. I am never a burden or an embarrassment. When is the last time you or John could say that?"

Georgia shook her head, choosing not to answer. Instead, she held out a hand. "Come home with me, Arianna. Take my hand."

"No." The response was forceful, assured.

"Honey–"

"*No*!"

The sound of her own voice jolted Arianna out of the hallucination. A dull throb worked its way across her forehead, muddying her thoughts. She was surprised to find tears in her eyes when she wiped a hand across them before taking inventory of her reality.

A blanket was draped across her, made of smooth waterproof leather that kept her warm in the dampness of the cave. Pulling back that blanket, she saw that her right leg was bandaged, the pant leg cut up to her thigh. Blood stained the bandage.

Arianna groaned and shifted to her good knee, taking in the rest of her injuries. Her hip ached and the gash bandaged at her shoulder stung, but she was alive, as alive as one with a bullet wound and three nearly matching wounds still struggling to heal could be.

It took her far too long a time to walk to the mouth of the cave, shuffling across rock, bracing herself against the wall and breathing hard with the effort. She couldn't tell if it was dusk or dawn by the clouded sky, but knew by the raging sea just beyond the lagoon that Malachi, wherever he was, was very, very upset. Sheets of freezing rain poured down in torrents, blowing every which way in the fierce winds. The rain bit at her face as she peered out, gales blowing her back against the rock.

This was no average storm, but the floodgates of a heart torn open.

A splash to her left had her looking away from the sky. The woman of white had appeared, half out of the water and braced against a rock. Arianna nodded to her, not wanting to move from her place braced against the cavern opening.

"Thank you," she said, holding the wound on her side and putting most of her weight on her good leg. "I was worried you wouldn't come since we were so far out." The woman only watched her with a calculating expression. "I think…I think I failed. I wanted to learn all of the captain's secrets but just got shot instead." Arianna laughed bitterly. "I let my weakness win. I was an idiot and now everyone suffers because of me."

That truth hit the hardest. She let more than her weaknesses win. She allowed herself to be seduced, even knowing of the captain's ability to do just that. And worse, she *wanted* to be seduced. The thrill of battle, the freedom of the open sea, the sensation of being untouchable, all had led to her downfall.

The creature seemed to know that too, for she looked at Arianna with so much disdain that the wounded woman took offense. "You know, you remind me of my mother." It was more than just the appearance, with the angled features and willowy build. "You're beautiful, exotic, mysterious, and jump at the chance to destroy the only part of me I have ever tried to embrace." She laughed to herself, shaking her head. "You look at me with that same expression, like you just can't believe you have to put up with me." She'd seen that expression so many times since her childhood, that look of regret and shame masked by a smile.

"I'll make this right," she promised, pushing herself off the wall with a wince. "I don't know how, but I will. Oh." Arianna reached into her pocket, relieved that the red stone was still there. "But, I did find this, the rock you showed me in the vision. I knew it belonged to you as soon as I touched it. I can hear music within the stone and feel The Never within it. I know it was part of the deal, but it's all I can offer you in return for saving me."

She tossed the stone over, and the woman snatched it greedily from the air. The woman of pink nearly leapt out of the water at her side, taking the stone gently and disappearing under the water. Arianna waited, wondering what would happen next, where she was going. In answer to her silent questions, a pulse rippled throughout the lagoon, one of gray light that disappeared as quickly as it made its appearance.

But the light brought something else, Arianna noticed. The feel of the air was different, cleaner, happier. The water cleared beneath the raindrops, its sparkle returning even under the cover of a clouded sky. Dozens of sea creatures surfaced, looking around in wonder, grasping one another in grateful hugs.

"You did not fail after all, Star Jumper."

Arianna jumped at the low, somewhat raspy voice. Her eyes widened when she realized it was the sea woman of white who had spoken. "You…you can talk again. How?"

The woman gestured to the water. "The Hunter stole more from us than he realized, silencing us so that we could not sing, and if we could not sing, then we could not bring peace to The Never."

Arianna remembered their songs, beautiful melodies that rang out across all of The Never. "Is that what's happened here? The storm, the darkness?"

"No." The woman's eyes were forlorn, her expression full of regret. "This is the Wild One's doing."

"Malachi? Why?"

"You were brought here under the cover of night, nearly five days ago. Word has spread of the attack and we could not speak to tell the truth. He thinks you are dead."

ARIANNA LEFT THE lagoon immediately, taking flight despite the pain still radiating throughout her body. She was weak, not having eaten a full meal since her rescue, and exhausted, making her flight unsteady and almost laughable. The rain and wind slowed her down considerably, the storm increasing the longer she flew.

Cold, stinging water slammed against her face as Arianna searched The Never, spotting the center of the maelstrom over the Fae Forest. It was there that she headed, flying over treetops, fighting for balance even in the air. Her breath tore from her lungs, wounds burning, until at long last she reached the clearing.

The landing was clumsy, Arianna stumbling to her knees with a cry as she hit the ground. Ferocious wind gales knocked her sideways into a log, which cracked at the impact. Bracing herself on an elbow, Arianna peered through the dark, a strike of lightning illuminating a man's form on the earth not far from where she fell.

The shirtless figure was squatting down in front of a soaked and burned-out hearth, hunched over, hands gripping his head. He didn't seem to notice the soaking rain or howling winds, locked in his own prison of grief. Even from behind Arianna could see the tension in his shoulders, the strain for control in his back. It hurt her to let him go on in such pain, and so she ended his misery.

"Malachi."

She saw the change in him when he heard her voice, the way his muscles tensed and his hands unfisted. For a moment he remained in that hunched position, but then he turned, seeing her standing unsteadily a few feet away.

Malachi rose, disbelief spread across his face. In one hand he held a knife, his grip wavering in the storm as though he were struggling between accepting the sight before him or believing it to be a trick. His jaw was clenched tight, shoulders shaking, and she saw the effort it took for him to speak.

"They…they said you were dead, that the pirates shot you when you tried to escape. Are you a ghost?" His question was so innocent, so full of fear, that Arianna smiled.

"Of course not," she answered, her words nearly lost in the roar of the wind. "The merfolk found me, cared for me. I–" She was cut off by Malachi's hug. He swept her off her feet, spinning in a circle, holding on so tightly that she cried out in pain.

"What? What is it?" He pulled back, noticing the red-stained bandages. "You are injured."

"Still healing," she corrected, resting her head against his shoulder and closing her eyes. "Take me home, Malachi."

The Life-Force of The Never

THE STORM CLEARED during the flight back to their treehouse, a light rain drizzling by the time Malachi touched down. He held an exhausted Arianna in his arms, and didn't let go until they were inside and he had laid her down on the bed.

"Where are the boys?" she asked as he started to unbutton her wet yet blood-crusted shirt.

"They roam the land now. The boys have gone savage, their minds overcome with evil as The Never succumbs to the darkness." Malachi hissed when he removed her shirt, seeing the bandages on her stomach and neck, another around her wrist. "They did this to you."

"Well, I *was* trying to escape with their treasures." They both laughed at that, nervously. "The wounds were cleaned and stitched. I just reopened them a bit during the flight." She allowed him to remove her pants as well, welcoming the blanket he pulled over her to keep her warm.

"I will take care of you." Malachi removed the used bandages and gently cleaned her skin, then re-stitched the areas that had come open again, doing his best to keep her out of pain though the needle and thread were thick. He worked quickly and efficiently, used to tending to injuries caused by knives and guns. Even though she could have done so herself, she let him, for the moment, believe that she was too weak and injured to take care of the injuries.

"There," he said, patting down the last bandage on her thigh. "Good as new."

"Just with a few more holes in me," she joked, face turning somber when Malachi only pressed his lips together and avoided her gaze. She touched a hand to his cheek. "Hey, I was only kidding."

"My Arianna." He took her hand and held it against his forehead, swallowing hard. "I thought I lost you."

"But you didn't." Arianna moved over, gesturing for him to join her on the bed. He did so, laying back and staring at the ceiling crisscrossed with tree roots. Together they rested side by side, holding hands, thinking of what they could have lost and cherishing what they still had.

HOURS LATER, THE two enjoyed a meal that Malachi cooked himself, and proudly so. He displayed the spread of meat and vegetables with a smug grin, hands on his hips.

"Figured out how to cook all on your own, did you?" Arianna teased, slowly taking a seat on a crudely carved chair.

"They say I am a clever one," he retorted, handing her a plate.

She accepted eagerly and they tore into the food. The meal rejuvenated her tired and weak body; she ate with passion, sharing bites with Malachi until there were but crumbs left on the table.

Malachi sat back, chewing the last of his food thoughtfully. "You look different," he observed. "You look like a true warrior. Like when we were children, just…older."

"You saying I'm old?"

"No, not at all," Malachi said quickly, grinning when he saw that she was only teasing. "Just…tougher, is all."

"I had to be," Arianna replied. "I had to be tough. I…I thought I would enjoy being a pirate. As a kid I imagined being one and thought it would be fun to sail the open seas and take whatever I wanted. And for a while, I did have fun." She noted the look of wariness on Malachi's face. "But it's not who I am. I'm not some tough sword-fighting pirate and I don't like what being a pirate does to a person. I don't belong on the sea. This is my home."

"I'm glad you no longer look like a pirate." She had slipped into her old clothes upon rising, ones that matched his own. "Although this is interesting." He reached out and touched her arm and the vine wrapped around it.

"Oh, that." In the chaos of the past few days, she'd forgotten about her newest accessory. "It's a spoil of war that the captain needed for whatever he's doing. It's part of the reason why they were shooting at me, because I got away with it."

"What is it?"

"Some kind of vine." Arianna waited while he observed it, tracing his fingers over the curved lines that wrapped around her arm. "The captain couldn't get to it himself. I cut it off a tree and it decided it liked me. Wound itself around my arm and hasn't let go since."

Malachi tapped the vine with a fingernail. "Mischievous little vine," he commented playfully. "Sent to suck the life out of its captor."

He said it light-heartedly, but the comment made Arianna pause. She repeated his words to herself as Malachi continued to talk, not hearing what he said, her mind racing through her time on the pirate ship.

"You cannot take our hope, our power, our life." The crystal from the stone isle was more than a mere trinket.

"*The Hunter stole more from us than he realized, silencing us so that we could not sing, and if we could not sing, then we could not bring peace to The Never*." The red stone belonging to the sea creatures was more than a mere rock.

The golden vine, the one wrapped around her forearm, was more than a mere plant.

Everything they'd taken, everything she'd helped steal, the seemingly innocent possessions closely guarded by the people—they held the power of the land, the life-force of the ones who regarded them so dearly.

"That's it," she whispered, cutting into Malachi's one-sided conversation. "That's why The Never is changing. Don't you see?" She held up her arm. "The pirates, they are taking the things that power each people, each land, each different...civilization that makes up this entire realm, and corrupting them."

"The other lands never had any bearing on us in the past."

Arianna shook her head. "I don't think that matters. He's not just going after our home. He's going after all of them. We always knew there were others out there, different islands, but couldn't reach them. The Never is just a part of this world, the hardest one to overcome. They are destroying peace, and life, and hope...but to what purpose?"

Malachi listened intently, his eyes on the golden vine. "To take over The Never. To fulfill his father's vision of controlling our land and turning it into a place where the pirates can thrive. To find a way to other worlds."

Her brow lifted at that. "To other worlds? Like my world? Where I come from? How would they reach my world by destroying The Never?"

"My Arianna." Malachi regarded her plainly. "If what you say is true and they are taking the life-force of the lands surrounding The Never, then why do you think the captain wanted you?"

The truth sunk in slowly, disbelief creating a sense of fright within her. "So you're saying..."

"You are the life-force of The Never."

They were quiet, assessing this discovery and what it meant for their land. The Never had always responded to Malachi as a child, growing up with him when she left that final time as a child. Now it also responded to her, torn between two halves that made up a whole. But *she* was what gave The Never its life. Malachi was but a temporary keeper, watching over what she had created when she couldn't be there.

In turning her own mind against her, Jim could achieve his ultimate goal—to destroy The Never. Arianna's land was a world of hope and light and life, one that celebrated the unique and believed in the impossible. There was no place for evil, and yet, she let evil taint her heart and soul. In doing so, she broke her connection to The Never, and could only hope that bond could be repaired.

"That's why he wanted you," Malachi continued, connecting the pieces. "To take you away from The Never. To corrupt you. To seduce you."

To seduce you.

Arianna shifted uncomfortably, memories of that night flooding back to her. She cleared her throat, running her hand over the vine for courage. "Malachi, about that…"

"About what?"

"About…the captain wanting me. To seduce me." She couldn't meet his stare, but out of the corner of her eye she saw his hands clench, saw the fight for control.

"You were intimate with him."

It was said with such controlled rage that it nearly frightened her. "No," Arianna said quickly. "I…he, we, it wasn't–"

"*What*?" Malachi shouted, leaping to his feet. "Wasn't *what*? Did he touch you?" Her silence confirmed his question. "Did he kiss you?" Another silent affirmation. "Did you enjoy it?"

"Malachi!" She reached for him when he attempted to brush past her. "I *stopped* it before it got too far. I told him I couldn't be with him, that I *wouldn't* be with him. Because I love you, not him."

He jerked his arm free and regarded her with a disdainful smirk. "It's love now, is it? Love made you stop. Love made it wrong for him to touch you, kiss you, pleasure you."

There was no justification for what she'd done. Arianna knew that and could only hope she hadn't broken the bond between them. "I have no excuse, Malachi. I can't even explain how it happened. It was like something in my head just snapped awake and realized where I was, what I had done. You told me the captain had a darkness about him, a seduction, and I didn't believe you. I let it happen and I'm sorry. It's unforgivable, and I don't know what to do to make it right."

Though she tried, Arianna couldn't look him in the eye after her confession. In staring at the floor, fighting back tears, she didn't see the expression on his face change to something of furious curiosity.

Body tense, nerves on edge, Malachi took a step forward. His movements were slow, deliberate, and yet, unsure. "And did you enjoy being seduced?" His voice was deep, hoarse, hurt. Another step closer, until he could all but smell the regret on her breath. "Did you enjoy his touch?" When she lifted her head, eyes full of remorse, Malachi took her by the waist, hand grabbing a fistful of shirt at her back. "Did you enjoy the feel of him against you?"

She was breathless against him, her body pressed to his, her hands on his strong chest. Her mind formed a response, but her mouth couldn't put the words together.

"Does he know every part of you, the parts that you have kept hidden from the world?"

Teeth nipped at her earlobe, then her neck. Arianna's fingers dug into his shoulder when those teeth clamped down. Not enough to hurt, but just enough to get her heart racing.

"Does he make you breathless with a single touch?"

Her skin tingled as his hands grazed across her shoulders, down her arms. It made her heart flutter that he carefully avoided her injuries, even when he lifted her, one arm below her backside. Arianna barely felt the stinging wound in her thigh as she locked her legs around him, holding on tight when he sent them floating off the ground to the bed, where he laid her down gently.

"Did you give into him, like you give in to me?"

With one swift flick of his wrist, Malachi removed the thin material covering her body, tearing it down the middle. He lowered himself to her, applying soft kisses along her collarbone, down the center of her stomach. He traced his hands from ankle to hip, grazing around the bullet wound, sliding his palms beneath her. She gave in to him as his kiss moved to the inside of her leg, to her hip, to the part of her she kept hidden, even from the captain.

She indulged herself in the feel of him, his mouth against her, his hair tangled in her fingers. He indulged himself in the taste of her, the way her body responded to him, the barely restrained sounds of passion escaping her.

Her world became just the two of them, a solitary island surrounded by an unbreakable void that forced them together and kept them whole. There were no words, no apologies, no proclamations of affection. Only them, the dreamer and her savior, together as one.

When Malachi pulled back, Arianna opened her eyes to see him resting on his knees in front of her. The rage that had filled his face earlier was gone, replaced with tenderness and just a hint of sadness. She rose to meet him, wrapping her good arm around his neck and drawing him back down with her.

Wordlessly, she pushed him over, lowering herself just as he had done, removing his clothes just as easily. Her mouth found him, ready and eager, giving what she had been given, taking control of her body and his, bringing him to the edge.

Malachi stopped her on that edge, restraint showing in his face as he guided her back up. One arm slid around her back after she lay atop him. The feel of warm skin against warm skin, the scent of want and need in the air, wrapped around them.

Malachi cupped a hand to Arianna's cheek, a hint of a smile forming when she leaned into his touch. "Does he love you the way I do?"

The question needed no answer.

No, it wasn't like this with the captain, Arianna thought as she kissed him, hoping he never let her go. It was never like this with anyone but Malachi.

Thirty-One

The Never Is a Cruel Beauty

THE TIME FOR games was over. The time for planning had passed. Now, it was time for action.

Arianna and Malachi tracked the boys down one by one, pulling them from battles with the natives, yanking them out of trees, all but tying them down back at their treehouse base to force them to listen.

"We want to fight!" Caps shouted, swiping his knife at empty air.

"We want our freedom!" Shooter yelled, pointing at Malachi.

"It is dreadfully suffocating in here," Solemn Sam put in, shuffling his feet.

"You will get your freedom!" Arianna answered their cries. "But first you must fight!"

"Who are we fighting?" the boys asked in unison.

Malachi leaned closer, a malicious glint in his grin. "The Sea Killers."

The boys cheered, racing to their respective bunks to gather whatever weapons they had. Some produced crudely made axes and spears; others had fashioned bows and arrows. Arianna also saw a mix of silvery canisters and had a sneaking suspicion that they would explode when lit.

Their plan was simple—the boys would storm Pirate Port, taking down as many enemies as possible and scaring away the rest, while Malachi and Arianna snuck aboard the ship to find the captain. Any loyalty she may have felt to Jim had vanished, betrayal settling in its place the more her mind cleared, the more she realized what kind of hold he had over her.

For that reason, she was going to take all that he'd tricked her into stealing, and everything else. Malachi had already fashioned a room for her paintings, small but enough to store them until they could find a more permanent fixture. The rest they would sort out later.

Malachi went over the plan with the boys after they exited the treehouse. Arianna listened intently, thinking of all the ways the plan could go wrong and all the ways it could go right. With an army of children led by two grown-ups, their chances of failure were high. She wasn't sure she could handle losing any more of the boys, but what choice did she have? It was either fight the pirates now while the children were still loyal to Malachi, or let them pick each other off one by one until none were left.

The boys cheered at something Malachi said, but before Arianna could join in, she was distracted by movement on the edge of the woods. Frowning, she went to investigate, stepping back when several figures emerged from the trees.

"Natives," she whispered, unsure if they were friend or foe. A line formed in front of her, men and women alike armed with spears and daggers. They were dressed for war, with guards on their chests and stomachs and legs, weapons belts around their waists. Faces were painted black, blending them in with the oncoming night.

One of those figures stepped forward - the chief, Arianna realized. "We hear you gather boys to fight Sea Killers. We fight with you," he announced. "We bring peace back."

She looked over his shoulder, eyes widening at the numbers. Both the north and south tribes had banded together, fighting for a common cause - to protect the land they called home. There were subtle differences in the two tribes, changes in facial structures, height, clothing. But when dressed for war, they were united as one.

“Let’s kill us some pirates,” Arianna replied, leading them to where Malachi and the boys waited.

Their forces were now more than tripled, giving Arianna a sense of relief from the tension she hadn’t realized was carried on her shoulders. Their chances of winning were slim, but with the natives on their side, they may actually all come back in one piece rather than several.

“We could die, you know,” Arianna said to Malachi just before they left.

Malachi took her hand. “Die?” he repeated, a grin forming. “Sounds like quite the adventure.”

NIGHT HAD FALLEN by the time they reached Pirate Port.

They stopped on the outskirts of the port, an army of lost Never souls looking for salvation. Arianna and Malachi led the pack, weapons drawn. A bag was slung across Arianna’s shoulders, heavy with a container given to her by one of the tribes’ medicine women. Only she and that tribeswoman knew what the container held, and only they would know until it came time to open it. Malachi also held his own weapon, though it was not nearly so secret. An explosive made by his own hands, it would be used to take what they wanted, needed.

As planned, Arianna left the group before the attack. Malachi grabbed her before she took off, kissing her hard and fast enough to make her head spin. No parting words were offered - they had no delusions about what may happen this night, but would not speak of the possibilities to one another now.

She flew around the port, landing gracefully on rooftops and empty balconies, skirting along the edges of light until she reached the dock. For the occasion she had dressed like the pirates, with big black boots and an oversized black coat that swished around her feet. The collar was propped around her neck, and the hat that topped her head hid her from prying eyes. She moved easily from the dock to the ship, undetected by every man she passed, knowing that as soon as the native scouts saw her head below deck, chaos would erupt.

That chaos sounded as her footsteps echoed on the stairs. Gunfire rang out, sword clashing against sword, men shouting at each other to kill the Wild One and his horde of attackers. Arianna didn't allow herself to worry, but did duck into an alcove when she heard the crew rushing to be part of the battle. They raced past her in a blur of drunken squalor, eager to fight and kill.

But the captain wasn't with them, she noted.

After she was sure the last of the crew had run by, Arianna slipped out of her hideaway and made her way to the bunks. The stench alone nearly had her turning back. With a hand over her nose she pushed forward until she was in the center of the bunkroom surrounded by unmade beds, filthy clothes, and days-old plates of food. The rest of the ship was kept spotless by captain's orders, but here the pirates held not a care.

In the center of the room was a lone table cluttered with empty mugs, playing cards, and random pieces of past battles. Taking off her pack, Arianna reached inside and removed the metal container, setting it down in the middle of the table. Quickly she released the clasps and pulled off the top, revealing a thick, round cake baked by the medicine woman. Arianna was careful not to touch any part of it, not even to fix the green frosting that had been smeared during her flight. The pirates wouldn't care what the cake looked like, only that it was there.

Her delivery complete, she made her way out of the room and took in a fresh breath of air. Then she squared her shoulders and went to the only other room she needed to visit - the captain's quarters.

A dim light shone from beneath the door when she approached, which she had expected. The captain wouldn't be in the middle of the fight outside. He was too smart for that. No, he would be here, protecting his treasures.

She wasted no time in pushing the door open, sword ready, prepared to duck at the first sign of gunfire. But no struggle met her as she entered. Arianna lowered the sword when she saw the captain sitting at his desk, leaning back with his feet propped up on the desk, drink in hand. The sword hung across the back of the chair by its scabbard only heightened the feel of darkness that surrounded him. He looked so much like his father that she stared in wonder rather than speaking.

"You've caused quite a commotion out there," Jim said casually, breaking the silence. "Thrown your lot in with the natives and wild boys, have you?"

"Always have."

He eyed her with amusement. "Then you are a fantastic liar. But can your sweet someone forgive you so easily? Can you forgive yourself?"

"We both know what was done to me. What you did."

"Oh, little Star Jumper." His tone reminded her of a scolding parent. "Do you take no responsibility for what you've done? You are no longer a child. Stop acting like one."

Anger burned, mixed with embarrassment. "How quickly your own affections fade, Captain."

The derision in his face deepened. Setting his feet to the floor and sitting up, Jim asked, "So you have come to kill me, then?"

"No. I've come to save The Never, and that starts by taking back the spoils of war."

Jim rose to his full height so that he could glare down at her from the other side of the desk. "Now that, I cannot allow you to do."

Arianna braced herself as he walked around the desk, surprised to see that he had no weapon on him. Nevertheless, she held hers tighter, fighting against the dark thoughts that crossed her mind suddenly, the desires to put down her sword and make herself at home with a cigar and glass of rum.

"You don't have a choice," she told him. "We will take them."

"You and your little boys?" Jim smirked. "Against my men?"

"And the natives." She knew she caught him unprepared with that revelation when he paused. "Did you think we would come alone?"

"I did not think you would come at all."

The confession surprised her. "Why not?"

Jim leaned one hip against the edge of the desk, glancing down at her sword, then back up at Arianna. "Do you know what my father told me, the last time I saw him?" Arianna hesitated, then shook her head. The sounds of battle disappeared as she listened, giving him her full attention. "He told me that the captains of this ship lead great lives full of riches, but that all riches come with a price. And that price, love, is the company of the ones we hold dear. My father was a lonely man, Star Jumper, surrounded by people but always alone. He was right."

She let his words sink in before responding. The captain had, indeed, been a lonely man. Even as a child she'd sensed that, and tried her best to fill his days with laughter and fun. She wanted to be the company he kept, but he wouldn't have her.

"The last time I saw your father, he told me that The Never belonged to me, and that to save it, I had to leave. At the time I thought he meant I had to leave The Never, and so I did. But now I realize he meant I only had to leave his ship, to save myself from X and from the one who would captain it next. He must have known what the prodigal son would become."

"The Never is a cruel beauty," Jim said, crossing his arms. "And that is why she must be destroyed."

"Now that, I cannot allow you to do." Arianna lifted the sword, the hint of a smile on her face.

He didn't seem frightened, only bothered. "This is not a game, Star Jumper. You cannot play everything away with illusions of fun. My father was willing to indulge in your childish fantasies, but not

I."

"Well if you aren't willing to play," Arianna lowered herself into a fighter's stance, "then perhaps you're willing to go to war."

The leer that crossed Jim's face encouraged her forward. She lashed out with the sword, only to be blocked by a hidden dagger he produced from his side. Jim spun gracefully, grabbing his sword from its sheath and meeting her next attack.

Metal against metal clanged between them, grinding and sparking when he slid his blade against the length of hers. There was nothing playful in his expression, even though Arianna couldn't help but smile. She loved the feel of battle, the excitement that filled her bones, the shock of adrenaline every time her sword connected with his.

She swore she saw sparks as they danced across the cabin, Jim's fancy footwork easily overshadowing her quick and jumbled steps. Her back hit the wall and she spun, barely feeling the slight sway of the ship as she dodged his next attack by moving behind the desk. Jim wasted no time in leaping atop that desk, knocking maps and empty glasses to the floor, giving no care to the mess as he followed his prey. His heavy boots thudded against the wood floor when he leapt down and cornered her again.

Arianna lunged again, the tip of her sword catching him along the top of his hand. Jim snarled, kicking her knee and sending her to the floor, smacking her with the hilt of the sword as she fell.

"Really, Star Jumper," he said calmly as she wiped the blood from her mouth, "I thought you'd be better at this."

Jumping to her feet, Arianna blocked his blade from slicing into her gut, already breathing hard. Malachi was the swordfighter, not her, though at one time she'd been able to hold her own in a fight. But she was out of practice, barely able to predict his next move. Jim parried, she advanced; he arced the sword down toward her throat, she dropped to her knees and lifted her arms, blocking and escaping with a roll to the side.

"Fancy." Jim smirked, twirling the sword in his hand. She was no match for him and they both knew it, just as they knew she would never admit defeat. "Why did you come here, Star Jumper, if you cannot beat me by the sword?"

"I don't have to beat you," Arianna breathed out, chest heaving, spitting a mouthful of blood. "I just have to delay you."

A sudden explosion knocked them both off their feet. The ship lurched sideways, righting itself unsteadily. Jim tumbled into the desk, collapsing when his head collided with the sharp wooden edge. Arianna used the fall to her advantage, leaping atop him and striking him hard, dazing him enough so that he was content to lie on the floor rather than resume the swordfight.

In the moment of fogginess, Arianna grabbed for one of the shorter chains still staked to the floor and clamped it to his wrist, then ripped the key from around his neck. The captain came to slowly, blinking through his groggy vision to see his enemy rapidly collecting items from the cabin. Into her pack went the blue crystal, the ruby necklace, the silver statue, the Scroll of Life, all of his treasures disappearing before his eyes.

"Wench," he growled, leaping to his feet. "Put them–"

Jim jerked back when the chain caught him, not allowing him to reach her. He pulled against the restraint as she finished her collection and moved to the open window. "I will slice you open for this, as I should have done when you first came aboard. Mark my words, you will suffer."

"Such sweet promises, Captain." Arianna gave a mock bow, weighed down by the treasures, then climbed out the window and disappeared into the night.

She didn't go far.

Arianna met Malachi at the side of the ship, where he had blown a hole in the only gallery wall without paintings. Already he had removed the canvases from their holdings and stacked them, prepared to carry as many as he could.

"You got them?" he asked when she landed in the room. Arianna gestured to the now-bulging pack, not wanting to waste time on words. Together they divided up the paintings, managing to take them all between them both, then flew from the ship before the first pirate burst through the gallery door.

A Battle Well Fought

THEY SECURED THE paintings in a temporary hiding place among the trees before returning to the battle. From the forest edge they could see outlines of fire and smoke, and as they got closer, those outlines turned into chaos. Bodies littered the ground they flew above, natives and pirates and women of the night. But not, Arianna noted thankfully, any children.

Smoke plumed above buildings and trees. Flames reached high into the sky. Blood stuck to Arianna's boots when she touched down, Malachi at her side. Immediately they were surrounded by pirates, sucked into the war once more.

And they were outnumbered.

"Together, Arianna of the Stars," Malachi stated, pressing his back to hers. Though she was exhausted, Arianna met his stance and drew her sword.

The pirates advanced, but they too were tired and slowed down by drink. The duo cut down each man that attacked, slicing sword through stomach, leaping high in the air over the pirates when they got too close.

In flight, Arianna kicked at one man's head and landed atop him when he fell, feet perfectly balanced on his back. From her make-shift pedestal she fought with sword and dagger, ducking beneath a steel blade and lashing out with her knife, connecting with an enemy's knee. The man collapsed with a cry and she left him there in his pain, racing to help Shooter when she saw him in a fistfight with Tats, one of the Sea Killers.

Arianna snuck up from behind and took Tats down, tossing her knife to Shooter at the same time. "Go kill some pirates, kid," she shouted, then looked at Tats with her sword to his throat. "I don't want to have to stab you."

On the ground, Tats held out his hands. "I'd much rather ya didn't, lass."

"Good. Then take your men and go back to the ship, or else we'll burn this port to the ground and slice every one of you open."

"Ya forget who ya talking to, lass. The Sea Hunters never surrender."

Arianna pushed the sword against his skin, drawing a drop of blood. "Don't think of it as surrender. Think of it as letting the rest of the scum fend for themselves, or I'll personally make sure you never again have a port to call home in The Never. We will burn Pirate Port to the ground, and your ship along with it. And every time you try to rebuild, we'll be there with torches in hand." She knew the pirate realized just how serious she was when he let his head fall back against the ground. "Consider this battle lost."

Tats looked around at his fallen friends, at the natives who killed without mercy, and nodded vigorously. "Back ta the ship, lass. Ya got it."

She lifted her sword from his throat and let him run away, watching him grab pirates by the collar and shove them toward the ship.

"You have turned my men into cowards."

Arianna turned, surprised to see Jim behind her. An amused huff escaped when she saw the chain dangling from his wrist. "They were always cowards, hiding behind a tough-guy name." She pointed at him with the sword. "Come and get me, Hunter."

Jim drew forth his blade, but stumbled back and caught Arianna when she was thrown into his arms by another pirate who struck her in the back. They both tumbled to the ground, Arianna rolling to her side and biting her teeth together at the pain in her side.

"No!" she heard Jim yell, and looked up to see the pirate standing above her with a dagger held above his head. Jim shoved the man aside. "This one's mine."

Arianna grinned a malicious grin and rose unsteadily, the other man giving up the fight and turning his attention to one of the natives. "You should have let him kill me."

"That satisfaction will be mine, Star Jumper."

Favoring her injured leg and feeling blood running down her thigh, Arianna allowed herself a moment to rest and prepare for the impending fight. A shout to her left distracted her for only a moment and she saw Caps running away from a building. That building erupted in flames when he was only steps away, the heat of the blast lifting the child from his feet and sending him into a wall of fighting pirates. Inside the burning building men and women screamed; outside those who weren't battling ran for water.

Arianna could smell the stench of roasting flesh, but what concerned her most was Caps, whose hats had both been knocked off upon his rough landing. The pirates he collided with had turned and set their sights on the boy.

"You can't save them all, Star Jumper," Jim cut in. "You will leave this night knowing you caused his death…if you leave this night at all."

Because she already knew she couldn't beat him, Arianna didn't try to fight. When he lunged for her, she wrapped her arms around him and sent them both into the sky, high above the battlefield. Jim struggled in her grasp, trying to gain enough leverage to use his blade against her, then clutched at her when he realized what Arianna was doing. His sword fell from his hands, landing in the shoulder of a pirate far down below. Neither of them noticed when that pirate dropped to his knees, his life spent.

When they had reached past the tree and building tops, Arianna stopped her upward flight. She had her arms gripping his waist and felt his own around her shoulders. The captain, the feared Hunter, looked frightened but was trying to hide his panic with narrowed eyes.

In that moment she nearly felt sorry for him, and gave him a second chance. "What makes you happy, Jim?"

Not understanding the question, Jim sneered at her. "Just another game?"

"No," she answered quietly, only the sound of her voice heard this high in the sky. "You've ended game-playing in The Never. I'll do what I must to restore this land, even if that means taking your life."

Jim's jaw clenched and a huff escaped his lips. "You fight dirty, Star Jumper."

"Whoever said a pirate fights fair, Captain?" Arianna asked, her question panicked and tearful, her voice weak.

Then she released him.

She didn't watch his fall. She didn't want to see where he landed, how he landed, wasn't sure she could handle the sight. After sending him into his tumbling demise, Arianna turned and raced for the battlefield again, her sights set on Caps. The boy was struggling to get away, weakened by the blast.

Arianna pressed her arms to her sides to fly faster and grabbed hold of Caps by the shirt collar, pulling him from the ground just before the first sword could cut through him.

"You saved me!" the boy cried, hugging Arianna as best he could in flight.

"Of course I did, silly," she answered, and didn't let him go until they were on the outskirts of the port. Solemn Sam and Cowboy were already there tending to their wounds. She set Caps down next to them. "Stay here. I'm going to finish this."

She did just that, stalking through Pirate Port with a fierceness brought on by fear, anger, and adrenaline. The miscreants who called the port home had been overrun by her army's numbers and few were left, fighting for the place they called home. Those who weren't fighting were either dead or retreating to the woods for cover.

Arianna found Malachi standing over a fallen pirate, cleaning blood off his knife. "A battle well fought, Arianna of the Stars."

Her eyes glimmered and reflected the fires set by their own hands. Together they took in what was left of the port, let the retreating enemy get away with their lives, and when the natives celebrated their victory with chants and cheers, lifted their swords above their heads and crowed right along with them.

THE BATTLE WAS over, but Arianna still had a promise to keep.

Despite being exhausted by battle and wounded all the same, one by one she and Malachi returned what was lost. To the Cold Caverns they brought back the blue crystal, Arianna offering what apologies she could for her actions. To the sprawling coastal village they placed the ruby necklace back on its pedestal, explaining to the governor why it had been taken and grateful that he understood.

Arianna was surprised that so many of the keepers and leaders were understanding of her plight, and commended her for returning the pieces of power. She and Malachi were welcome at their tables and enjoyed many meals with villagers and townsfolk who celebrated the return of their light and hope.

Others, though, weren't so accepting.

Their last trip was to the island that nearly took Arianna's life as she tumbled to the ground caged in a falling tree. There weren't many natives left, but those who were there made it clear she was not welcome and that nothing she could do would make up for her actions. The tree had been destroyed, and with it, the vine's home. She was now its host, they told her, and she alone would be responsible for its care, a constant reminder of the pain and suffering she'd caused others.

Arianna did the only thing she could think of, and promised to be a host worthy of their tribe. The people had lost their light and many of their loved ones at the Sea Killers' hands, but she could keep some small part of their existence alive. It was her duty to preserve their culture and spend her years giving back to their land. It was also her penance, for should the vine ever be removed from her arm, she too would perish.

WHEN IT WAS done, and all the items were returned to their proper place, Arianna and Malachi allowed themselves a much-needed rest. They lay in the meadow side by side, staring up at the clouded sky. Arianna searched for shapes in the clouds and hoped Malachi would start the game, but neither of them could see past the memories of The Never's first war.

"Did we win?"

Malachi frowned. "Why would you doubt our victory?"

Arianna watched the sky. "The sun, it still hides from us. The air is cold. The boys ran off. Why aren't things back to normal?"

"Maybe The Never is healing itself, adjusting to peace after the darkness."

"Maybe." She wasn't convinced, but was afraid of what the alternative would mean. They had returned the stolen treasures, offering what amends could be made for such an action, but hate and distrust still reigned heavily throughout the land. Arianna could only hope that she was forgiven for what she'd done, both by the inhabitants of The Never and by her own self.

Malachi took her hand. "Hey," he said softly, waiting until she had turned her head to meet his. "You did well. The Never knows your heart. It will return." Arianna saw the truth in his eyes, the belief in what he said. There was no doubt that The Never was safe to Malachi, and so she too had to trust that all would right itself.

The vine that had become part of her warmed a bit, but she ignored the sensation and accepted the gentle kiss Malachi pressed to her forehead. The comfort was welcomed, needed, and disrupted by the splash against her cheek.

Frowning, Arianna wiped at the spot, lips parting in surprise and confusion when her fingers came away red. "What..." Her voice trailed off when another splash connected with her forehead, and a third on Malachi's chest. They leapt to their feet, staring about themselves, up at the sky. "It's...it's blood," Arianna said, disgust and fear clouding her words. "Malachi..."

He grabbed her hand. "Into the trees."

They fled for the safety of the forest as the blood rain poured down. Beneath the cover of the thick canopy, only a few droplets made their way to the forest floor, and so they watched from the trees as the clearing was washed in a red-stained bath.

The rain lasted hardly longer than several frantic breaths, long enough to frighten the two standing by and leave the land looking like a bodiless battlefield. When it was over, an eerie red sky taking its place, Arianna spared a glance at Malachi, whose shoulders and face were smeared red as well.

"What the hell was that?"

Instead of answering, Malachi dared a step into the clearing. His bare foot squished into a thick mixture of blood and dirt. Squaring his shoulders, he walked further out into the clearing, investigating a mystery whose answer would not be found in the field. When he was in the center, looking around and up at the sky, Arianna turned her attention to the forest. It was quiet, dark, cold, matching how she felt, with a coppery stench that made her stomach heave.

Her blood-stained fingers brushed over a tree trunk, feeling the wood shudder beneath her hand. Horrified, Arianna pulled her hand back, sickened by the black mark her touch left behind. She looked over her shoulder to see the same blackness marking the trail she'd walked into the forest.

She was poison, her touch bringing death. Malachi was wrong. Something had changed, something had transformed within her and

The Never hadn't forgotten, hadn't forgiven. There was darkness in the world—and it was coming from her. Just as Jim brought evil to The Never, so too did she, but couldn't figure out how.

The pungent scent of smoke wafted past her, diverting her attention yet again. In the distance, black smoke rose from the treetops, billowing and hiding flames somewhere beneath the canopy. Malachi noticed the fire too, casting Arianna an accusatory glare.

"What did you do?" he shouted from the clearing. He ran back to the forest edge, seeing the black trail, the black handprint on the now-dying tree. "How did this happen?" Arianna could only shake her head, not knowing how to respond. "What did you paint?"

"Paint?" she repeated, snapping out of her state of confusion. "What do you mean?"

"You did this!" Malachi accused. "You painted this. You painted death!"

"Death," she whispered, hands covering her mouth. Blood staining the earth. The forest on fire. The Never forsaken for battle and bloodshed. "Death of an Enemy." He was right. What she painted was coming true, which meant she was right in her suspicions. The evil destroying The Never was crafted by The Hunter's greed as well as by her very own hand.

The horror of what she'd done brought forth a new question. "How did you know that I painted something? That all *this* is the result of something I painted?" The look on his face spoke of his guilt. "You knew about my art? That what I painted would come true? How?"

"I suspected," Malachi shot back. "The Hunter wanted you, collected your darkest art. There had to be a connection between what you painted and what The Never had become."

"And you didn't think to tell me? To warn me?"

"You had to discover the truth on your own."

The answer was a cop-out, and she knew it. But she didn't know what else he was hiding, and why he wouldn't tell her the truth now. If he wouldn't tell her, then she would discover it on her own. "I'll make this right," she declared. "Unless there is something else you've chosen not to tell me."

"Don't act like this is *my* fault," Malachi snapped. "You threw your lot in with *them*, and this is the result. *You* painted this death." He grabbed her wrist, recoiling instantly with a low cry when her touch burned his hand. Stumbling back, misery filling his face, he could only stare incredulously.

Arianna felt the same sense of shock and betrayal. She had become destruction, decay. The darkness she painted was within her, struggling to be freed, and so she did the only thing she could do to protect Malachi and the forest.

She left.

Death Comes to The Never

WITHOUT MALACHI, WITHOUT Jim, without the boys, she had no one in The Never. She was alone. But there was one who may be able to help, and so she went there, to Misty Marsh.

The water was clouded, though sparkling still, the sky hiding any sunshine the day may have offered. A few of the sea creatures were laid out on rocks, resting and enjoying time out of the slowly muddying waters. They hummed a low, haunting tune that matched the despondent mood currently flowing through The Never.

"Soon we will be forced into the open sea." Arianna had landed next to the woman of white, the one who reminded her so much of her mother. "We had hoped that the return of our life-force would restore us, but the lagoon is dying. We must leave The Never."

"No. I will make this right."

"So many promises made, Star Jumper. So many promises broken."

Arianna sighed. She wanted to argue, but the woman was right. How many times had she promised to fix the situation, and how many times had she only made it worse? "What do I do?"

"What you do best."

Lowering herself to the rock, Arianna observed the sea creature. Her translucent skin was even more so, revealing pulsing blue veins and the hint of sparkling blue blood beneath the surface. Her hair, normally so pure, was tinted gray and tangled at the ends. The fingers that gripped the rock were tipped with brittle and chipped nails.

"I don't know how," Arianna finally admitted. "I don't even fully understand what's happened. All this time I thought the pirates were killing The Never, but it turns out they were only part of it. It's like Jim needed me to paint one final piece here, in The Never, to turn me against the land for good."

"And have they succeeded?"

"I don't know." That scared her most of all. If The Never had become her enemy, then she had painted its death and had no way of correcting her mistake. She'd used the last of the paint on the ship, and her brushes were lost. "Even if I knew what to paint, I have nothing to paint with. I don't know how to fix it."

"Then death will come to The Never."

Frustrated and discouraged, Arianna straightened, stomping a foot on the rock. Something crunched beneath her heel. Fearing she had just killed yet another Never creature, she lifted her foot slowly and peered down.

A frown replaced the fearful grimace when she saw the crushed white shell. It had broken into a dozen pieces, shell powder mixing with water on the rock to form a thick paste. She leaned over and touched the liquid, rubbing it between her fingers. A painful throbbing formed in her stomach.

"Do you have more of these?" she asked.

The woman of white eyed her suspiciously. "We have plenty, in the depths of the lagoon."

"Bring them to me. As many as you have."

"Why?"

Arianna's hands clenched into fists, eyes grazing over the fires in the distance, tears forming and threatening to cascade down her blood-smudged cheeks. "Because I know what I must do, and how to do it."

IT HURT, WHAT she had to do. So much so that for a long while all she could do was sit in misery and stare at the pieces she'd worked so hard on, and loved so much.

She sat in the small room Malachi had fashioned for her paintings. It was meant to be temporary, this round room with clay walls and low ceiling and root-covered floor. Around the walls hung her paintings, side by side, one on top of the other, crowded close together so that they hung together in one panoramic portrait of her darkest moments.

The piece closest to her showed a young woman lying across a bed, wrist dripping red. She'd painted that one after one of her worst nightmares to date, filled with images of X as he touched, maimed, stole, while her mother sat in the corner with needlepoint on her lap.

The next was of the river and ripples signifying an approaching enemy. That one was the result of a fight with Georgia, a teenage Arianna pleading to be let off her medication, knowing they were doing something terrible to her mind, only to be sent to her room for sassing.

Another painting to her left revealed a mother grieving over the loss of her child. Arianna remembered the morning she painted it, and the dreamless night before dawn that left her feeling empty, like something unknown had been stolen from her.

At her feet was a canvas filled with dark trees that formed a cage around an unsuspecting sleeping figure. Despite her joy in the moment, Arianna had painted the piece the day after John proposed, his promise to never let her stray too far from reality ringing in her ears.

From childhood to adulthood, these paintings were of all the days she wished she could forget. There was a way to erase those dark moments, to start fresh, to save The Never, even if it meant destroying a part of her.

Destroying *all* of her.

Rising unsteadily, Arianna allowed herself one final look around the makeshift gallery. She trailed a hand across the paintings sadly, hearing claps of thunder in the world above her underground treehouse that warned her of what was to come.

She had to convince herself to reach down, pick up the bucket at her feet. The earth below her feet rumbled, sending her to her knees and the bucket clanging to the floor, spilling droplets across the roots. Arianna cursed silently, picking herself up, and again falling to the ground at the next quake.

The Never, in its confusion, was fighting against her. The land knew her heart, was connected to it, understanding only that she meant to destroy—and not that she meant to save. It didn't want her to hurt or be hurt, feared that she was, once again, leaving everything and everyone behind.

"I must do this," she whispered. Arianna braced herself between the roots, securing her stance. She dipped a hand into the bucket. Her eyes were full of sorrow, saddened still by the sounds of torrential winds and rains battling outside. Water leaked into her sanctuary, tricking down the walls, forming small puddles at her bare feet. Where water touched roots, they began to move, climbing up the walls, wrapping around the edges of the paintings, securing canvas to cavern and making each piece a part of The Never, forever.

In its confusion, The Never was harming itself more than helping, embracing the paintings that were killing the land. There was no more time for delays, for regrets. She had to act now, before The Never sabotaged itself and was lost to the darkness.

"I'm sorry," Arianna whispered, then lifted a hand and slung white paint across the paintings.

When the first drop hit canvas, she felt The Never shudder. But still she didn't hesitate. Arianna dipped her hand in the bucket again, grabbing a handful of white paste made from the lagoon shells. And again, she slung the mixture across what was once hers, covering color with white, coating her life's work in quick, uncoordinated, blurry strokes.

Tears streamed down her cheeks with each application, her head dizzy as she turned around and around, destroying each painting one by one. Her hands were covered with the white paste, which also crusted in her hair and stained her clothes, speckled the roots below and the ceiling above, until finally what was once a gallery of art was now a whiteout.

Arianna breathed hard, staring at the destruction before her, not noticing the silence that had fallen. There was no rain, no wind, no shuddering earth. White paste dripped from the canvases, paintings no longer depicting the darkness inside her, but rather, the emptiness.

She noticed that emptiness now, the silence that met her ears, the white walls and roots and ceiling, the hollowness in her heart. It weighed her down, frightened her so much that she was afraid to exit the treehouse gallery. For a moment Arianna could do nothing but stare at what she had done, the result of her failure, the consequences of rashness and stubborn cowardice. Years of hard work, hours of labor, night upon night of dreamland torture - all was for nothing.

Or perhaps, for everything.

A corner of one canvas that rested on the root floor caught her eye. Arianna kneeled, touching the single spot with a fingertip, frowning and wondering what it meant. It was the smallest of specks different from the rest, but potentially held more power than all the whitewashed canvas in the realm. She tucked that canvas behind another, hiding it until she could determine what to do with it, then braved a walk outside.

At first she thought she was blind. Then, slowly, she started to make out faint outlines. Gone were the fires. Gone was the smoke, the blood rain. Gone were the colorful flowers and towering trees. In their place was a whiteout, the entire world painted blank. She had entered into an unpainted canvas, a painting waiting to be filled with color, with life, with spirit. If she tried hard enough, she could see outlines of what used to be trees, rocks, rivers, meadows, all without color and defined only by the images left behind in her mind's eye.

She used those memories to direct her, first to the Fae Forest and then to Misty Marsh, finding both silent and empty. The lagoon's waters were thick, barely rippling when she touched a toe to the surface and pulled her foot back coated in thick white paste. Arianna checked other familiar areas, discovering no person or creature to answer her unspoken questions.

Finally, she made her way to Pirate Port. Here there were people, but not as she'd hoped to find them. Bodies littered the ground, white flesh against white road—the dead from a battle fought not so long ago that were yet to be cleared from the port. Arianna could barely see them in the whiteout, but she stepped carefully nonetheless, her footsteps the only sound in this eerie, empty world.

Making her way to the ship, Arianna boarded with the same carefulness, feeling her way through the white maze, wary of surprises. But all was quiet, to the point that she was starting to feel afraid. Her breath caught in her throat as she headed below deck, to the room she now dreaded seeing most.

Her hand shook as she pushed open the door to the pirates' bunk. Gone was the stench and the mess. But in their place was something far, far worse.

Bodies were spread across the room, barely visible in their white outlines, but part of the landscape as much as the dead men and women outside. Pirate after pirate laid collapsed on the wood floor, and if she looked hard enough, she could see some of them clenching their stomachs, others with their mouths open. And there, on the table, were the poisoned remnants of her special delivery.

Sickness rose in her throat, forcing her out of the room. Arianna searched the rest of the ship but it was empty, forcing her back to the deck as tears burned in the corners of her eyes. On deck, she spun in a circle, searching for someone, anyone, in this frightening blank world. But there was no one, nothing, just a vast canvas waiting for its artist.

"Malachi?" Arianna called out, her voice shaky. "Malachi! Where are you?" When only an empty breeze met her question, she tried again. "Jim? Anyone? Answer me!" The strength left her then and she sank to her knees, barely able to whisper, "Please, answer me."

"I am here, Arianna of the Stars."

Arianna spun around on her knees, gasping in relief. She leapt to her feet and rushed at him, grabbing Malachi in a hug. "I thought you were gone," she said into his shoulder. "I thought you left me."

"It seems neither of us did, Star Jumper," another man said behind her. Arianna released Malachi and turned to see that Jim too had appeared. Unable to reply, she shuffled her feet uncomfortably and tried to think of something to say, but a third voice saved her from a response.

"I thought you'd left me for good this time, Ari."

That voice caught her attention the most. Arianna turned slowly, seeing the man she'd almost forgotten standing a few feet away from Malachi. "John." She couldn't move, not even when he reached out to her. She realized then that she was standing in the center of the triangle the three men had formed.

Arianna observed them all in turn, trying to understand this strange and sudden apparition, if that's even what it was. There was Malachi, with his boyish enthusiasm mixed with an ages-old yearning for adventure. There was Jim, with his charming smirk that betrayed melancholy eyes. And there was John, with his wounded innocence battling a strong sense of betrayal.

She had loved and left them all. She was, in every sense of the word, a deceiver, and that fact shamed her. They stared at her as though expecting some kind of explanation, an apology for what she'd done, even when she couldn't explain it herself.

"I don't…I don't know what's happening," she finally admitted, locking her eyes on each of them as she addressed the man. "Malachi, you knew this was possible, that what I painted may come to life, but you never warned me. What I've done, it's…unforgivable.

It's my fault, because I always looked to someone else to lead me." Malachi only watched her, hands on his hips, neither denying nor confirming her accusations.

"Jim, you allowed me on board your ship thinking your father had done unspeakable acts, and then fed me to the wolves when I would not allow you to do those same things. You said you wanted to make up for what you thought happened, and for a moment there, you did. I was stupid enough to let down my guard and make myself vulnerable to a pirate." She saw the rage flicker on the other men's faces even when Jim's remained stoic.

"John, I always thought you never understood me and were keeping me from being who I am. I tried to be who you wanted me to be, and it scared the hell out of me that one day you'd wake up and figure out that you deserve more." Her fiancé frowned, trying to access the meaning in her words.

Silence befell the ship, an unbearable silence that Arianna couldn't stand. "Say something!" she snapped.

John was the first to step forward, holding out a hand pleadingly. "It was never a question of needing to understand you, Ari. We don't have to know and understand every part of each other. All we need is to be together. I've tried so hard to reach you, Ari. I argued with your mother that the meds were too much, but she turned against me, took back her decision to name me your primary care provider and I had to fight. It took so long, and resulted in so many new medications that just seemed to hurt you more, that I thought I'd lost you."

"Primary care?" she repeated. "You've talked to my mother behind my back?"

"For your own good, Ari. So that we could be together and be happy."

"She's happy here," Malachi growled, his body stiffening. He dragged his eyes from John to Arianna. "I told you what you needed to know so that you could reconnect with The Never, remember it like you did as a child. It was the only way for you to be one with the land. Some things you had to discover on your own, my Arianna."

"You kept me here under false pretenses."

"I gave you a choice. You were never forced to stay or leave."

"She was only driven away," Jim cut in. "Driven away by the ones who claimed to love her, driven to turn against her own kind and cut them down in cold blood."

"I did what I had to do after you turned on me, tricked me into one last painting, tricked me into severing my connection with the only place where I ever felt safe."

"I would have given you everything," Jim replied quietly, no longer appearing the intimidating captain. "From the moment I breathed in your scent, I knew you were meant to be mine. But then you turned against me, tricked my crew into their deaths, and tried to kill me, though clearly you didn't succeed."

"How…how did you survive?" The shame at what she'd done ate at her, the annoyance of his survival pushed it away.

"It doesn't matter how one escapes your clutches, or who comes to the rescue of those you have turned against. What does matter is that you left me there, alone, just like my father."

In that moment she saw what he saw, limping through the ship, searching for the rowdy pirates, finding them in their deaths after a sweet feast. In that moment she felt what he felt, an unbearable sense of loneliness, an ache that couldn't be healed.

She'd done that to him, her and no one else.

"Jim, I…" Her hand clutched her chest at the memory, and yet, she couldn't form an apology. *Was* she sorry? Did she regret killing the pirates as retribution for Jim's seduction?

"Perhaps you're more like me than you'd care to admit," Jim sneered, seeing the lack of regret for her actions. "You lie and steal, while pretending to be so pure and innocent. And that is why I will destroy The Never."

To her right, Malachi scoffed. "You cannot destroy The Never," he said scornfully. "It is neither here nor there. It is the empty void, the all-encompassing eye. It is the unattainable, except to those who belong to its very core."

"You talk like her," John responded, squaring his shoulders and making his presence known. "Another way to confuse her, trap her here."

Malachi turned his sights to the newcomer, sizing him up. John was shorter and not as well built, but held his own all the same. Both men met the other's scrutinizing glare. "I *freed* her, stranger. I showed her the truth in herself and nourished her imagination."

"She doesn't need your nourishment. She has enough imagination on her own." John's tone was stern, almost fatherly. He looked back to Arianna. "Ari, this has gone on long enough. Come home with me. Be with your family, with Lily, with me." When she only stared at him, he threw his arms out at his sides. "Have you even thought about me? About what happens when you disappear? They will throw me in prison, Ari."

"No, they won't," she whispered sadly. "I could make sure of it."

"Because you've shown such care before?" "John crossed his arms. "Come home, Ari. Where you belong."

"She belongs in The Never."

"Look around. The Never no longer exists," Jim cut in and sneered to Malachi, whose expression had lost some of its confidence. "The Never is nothing, just like the Star Jumper."

"*Enough*!" Arianna shouted when the three men made to lunge at each other. "Just…*stop it* and let me think!" She could feel their hate-filled thoughts swirling in the white air, confusing her even more. She didn't understand why they were here, *how* they were here, what they were trying to say in between their accusations. Their innuendos only angered her, made her long for freedom away from it all, even if for only a moment.

Something inside her broke, turned confusion into fury at the thought of once again being deceived. They called her a deceiver, said she was to blame for all of this, that *her* actions destroyed The Never. And yet, they too held their little lies, pretending to be something more or less than what they were, always keeping the truth from her just as much as she kept it from them.

Arianna laughed a derisive laugh, sending each of the men a scathing glare as she addressed them—John, Malachi, Jim.

"One who seeks to love me, so that he may imprison me," Arianna declared, thinking back on all the times John pushed more medication on her. "One who imprisons me, so that he may seduce me." All the times when Malachi hid secrets from her, to keep her here longer. "One who seeks to seduce me, so that he may kill me." All the times when Jim pretended to love her, only to sentence her to death.

"Jailer." The Fiancé.

"Liar." The Wild One.

"Executioner." The Hunter.

She stood before them now, a single beacon of strength slowly wilting into nothing. "I am who I am, and who *I* choose to be." Her gaze shifted to John. "Maybe good-bye is fitting after all."

Before he could reply, before any of them could respond, she left them standing there in their triangle, bending her knees slightly and launching off the deck to embark upon her newest journey of self-discovery. And the only one who could have followed her, didn't.

We Are The Never

SHE FLEW WITHOUT purpose until her mind settled and her thoughts cleared. It was a long flight, filled with worries of the future, confusion over her own self, anger over years and years of lies. Arianna wanted to believe that they all acted in her best interest, that they wanted only the best for her, but deep down she couldn't shake the feeling that she'd been deceived.

And the worst part was, she didn't have the right to be upset.

From the moment she'd entered The Never, she'd become a liar in her own right. She willingly left her life with John behind, leaving for another place with another man, never intending to go back. She willingly left her place by Malachi's side to go on adventures with the pirate captain known for his seductive power. She willingly let that captain seduce her and then balked at his advances. The judgments she would have cast upon any woman in her situation, the names she would have called another as an outsider looking in—Arianna had lost respect for herself just as the others had.

But she could make it right.

It no longer mattered what she wanted, what she needed. Arianna had once thought that The Never was about her desires, fears, wishes, dreams. That it was the place where innocence had been lost and freedom gained. But now she realized that like everyone and everything else, she was part of the land, nothing more than another piece of the landscape, nothing less than the heart that fueled the world.

She had to think about The Never now, and not about herself. Whatever would come from her next action would have to happen naturally, regardless of her personal wants.

There was only one place to go, one place to hide away from the world. Along the way she collected supplies, her mind focused only on the task at hand. In doing so, she discovered a new kind of game in this whiteout world, where pretend became reality as she willed colors to appear. She remembered what it was like to make paints out of plants and rocks, and encouraged The Never, as nonexistent as it appeared, to match her will and bring forth beautiful hues. By the time she reached her treehouse gallery, nothing else existed except the colorful image formed in her thoughts.

Holding back a sad sigh, Arianna closed the door and stepped carefully over the roots to the canvas she'd tucked behind another. She set it down carefully against the clay wall, lowering herself to her knees to observe it. The canvas was fairly large, more than an arm span in length and half as tall as Arianna when she was standing at full height. It once held a landscape of dying ocean life, a storm at sea and a sinking ship, but now there was not a trace of what once existed.

Except for that one small corner of blue.

In her chaotic destruction, she'd somehow missed this tiny portion of canvas, a beacon of hope in an otherwise lost realm. She cherished that diminutive blue speck, touching it softly, her heart aching for a return to the only place that felt like home.

"Out of nothing, we create something," Arianna whispered, then set to work.

Green leaves were crushed into fine powder, mixed to create a beautiful jade hue. Stones were ground into gentle blues and grays. Flowers turned into bold reds and glowing yellows that waited anxiously to be mixed from palette to canvas. Color stained her fingertips as Arianna dipped brushes made of stalks and stems into paint and crafted a whole new world from that single spot of blue.

The ocean was created first, with its sparkling lagoon. Mermaids basked on rocks, soaking in warm sunlight that glittered across crystal-clear waters. Their soothing song was clear even in picture, bringing peace to their land.

From the lagoon stretched the open sea, traveling into the bright horizon. And in the distance, a pirate ship sailed off to a brand-new adventure. A figure stood at the helm, proudly steering his ship into a land not yet known. This time, he didn't sail alone. A second figure was at his side, long hair blowing in the breeze, a woman ready to take on the world as his first mate and love to the one who hunted the seas.

The ocean gave way to a forest in the background, where white light shone through the trees even in the daytime. The spirits celebrated in their emerald woodland, souls rejuvenated by the rain of happiness and light, sparkling to one another in a carnival of color.

Brush stroked over canvas from forest to meadow, wildflowers dotting the landscape, imprints of where bodies once lay staring up at the clouds. Children ran around that meadow, little boys laughing and playing, their steps light and their smiles bright. Mischief was in their eyes, but innocence filled their faces.

Just beyond that meadow, a man was painted in careful, even strokes. His hands were on his hips, a smirk crossing his face that matched his artist's as he watched the boys play. There was a certain cockiness in his stance, a surefooted stature that he wore so well.

Over his shoulder, far in the distance and high in the sky, two figures departed, heading for the stars that shone even in the brilliant afternoon sun. One was strong and male, the other willowy and female, leaving behind their shadows that clung to the canvas in hopes of never being forgotten, even as they accepted their loss.

End to end, color reigned and darkness cowered in corners. A new world was born, a realm rebirthed from destruction in the eyes of the one who finally knew where she belonged. Behind that new world, on the back of the canvas, was a message from its creator.

The words were scrawled in black paint with a thin-bristled brush to form an explanation of this place and what it meant to her. She told anyone who would ever lay eyes upon her message why she loved The Never, why she needed to visit, why she couldn't take her medicine if she ever wanted to see her other-worldly friends again. In giving this final message, she hoped that no more questions would be asked, and that no one else would ever suffer because of her.

Finally, after hours upon hours of endless concentration, Arianna rested, allowing the world created by her own hand to finally come to light.

FOR THE FIRST time in weeks, perhaps even years, Arianna slept without dreams.

No longer was she tormented by memories of a hulking figure that ripped away her childhood innocence. No longer did she feel the weight of two worlds upon her shoulders. No longer did she struggle to remember who she was, where she belonged.

Even in sleep, she knew she made the right choice. It was why she slept so soundly, without worry or fear, and why she slept so long, without a care for what may happen when she woke. She'd painted The Never as she once knew it, before stress and anger and hate filled her heart.

When she awoke, her body refreshed and her mind restored, white had been replaced by black. After a moment of panic, Arianna realized she was merely in a dark room, not another world of nothing. She rose slowly, stiff from hours of painting, dreading what she would find when she exited wherever she had fallen asleep. In her exhaustion, she'd stumbled and wandered until her body finally found a suitable bed. Her hand shook ever so slightly when she found the door and pushed it open.

Sunlight met her eyes first. The bright golden light blinded her; Arianna shielded her eyes and squinted through the rays, ready to welcome the life she had finally chosen for herself.

Careful thought had been put into this life. And yet, it was a decision that fate seemed to have chosen for her. She supposed she had the choice, ultimately, to go where she wanted and to be with the person she desired, but there was something comforting in knowing that she'd always had her place here.

"Here" was the woodland that met her eye as soon as her vision adjusted to the sun. The light was different, filtered in a rainbow of color, almost palpable rays of color that warmed her chilled skin. Arianna smiled when the golden light touched her outstretched arms, when her bare feet walked over crisp green grass, when she breathed in the freshness of her own private forest.

Yes, she was home.

"Welcome back," a man said behind her.

Arianna smiled at the voice, lowering her arms and turning. "Some might say I never left."

"Oh, but you did." He took two steps closer, nearly toe-to-toe with her. "I missed you every day you were gone. That's how I knew you had left."

His words warmed every part of her, widening her smile. It was an honest smile, one she rarely displayed. When he cupped a hand around the back of her neck and drew her in for a kiss, she allowed herself to enjoy the moment, to bask in the scent of him, of home. "I'm here now, and never plan to leave again."

"You couldn't even if you tried. You're all mine now." There was something teasing in his tone, though his face sobered nearly instantly. "Where are the others?"

Her smile softened, but didn't disappear. "I gave them the lives they deserve. One sails for treasure with a woman worthy of being at his side, proving that he is not like his father after all. He will find the love he seeks without having to change his ways.

"One learns how to let go of a bond that cannot be rebuilt. He looks forward to finding true love in the heart of another, without mourning the memory of a woman once held dear. He will enjoy a freedom he thought he lost, and salvation in the written words of the one who released him."

Arianna shifted, looking up at him with teary eyes. "And the third I gave the entire world in the hopes that he hasn't forgotten the girl he once befriended. In the hopes that he is able to forgive the woman he once loved."

Sparkling eyes, that strong male form, a strangely hesitant stance—she took them all in as she awaited his answer. As was his way, he made her wait, letting that knife of fear work its way through her gut, sending a tremble through her chin. She'd taken a risk in returning to him, knowing she had no right to ask for his forgiveness, desperately hoping for his love nonetheless.

Just when she thought she couldn't handle the silence, he spoke. "You chose me."

"No," Arianna answered honestly. "I chose me."

Malachi leaned down, kissing her softly, wrapping his arms around her. Laughter glinted in his green eyes as they worked their way over her body, seeing the speckles of paint, smudges of color—remnants of the dream that crafted their very beings. He wiped at one of those spots, expression turning thoughtful when it stuck to her skin.

"You are the dream," he whispered, kissing her skin where his hand had just grazed, tracing a finger over the golden vine that had become part of her forever. Arianna's eyes closed at his touch, body leaning into his. "You are the reality." He moved her in a dance, lifting them both off the ground and spiraling them up toward the treetops.

"You are the eternal," he continued, twirling her out and back in, grinning when her laugh echoed throughout him. "You are the forgotten." Their hands clasped as their feet brushed the verdant canopy.

Arianna looked out over the land, her land, with its crystal ocean and shimmering lagoon, glowing Fae Forest and pale pink sky, natives roasting meats over fire pits and energetic boys racing around the meadow in rambunctious romps.

"We are the always," she said, wrapping her arms around Malachi, the Star Jumper and the Wild One molded together.

"We are The Never."

Stephanie North, for being an amazing and encouraging editor.

Cindy Circelli, for continuing to be my biggest fan and honest critic.

Nicole Pascale, for her beautiful cover, and for putting up with my crazy requests.

Kristi Strong, for providing insightful advice as a fellow author and friend.

My readers, for their continued support that lets me continue this crazy writing adventure

About the Author

(Photo by Kevin Radford Photography)

KRISTINA CIRCELLI IS the author of several fiction novels, including *The Helping Hands* series and *The Whisper Legacy*.

Her latest series, *The Whisper Legacy*, features *Beyond the Western Sun*. This book is what all fantasy adventures must strive to be: a complex, intricate examination of human emotion set within the context of worlds known only in our imagination. Melding fantasy and legend in an epic quest, this series signals the arrival of Kristina Circelli as a master storyteller and an important voice in Native American literature.

A descendent of the Cherokee nation and niece of a Cherokee elder, Circelli holds both a Bachelor of Arts and Master of Arts in English from the University of North Florida, where she also teaches creative writing.

To find out more about Kristina and her books visit:

Website
http://www.circelli.info

Blog
http://anawfullybigadventure-kc.blogspot.com/

Facebook
https://www.facebook.com/pages/Circelli-Books-novels-by-Kristina-Circelli/341115646710

Twitter
https://twitter.com/KCircelli